LAND WITHOUT SHADOW

Also by Michael Mewshaw

MAN IN MOTION (1970)

WAKING SLOW (1972)

THE TOLL (1974)

EARTHLY BREAD (1976)

Michael Mewshaw

LAND
WITHOUT
SHADOW

Doubleday & Company, Inc.
Garden City, New York
1979

ISBN: 0-385-14504-7
Library of Congress Catalog Card Number 78–69661

For Linda

I would like to express my
gratitude to the American Academy in
Rome for its hospitality and help
during the completion of this book.

M.M.

Integrity was not enough; that seemed
The hell of childhood: he must try again.
Now, galloping through Africa, he dreamed
Of a new self, a son, an engineer,
His truth acceptable to lying men.

"Rimbaud"
W. H. Auden

Where they make a desert, they call it peace.

Tacitus

LAND WITHOUT SHADOW

Book One

CHAPTER I

Jack Cordell could see his breath as he knelt at the wood stove and stacked the kindling in a pyramid. Striking a match on the wall, he lit Tucker's telegram and touched it to the dry slivers. Once they caught, he laid on a spidery vine root that shriveled quickly in the flames, its tendrils reddening and curling into rings of fire.

When he tossed on the first slab of oak he recognized the tense, expectant feeling in his chest. It used to be this way whenever he painted. Now building fires seemed to be the ultimate expression of his artistry—a consoling ritual, half pagan, half religious, yet altogether practical.

About the telegram he had no sense of urgency, only a little curiosity. It had read:

> DESPERATE. SAVE MY LIFE. MEET
> ME AT THE CARLTON HOTEL, CANNES.
> IMMEDIATELY.

Jack doubted Tucker was desperate. The breathless tone betrayed his tendency to exaggerate the most mundane problems; under pressure he was usually deliberate and eerily calm.

He could guess where Tucker had gotten his address. He must have had the telephone number too and learned the line was disconnected. Now if he didn't drive down to Cannes, Tucker

was liable to come up here, and he didn't care to have anyone
see yet what he had accomplished living alone.

Except for an overstuffed chair and a mattress in the corner,
the room was stripped of furniture. He had stored it all downstairs, along with the books, steamer trunks, and other personal
belongings he didn't want to bother about any more. In this huge
drafty room, Jack cooked his meals over the fire and painted
whenever he could. But the light was bad, sometimes so bad he
could barely distinguish colors. He had hung army blankets over
the larger windows to cut off the icy currents of air, and there
was only one small opening onto a Cézanne landscape of olives
and cypresses.

The house was an extraordinary example of something or
other, the real estate agent had claimed, but Jack's French was
shaky and the agent's honesty suspect. The architect was said to
have been internationally renowned; Le Corbusier's name was
invoked. But at the low price Jack was paying, it had to have
been a disciple who had imitated the master's hallmarks—wide
windows, skylights, and an intricate arrangement of space into "a
machine for living."

In winter, however, the "machine for living" had become as
cold as a crypt, a jumble of concrete boxes where a tenant could
freeze to death amid the consolations of symmetry. Before hanging the army blankets Jack had caulked the window frames with
paint rags and shut off one refrigerator of a room after another,
burrowing toward the center of the house in his search for
warmth. Still a fierce chill penetrated everywhere, and the tile
floors felt like iced-over ponds. Finally he had had to install the
wood-burning stove, which scorched the whitewashed walls,
fouled the air with smoke, and made the light worse. As he
transformed this marvelous example of modern architecture into
a slum, he had realized that, whatever else you might say about
a work of art, it was difficult to live in one.

Most of his own canvases faced the wall. He regarded them as
exercises, not art—forced marches in the attempt to loosen up
and stretch his limits. Because he believed his painting was too
static, too detailed, too rigidly controlled, he had sometimes
worked left-handed, or with his eyes shut, he had splattered
paint like Jackson Pollock, anything to convince himself he was

an artist, not an illustrator, not a draftsman. Much as he feared that years of teaching and money troubles and domestic tirades had not diminished his talent—much as he suspected they had only distracted him from the realization that he had damn little —Jack went on working. The greater his doubts, the more he drove himself. With nothing and nobody to interrupt him now, he told himself this was what he had been waiting for.

Then, before she left, Sybil had been sick and spent four days in the hospital. Weeks later, when she and their son David were back in Texas, the doctor's bill had arrived along with the X rays of her upper torso. Tossing the unpaid bill into a box with all the others, Jack had studied the X rays, intrigued by the shape of the rib cage and the contrast between the shadow of her lungs and the sleek white curves of her skeleton. Certain he had seen something—or rather had sensed something he couldn't see—he had started to copy the X ray in acrylics. Then he had begun to put flesh on Sybil's bones. Now he wondered where to go next.

If he stopped, she would resemble a cadaver on an autopsy table. If he went on, he would reproduce one of the earnest, nearly photographic nudes he had done before they were married. The precise shape of her breasts, the ruddiness of her skin, the prominent pelvis and auburn hair . . . Jack didn't need a picture.

There was nothing around to remind him of David. No toys strewn up and down the stairs. No coveralls drying on the shower rod. Above all, there was no noise. But it seemed to be this nothingness that prevented him from forgetting. At night when he came home alone, he sometimes caught himself walking on tiptoes, remembering how, whenever Sybil and he got in late, one part of him had always hoped the baby wouldn't wake up, while another part wished that he would so that he could take David in his arms and talk to him until he nodded back to sleep.

Jack knew it did no good to think about David and he made himself move. Going into the bathroom, he shaved a week's stubble from his chin and, as usual these days, was shocked by what he saw in the mirror. After months of skipped meals, too much drinking and not enough sleep, he expected everything to show in his face. But as if to mock his foul mood, his color had seldom been rosier, his health more robust. Wood chopping and long walks through the hills had left him stronger than at any time since college. He had lost weight, but thought he looked better for that; it exaggerated the sharp lines of his face which, along with his dark hair, had led some people in Texas to accuse him of having a touch of Indian or Mexican blood.

Putting on a black corduroy suit, Jack went downstairs, past the stacked furniture, and stepped outside.

A mistral had blown all night, rattling the shutters, driving clouds out to sea, leaving the air sharp and still. Mimosas were in bloom, and a haze of yellow and a cloying scent hovered over the valley. Nearby, in the tiny hillside village, dead vines dangled from the walls like fishnets drying and when the church bell rang three o'clock they appeared to tremble.

At this time of year there was little traffic, and once out of the foothills he followed the coast road along the choppy blue Mediterranean. Two white cruise ships yawed at anchor a mile offshore—the colors intense, the scene as flat and explicit as a child's sketch of his day at the beach.

On his infrequent trips to Cannes, Jack usually headed for a sleazy foul-guttered area near the *gare* where the air smelled not of flowers or Bain de Soleil, but of cheap wine and stale Gauloises. There, in bars that reminded him of Mexican border towns, he felt almost at home. But today he parked in front of VanCleef and Arpels' and sat with his hands on the steering wheel, wondering.

He hadn't seen or spoken to Tucker Garland in six years. There had been no specific disagreement, no dramatic break, just a gradual drifting apart. At first he thought it was Tucker's fault and agreed with friends who claimed Tucker had dropped them.

Now he wasn't so sure. Perhaps he had quit listening before Tucker quit talking. Who was to say when a man stops being thrilled and starts feeling threatened by his old friend's success? Or when that friend stops being sympathetic and starts being bored by the other man's failure?

Leaving the car, Jack set off for the frothy white confection of the Carlton. In the shade it was chilly; even in full sunlight the season seemed unsure of itself. Although gaudy spring flowers were banked around the hotel entrances, the plane trees were bare.

Still, a swarm of Germans and Swedes sat outside the Festival Bar, nursing *cafés crèmes,* their faces tilted toward the sun. Ragged blacks and North Africans prowled among them peddling wood carvings and jungle scenes painted on velvet. There were no buyers.

At the Carlton, the desk clerk said Mr. Garland was waiting in the bar, and Jack paused at the entrance, glancing around, not caring to take Tucker—or himself—by surprise.

One customer sat by a window, gazing at the sea and the thorny promontories of the Estérel. It was his old friend all right, but he bore about the same relation to the man Jack had known as an enlarged color photograph does to a wallet-size snapshot in black and white. This Tucker was florid, bigger, and bristling with inner agitation.

In college they had both had coarse black hair and resembled each other enough so that everybody referred to them as Big Brother and Little Brother. Jack's hair was still dark, but Big Brother had gone gray and grown a beard speckled with white.

Shifting his weight, Tucker swung around in the chair, smiled, and said as though genuinely surprised, "Jesus Christ, look who's here. Hidy, bubba." He bounced to his feet and pumped Jack's hand, his movements as brutally quick as they had always been. Despite his size and the slow country cadences of his speech, Tucker had the metabolism of a jockey. "I been trying to get in touch for days. Afraid I was going to miss you. Hope I didn't interrupt your work."

"No. I was at the end of something."

"Good." He grabbed Jack by both arms. "I swear I can't believe it. It's been too goddamn long since I've seen you. Sit down, have a drink."

"I can't say you haven't changed," Jack said.

"Christ, don't I know it. I've put on about thirty pounds."

"I mean your hair, the beard."

Tucker combed his fingers through the beard and grinned. "My new image. I got tired of coming on as a Texas cowboy.

Now I'm an *artiste*. Nobody with any self-respect calls himself a director any more. I'm an *auteur*."

As soon as they sat down a waiter came, and Jack ordered a whiskey with Perrier and ice.

"You, you're looking terrific," Tucker said. "All except that suit. Makes you look like a mortician."

"And what are you supposed to be in that get-up—a big game hunter?" Tucker wore a beige safari outfit with big patch pockets and a belt that dangled unbuckled at the waist.

"Matter of fact I am on my way to Africa. Going down to Maliteta to shoot a film."

When the waiter brought Jack's drink, Tucker insisted on signing for it. "It's all out of EPC's pocket."

Jack raised his glass. "Here's to the new film."

"Ah, the hell with that. Here's to your work."

As they drank, a black in a tattered dashiki appeared at the plate-glass window, holding up a few fertility gods for their inspection.

Jack was watching a bellhop chase him away, when he asked, "Who told you where I live?"

"On the way over I stopped in Texas to see Daddy. Then I cycled"—he pronounced it "sickled"—"on by Austin and called Sybil."

Although he expected more—wanted more—Tucker didn't supply it. Jack fought it but felt his irritation growing. He didn't like this game—making the other guy ask all the questions. Tucker was too good at it.

"The telegram?" he finally said. "You have problems?"

"Nothing serious." Tucker sounded cheerful. "Just my career and my bank account racing to see which one goes down the drain first."

"I don't get it. This new film, what is it, your fifth?"

"Sixth. The last one never was released. None of them made any real money. With that kind of track record it's hard to get backing."

"Come on! Ever since *Traveling Light* you've had it made."

"Nah. It hit at the wrong time—just when the market for small, quiet pictures was drying up."

"But it got terrific reviews."

"Not bad for a first movie, but that doesn't mean a damn thing."

"Sure it does. It gives you a reputation, something to build on."

"That's not how it works, bubba. It's not logical, not some kind of escalator. Every time out it's a roll of the dice and you either make your point or crap out. I keep throwing losers, you'll have to set me up with a teaching job."

"Take mine."

"Don't think I wouldn't, if I could paint."

"You don't have to paint. Just praise everybody and be patient. Ever consider going back to New York and directing plays?"

"There is no New York. There aren't any plays. Anyway, I'm hooked on movies now. Just stubborn, I guess. And stupid. It's like anything else. You gotta be smart enough to know how to do it, but dumb enough to think it matters."

"Maybe this new one'll turn things around for you."

"Yeah, maybe." Tucker unbuttoned a pocket on his bush jacket, stuck in a hand, then brought it out, empty. "It's called *Terms of Peace*. Ever read the novel?"

"No, just a few reviews. Something about a draft dodger in Canada, wasn't it?"

"Yeah, but the story wouldn't work the way it was. Not with the war over and everybody sick of Vietnam. The central character's a Peace Corps volunteer now. I don't think we lost much and at least we don't have to face that crummy weather in Canada. Maliteta's in the Sahara; sunny all the time."

"You've been there?"

"No. The people I sent to scout locations have been sending back pictures. Looks great. Only problem is, we kind of got our plow stuck in hard ground before we even started. It's a Moslem country, you see, and some Jews in the industry, they're jumpy about working there."

"Maliteta won't let Jews in?"

"Nothing like that. There hasn't been a bit of trouble about visas. But the other day my art director, fellow by the name of Liebermann, got a wild hair and quit." Tucker grimaced. "Now ain't that just like a creative type? Too sensitive to put up with a little heat and dust."

"And maybe some Jew baiting."

"No, he just didn't dig the location."

"That's too bad."

"You bet your ass it is. We're on a tight schedule and I was counting on Liebermann's continuity sketches. You grope around figuring out what to shoot next and you might as well flush the budget. I need to find another art director damn quick."

"Sounds like it." Jack dipped a finger into his drink, flicking the ice cubes. "But I'm not your man."

"Don't make up your mind till I finish what I have to say."

"I don't want to hear it."

"Why not?"

"Because I'm not in the movie business, I'm not in the job market, and I'm not in the breadline."

"Nobody said you were."

"Don't do a number on me, Tucker. I know why you tele-grammed."

"Yeah, I need help. What do I have to do, fall down on my fucking knees and beg?" Though he was still grinning, he sounded serious and seemed ready to push away from the table and kneel. Tucker had always, even at the worst times, had this melodramatic exuberance, a kind of self-intoxication, that was what attracted some people to him and also was what their attention fed in him.

"Just tell me," Jack said, "did Sybil call and ask you to put me on the payroll?"

"I phoned her."

"Why?"

"I was calling *you.*"

"After six years?"

"Should I have waited twelve? I wanted to get in touch."

"Okay, now we're in touch. Let's stay that way. But that doesn't have anything to do with me working for you."

"Is that the problem? Working for me? I suppose you'd rather work for those cretins at that jerk-off school in East Jesus, Texas."

"I don't intend to work for anybody again until I have to."

"Meanwhile who's going to pay your bills?"

"Don't bullshit me," Jack shouted. "That's right out of Sybil's mouth. She sent you here."

"Nobody sent me. It wasn't till Liebermann quit that I got this idea."

"She didn't tell you I was late with the support payments? She didn't swear the instant I set foot in the States she's going to have me hauled into court?"

"Chrissake, bubba, hold it down. Those guys at the bar don't have any right to know your business. Let's go to my room."

"You won't change my mind."

"To hell with changing your mind. Come upstairs till you calm down."

He saw no sense in it and was about to say if Tucker intended to talk any more about money or a job he was leaving. But then, as Tucker headed for the elevator, he noticed the splotches of perspiration that had soaked through the shoulders of his safari jacket, and it startled him to think that Tucker might be more upset and in greater need than he was.

In the room both beds were unmade and between them, on a night table, stood a movie projector aimed at the wall. An Eclair camera rested on one chest of drawers, a stack of film canisters on the other.

"Sorry about the mess," Tucker said. "All this gear spread around, I don't let the maids in."

Jack took a seat with a view. Along La Croisette palm fronds were flapping in the wind and cars were cruising toward the winter casino. As the lights came on at dusk, Cannes was a canvas by Dufy. "There's nothing like going down the tubes in style," Jack said.

"It's all out of EPC's pocket."

"Who's EPC?"

"The studio behind this film."

"Whoever's paying, I'd say you're making out all right."

"You remember the old line—it's a quick ride from the penthouse to the outhouse. Believe me, you can go just as broke on a hundred thousand a year as you can on ten."

"Not *just* as broke. You've forgotten what it's like to be tacky poor."

"I'm fixing to get a reminder if this film doesn't make money."
He went to a cabinet. "Want a drink?"

"No."

"Neither do I." But he poured one anyway, then sat facing
Jack. "You were right. Sybil did say you were three months
behind in your support."

"I've been sending money for David. I can't afford all she's
asking for herself."

"She swore she'd sick the law on you when you get back."

"The way she's going, she'll wind up forcing me to stay here.
Which is fine by me. I like it a hell of a lot better than Texas."

Tucker shrugged. "I suppose it's your business."

"Exactly. And I'll take care of it."

"How?"

"Maybe I'll sell a painting. You in the market?"

"I couldn't afford to buy a toothbrush. But I can give you a
job."

"Look, Tucker, I'd like to crawl out of the corner I'm in—but
not by backing into another one, not by putting things off again.
That's part of what caused trouble between Sybil and me. For
years I wanted to take off and paint. So I taught full time at
school and part time at a community center and I did portrait
commissions and scenery for the drama department and signs for
local businesses and any other damn thing people would pay for.
By the time I got here, I was empty and had to wait till I filled
up again. Then just when I was feeling half right, Sybil said she
was ready to go home."

"I understand and I'd like to help."

"I don't mean to sound like a prick. But why don't you look
out for yourself, and I'll worry about me."

"I *am* looking out for myself." Tucker hunched forward, elbows on knees, and rolled the glass of scotch back and forth
between his palms. His hands were small, almost delicate, unlike Jack's, which had hardened with paint and resin and were
rubbed raw at the knuckles. "If I could find an experienced art
director—a guy I trusted—I'd damn well hire him. But there isn't
time. And my fat ass is caught in a very tight crack. I got the
studio breathing down my neck, a ballbreaker of a producer
looking over one shoulder and an accountant over the other.

The leading lady is coked up and the leading man is twenty pounds overweight, and neither of them is satisfied with the script. If the first batch of rushes isn't absolutely perfect, I'm going to be yanked off this film so fast my eyes'll drop out. So I'm not doing you any favors, bubba. I need help."

Tucker had said all the right things. Jack didn't care to be manipulated, long distance, by Sybil and he didn't want charity from anybody, especially Tucker. Still he wasn't convinced. "I don't even know what an art director does."

"Don't fall out over that. You could learn." He set his drink on the table beside the projector. "What do you make on this sabbatical you've got?"

"Half my regular salary stretched over a year."

"Meaning what, about eight thousand bucks?"

"That was quite a conversation you and Sybil had. Did she show you my income tax statement and checkbook too?" Despite his sour smile, Jack spoke with no real rancor. He was used to having deans, department chairmen, loan sharks, and car dealers compute his personal worth down to the last dime.

"The deal with me is I'll cover all expenses and pay you fifteen hundred a week. We're scheduled for ten weeks, but it wouldn't surprise me if we ran over. What we're talking about is more than two of those fellowships. But the real kicker," Tucker said, "is we can let you have it in cash. No way the IRS'll know."

"I don't need that kind of trouble."

"No trouble. Now I don't know what you're supposed to be sending David and Sybil, but . . ."

"Sure you do. Don't start acting discreet now."

"But you should come out of this with enough dough so you don't get slapped with a subpoena when you go home."

"I'm not going back to Texas."

"Fine. Stay here and paint. That's my point, bubba. Take this job and pay off your debts and you can do whatever you damn well please." Damp splotches had blossomed on the front of his shirt. "It's the same deal Liebermann had. Ask anybody."

It wasn't just the money that appealed to Jack. There was the escape from his dank studio and the stillborn canvases. In a few months his frayed nerves would reknit and warm weather would return to the Riviera.

"What are continuity sketches?"

"First tell me is the money okay?"

"No. My agent said to hold out for a percentage of the profits."

"Son of a bitch!" He cuffed Jack's arm, then stepped over to the bureau, the one with the Eclair on top, and steadying the camera, he opened the bottom drawer and took out a loose-leaf binder. "Here's the book for my last film. It'll give you an idea what you'll be doing."

While Jack leafed through it, Tucker stayed beside him, kneading his shoulder. "Mostly it's a matter of filling in blanks. You gotta help me visualize what the characters are doing when they deliver their lines—how they're standing, where they're looking, what kind of cross action. Usually I don't depend so much on story boards, but this time I'll be hustling to stay on schedule and keep the male lead from eating himself right out of the role."

Jack chuckled.

"It's no joke. A few more pounds and he'll be fatter than an old sow."

When he continued laughing, Tucker's hand slid from his shoulder. "What is it?"

"This." Jack riffled through sketches of a boy and girl strolling down the main street of a small town, staring into a jewelry store, kissing under an apple tree. "It's a comic book. All that's missing are conversation balloons over their heads."

Tucker plucked at the damp patches on his shirt.

"You have to hand it to Sybil," Jack said. "She conned you into paying me fifteen thousand bucks to do cartoons."

"She didn't con me into anything."

"I haven't made that much on all my paintings put together. Maybe I've found my true calling."

Tucker glanced at his watch. "Look, I have to meet somebody for dinner. Why don't you come along? I'll get you a room here and we can start work first thing in the morning."

"There's all my stuff to pack." He stood up. "And the house to close."

"Okay, check in tomorrow. We don't have much time, and there's a lot of talking to do, a lot of things to catch up on." He smiled then, and it would have been the same smile Jack remembered from so many parties and double dates and amiable marathon-length conversations if it hadn't been for the gray hair, the grizzled beard, and the webs of tension and weariness around his eyes. "Hey, listen, bubba, leaving aside any misunderstandings in the past and all your hassles with Sybil and mine with a lot of people, I want you to know how great it is to see you again. We're going to have a hell of a time down there."

CHAPTER II

A Mercedes 600 sped them through a downpour toward the airport in Nice. While Jack and Tucker lounged on the plush back seat, Hal Nichols, the company PR man, crouched on a jump seat and switched on the TV set mounted in a console above the bar. There was a rerun of "Bonanza" dubbed into French. An Indian on horseback trotted up to Little Joe, raised his hand, and said, "*Ça va?*"

"Turn the fucking thing off," Tucker said.

Nichols did what he was told.

In spite of the air conditioner, Tucker was sweating as he drummed his fingers on the copy of the script in his lap. Jack still hadn't read it. Although he had moved into the Carlton and he and Tucker had been together constantly, they had done little work. In fact, they seldom spoke about the movie. Most of their time had been taken up by long dinners and lunches, and late nights at the casino in Monte Carlo and clubs in Juan les Pins. As Tucker had promised, they had a lot of talking to do, a lot of things to catch up on. Maybe it was his way of making up for the six years of silence—even though neither man mentioned, much less tried to analyze, what had kept them apart.

Tucker's assumption seemed to be that they were together again, close as they had always been, and no more need be said. At the Carlton, having a nightcap, he was liable to laugh as he signed for yet another bill. "Life's a funny old dog, ain't it, bubba? Who'd have figured us to end up doing the *Riviera* together?"

Although his tone was broad with irony—words like "Riviera" were always in italics—Tucker clearly believed life was rich with possibilities, with sudden pleasant reversals. But Jack, cursing his own petty suspicions, couldn't stop wondering why Tucker had hired him.

"About the script, bubba. I'd like you to read it straight through. Don't get hung up on details. Then let me have some honest feedback."

"Sure."

"I mean, it's not great literature. It's not chiseled in stone. We'll be changing it right up till the time we start shooting. Maybe you can come up with some fresh ideas."

Jack took the script from Tucker.

"Don't look at it now. I don't want to stare over your shoulder and influence you."

"You're going to love it," Hal Nichols said. "This script is pure gold."

Nichols wore snug denim trousers and a black leather jacket glittering with chrome studs and zippers. He was well over fifty and his dark hair, dyed and sculpted into lacquered flaps, might have been a toupée. "So this is the Riviera," he said as they coasted off the autoroute into the clutter of gas stations, motels, and snack bars in Cros de Cagnes. "Gimme Laguna Beach any time."

"It's better back in the hills." Jack found himself defending an area he was glad to be leaving now that the weather had gone bad.

"Ever see Topanga Canyon?"

Tucker sighed. "Jesus, Nichols, take a couple of hours off."

The PR man grinned. His teeth were capped. "Just sticking up for the home town."

"Why? The LA Chamber of Commerce have you on retainer? Better save your juice for this picture."

"Sent off a story last night about Barry Travis' new diet."

"Great. I hope he stays on it."

"I'm doing a thing now called 'Lisa Austin Talks to Teens about Acne.'"

"She didn't break out again?"

"No, she's been fine since she had her face planed."

At Nice International they splashed around behind the terminal to a chain-link fence where the chauffeur honked the horn until a security guard came out and glanced at their papers. Then the guard unlocked the gate and let them drive onto the tarmac to the rear stairway of an Air France jet. A customs officer and two stewardesses were waiting in the rain to check them aboard.

The back of the plane was noisy; the passengers, most of them French, had obviously been drinking a long time. Since they wore bright, summer-weight clothes, like tourists on their way to a tropical resort, Jack figured the film company was sharing a charter flight as far as Marrakech. But Nichols said no, they were crew members—grips, gaffers, and sound men. "Orangutans," he called them. "The creative types sit up front."

The creative types were quieter and dressed like day laborers in canvas and denim, leather and khaki. Hurrying along the aisle, Nichols introduced Jack to a blur of faces—the accountant, the production manager, the first assistant, and several slim, tanned bit-part players. While Tucker stayed behind to talk to the director of photography, they moved on to Barry Travis, the male lead.

Jack wouldn't have recognized Travis, he had gained so much weight. In the sixties he had played high-strung, hollow-cheeked rebels; Barry had been on speed back then. Now he was off amphetamines, Tucker had explained, and cultivating a new image. But heavy drinking had left him looking like a dissolute cherub with damp unfocused eyes. Attached by earplugs to a portable cassette recorder, he might have been undergoing an electroencephalogram test and he scarcely acknowledged Nichols' introduction.

Meeting Lisa Austin was like encountering a living billboard. For years before she went into films, she had been in all the ads for hair spray, shampoo, lipstick, toothpaste, and bathing suits. She smiled, showing all thirty-two perfect teeth, and introduced Roberta, her hairdresser, and Phil, her bodyguard, who looked like a bouncer and had a conspicuous bulge under his left arm.

When he turned to Helen Soray, Nichols sounded as if he were quoting from a press release publicizing the Obie she had just won for her performance in a Chekhov play. Marking her place in a paperback, she waited with some embarrassment for him to finish. Unlike Lisa who, Jack thought, was symmetrical to the point of vacuity, Helen had interesting angles and imperfections. Her dark hair was hacked off short, her mouth too large, her nose thin and slightly crooked. She was tall and had long arms and legs which made her look coltish, young, but Jack knew she was well into her thirties.

"What's the book?" Nichols asked her. "*Terms of Peace?*"

She showed him the cover of *The Sheltering Sky* by Paul Bowles. "I've been reading everything I could find about the Sahara." She snapped a finger against the copy of the script Jack held. "Too bad these writers didn't. They got all their ideas watching reruns of *Lawrence of Arabia.*"

"Don't listen to her." Nichols urged Jack into a seat across the aisle, next to Phil. "Helen's a typical stage snob."

Within minutes of take-off they were far out over the Mediterranean, bumping and shuddering through the clouds. Phil lifted a hand to the throat of his shirt and touched the tiny gold cross he wore around his neck. He grinned at Jack. "Just superstition."

Once they were above the bad weather and the seat belt sign blinked off, Jack opened *Terms of Peace,* eager to read it straight through as Tucker had asked him to. But from the first scene he had trouble and thought he must be missing significant transitions. Every few pages he had to backtrack to pick up the thread of the story or pause to reread a line of dialogue. Though he felt disloyal for doing it, the next time the plane ran into turbulence, he closed the folder.

"Terrible, isn't it?" Helen asked.

"Don't poison his mind," Lisa said.

"Oh, come on, you know nobody talks the way these characters do. And Barry, he plays a twenty-two-year-old Peace Corps volunteer."

"Bet that's been wonderful for his ego," Lisa said.

"Maliteta kicked out the Peace Corps ten years ago."

"No one else knows that. They wouldn't care if they did."

"That's just it," Helen said. "Nobody cares."

"Why'd you take the part?" Roberta asked.

Resting a hand on her leg, Helen spread her fingers and appeared to be examining her nails, which were untinted and cut short. It was a hand shaped by exercise or work, and it looked strong where it joined a surprisingly thick wrist. "Two kids in private schools, an apartment in the city, a farm in Vermont . . ."

Phil leaned forward, looking around Jack. "Like they always say, Hollywood's a factory town. Whatever else it does, it keeps a lot of people working."

"It isn't just the money," Helen said. "I was really ready for the desert."

"You should have gone to Palm Springs," Roberta said.

"I mean real desert—not split levels and plastic cactus and Jacuzzis."

"Soon as I heard we'd be shooting in the Sahara," Lisa said, "I right away thought of all the back light there'd be. You know, through my hair. That's how I always see myself."

"Why are you on this film?" Helen asked Jack so suddenly it sounded like an accusation.

"Guess I was ready for the desert too."

After skirting the coast of Algeria the Caravelle flew inland over Morocco, crossing the Rif Mountains and their deep gorges and peaks of snow. Then south of Fez the landscape flattened, resembling a rumpled beige dropcloth flecked with gray.

Jack plowed back into *Terms of Peace,* skimming much of the dialogue. Tucker would have to worry about it; somebody should. But he found that by focusing on the stage directions he could break the action down into abstract forms and treat the characters as objects arranged in space. Since he knew nothing about Maliteta, the background remained vague, but at least he felt a bit surer of the foreground.

Nudging Jack's elbow, Phil nodded out the window. On the drab plateau there was a sudden splurge of vegetation—the oasis around Marrakech. Encircled by walls, the town was made of rose-tinted mud and looked like the meat of some exotic fruit set in a green rind. Jack hoped for such a background in Maliteta.

The plan was to switch planes in Marrakech for the flight to Tougla, Maliteta, but once the baggage had been unloaded, they learned the Air Maliteta charter hadn't arrived. No one knew why. Word was there would be a five-hour wait, and the crew began grumbling.

Jack spotted Tucker at the far end of the terminal, looming over the production manager, Marvin Tallow, talking into his face and punctuating each sentence by jabbing a finger at his chest. While Tallow rushed off, Tucker stared at his watch as if timing a hundred-yard dash, and when the chubby fellow returned and panted out the news, he cut him short, called for silence, and said they would all go into town and wait at the Mamounia Hotel.

The first taxis took the creative types in order of importance, as determined by Marvin Tallow. As Jack's cab pulled away from the airport, the orangutans were standing out front, blinking in brassy sunlight, slowly sobering up. Surrounded by suitcases, golf bags, tennis rackets, and swim fins, they looked like furious tourists from one of those discount charter groups that go bankrupt every summer. A bus was on its way to pick them up.

"A thing like this should never happen." Although it was blisteringly hot, Nichols hadn't unzipped his motorcycle jacket.

"Couldn't be helped," Tallow murmured apologetically. "An afternoon in Marrakech won't kill you. I've heard the Mamounia's like the Beverly Hills Hotel."

"That's all I need. Five hours in the Arab equivalent of the Polo Lounge."

In the lobby of the Mamounia local color was laid on by the yard, but this didn't inhibit the German tour group that bellowed *Bierstube* songs and drove Tallow, Nichols, and Jack into the bar. It was a dim, neutral space with a single purpose, and they had ordered two rounds by the time Joel Schwarz showed up.

Shrunken and sunburned with a face as leathery as a baseball mitt, he had gone bald at the crown of his head but sported bushy white sideburns. "Where's everybody?" he asked.

"I got the principals a suite upstairs," Tallow said.

Pulling a cigar from his breast pocket, Schwarz passed it beneath his flared nostrils and squinted at Jack. "I worked with you before, didn't I?"

"No."

"I must have. I been in this business exactly thirty-six years about. I worked with everybody."

"Not him. He's a friend of Tucker's," Nichols said. "He's the new art director."

"What happened to Liebermann?"

"Got freaked out by the A-rabs. Claimed it was no place for a nice Jewish boy."

"Me, I work anywhere." Schwarz lit the cigar. "Numbers are the same all over the world; accounting's the international language. Am I right? I did pictures in Iran, in Turkey, in Tunisia, in a couple of Mickey Mouse countries I forget. What's the big deal about Maliteta?"

"No big deal. It's just at this rate we're never going to get there."

"We should have shot in Arizona," Tallow said. "I know the perfect place near Tucson."

"Why don't we do it here," Nichols said, "and call it *Marrakech-22?*"

Schwarz made as if to brand him with his cigar. "Don't even joke to me about *Catch-22*. You got any idea how far over budget it came in at?"

"What's a few million to you? It's not out of your pocket."

"It is if I can't account for it."

"Fat fucking chance of that. Just once in my life I'd like to find a pussy as tight as your budgets."

The discussion circled dizzily through the afternoon, growing listless and slurred after a few more rounds. Jack said little and for long periods didn't listen, but he didn't get up and leave either. Some of what they said was corrosively funny, much of it was foul and stupid, but all of it was better, he believed, than silence. Although he knew he was just killing time he had no delusion that the hours would be less dead if he were thinking about David and Sybil or fretting about himself.

They returned to the airport at dusk, boarding a Caravelle identical to the one they had arrived on. The single difference was that Air Maliteta had replaced the stewardesses with stewards—friendly inefficient black men who resembled gas company employees in their baggy gray uniforms.

East of the High Atlas Mountains they flew into night and were soon over the Sahara. Although they couldn't see the desert, they could feel it as the jet shuddered from one trough of clear-air turbulence to the next. The captain advised them to keep their seat belts fastened, and while all around him people gripped the armrests, Phil clung to his gold cross. Finally he asked Jack to switch to the window seat.

"What's out there?" Jack said.

"Nothing. I've never seen so much nothing."

Flicking on his reading light, Jack finished *Terms of Peace*. The last scene had been rewritten, but the original draft remained in the folder.

In the first version an idealistic Peace Corps volunteer (Barry) met and fell in love with a fashion model (Lisa) who had come to Maliteta with her friend and agent (Helen) on assignment for *Vogue*. When the lovers discussed marriage, the Idealist sadly discovered that the Fashion Model expected him to abandon his unspecified humanitarian project and live with her in New York City. Breaking off the romance, he claimed he'd always care for her, but drove back to his post in the remote Sahara.

In the revised version the Fashion Model told the Idealist she wanted to help him with his work and she thought she could do this best by accepting an occasional modeling assignment to raise cash for the project. Dedicating themselves to one another and to humanity, they set off by jeep for a honeymoon at his post in the remote Sahara.

Jack was tired, and the drinks, the bumpy flight, and the script had left him feeling queasy. He didn't bother asking himself why he and the others were traveling such a great distance to film this witless story. He had his reasons and assumed they had theirs. But he did wonder about Tucker and believed he knew now why his friend was in a perpetual sweat. He must indeed have been desperate if he had clutched this frail reed and expected it to keep him afloat.

He wished he could explain to Tucker the advantages of letting go. It dried you up. You didn't need to cling to a gold cross. You could gaze into the desert night and experience no desire to fill the darkness with consoling shapes or the illusions of light.

When the Caravelle stopped pitching and yawing, some passengers clicked their seats back and slept. Jack stayed awake and felt the plane bank and cut its power. Then he noticed lights at the landing strip in Tougla. A double strand of orange dots against the immensity of desert, they appeared to be no larger, no brighter than rows of glowing cigarettes. But the plane made a smooth descent and touched down so gently the sleepers didn't stir.

At the far end of the runway, the pilot swung around and taxied toward the terminal, announcing that they had arrived in Tougla, asking them to remain seated, thanking them for flying Air— His voice broke when he saw what Jack had seen.

A red stripe flared from the darkness like a match struck against the flat slate of sky. Arching over the nose of the Caravelle, it was followed by a second spurt of flame. "A welcoming committee. They're shooting off fireworks," Nichols said an instant before they heard two distinct explosions. Waves of aftershock rocked the plane.

The engines shrieked in acceleration, snapping everybody upright, then slamming them back in their seats. The overhead lights went out, but the intercom was on and the captain screamed in Arabic at the co-pilot, the tower, somebody. At the speed they were going, Jack thought he intended to take off, but they thundered from the runway onto hard-packed sand. Gravel torn up by the tires rattled against the fuselage. Over the whine of the jets and the outcry of the crew, Jack heard a third explosion and felt the plane go into a skid, wobbling on its undercarriage, the wings nearly scraping ground. He knew the fuel tanks were in the wings and if they cracked, the Caravelle would erupt in flames.

Struggling to his feet, Tucker hauled himself from seat to seat to the cockpit door and was pounding on it, shouting. But no one opened it, not even after the plane had shuddered to a halt and the engines died.

"What the hell was that?" Nichols screamed.

"Somebody shot at us."

"Those were rockets, not bullets," said Phil, scrambling out of his seat.

"Quiet," Tucker shouted. "Everybody calm down and keep quiet."

"I'm getting the fuck off this crate before it blows up."

"Stay in your seats," Tucker said. "Where are the stewards?"

"One's here on the floor."

"Ask him what to do."

Jack started to translate, but the steward panicked, got to his feet, and ran to the rear. Before anyone could stop him, he had opened the hatch and clattered down the staircase into darkness.

Several French crew members clambered into the aisle and looked as if they might follow the steward. But Phil rushed back, unholstering his pistol. "Shut that door. Don't go out there."

Jack released his seat belt and looked out the window. Suddenly he was as flushed and damp as Tucker. He might have ceased to care about certain things, but he wasn't ready to die. Not here, he thought, not like this, for no reason.

"Who knows how to shut this thing?" Phil kept shouting.

Tucker continued pounding the cabin door until someone let him in.

Jack saw flashes of light—bright flickering red blips—before he heard the gunfire and realized what it was. When it hit, it didn't sound much different than the gravel had, but slugs punctured the fuselage, ripping out wads of paneling and upholstery.

"Get down," someone hollered, and Lisa, Helen, and Jack fell tangled in the aisle.

Then there was shooting inside the Caravelle. Stretched out on his stomach, Phil fired down the staircase, spacing his rounds, not wasting any shots. "Tell them to start the engines," he hollered.

When he saw nobody else moving, Jack crawled over the heaped bodies to the cabin.

"They're coming up the back steps," he told Tucker. "Phil says start the engines."

The pilot revved the jets, and this set off a roiling sandstorm outside. Then he eased the plane forward, trundling over the desert, dragging the rear staircase. After a few minutes he brought the Caravelle to a stop but kept the engines on.

Jack fumbled his way back up the aisle and huddled where he had been before. He could no longer hear gunfire. Even when the engines died, he heard nothing until Phil said, "Stay down. Everybody just stay flat."

Now Jack thought the hammering of his heart had to have been audible. He heard Helen breathing and felt the warmth on his neck. In the cabin the pilot was whispering in Arabic.

Finally Tucker said, "Okay. Everything's all right." He tried to make his voice firm, commanding, but it had a quaver that kept it from being altogether reassuring.

Slowly they unpiled. Jack pulled Helen and Lisa to their feet. There were a few bruises and scrapes; nobody had been wounded. But several women started crying and some men angrily demanded what the hell was going on.

"Take it easy," Tucker said. "We'll have you off here in a few minutes. The Malitetans think they got everybody. But we'll sit tight till they're sure."

"Then what?"

"Then we'll go to the hotel and start making a movie tomorrow morning."

"After almost getting killed?" It sounded like Barry Travis.

"Come on now," he pleaded, his beefy shoulders silhouetted by a bluish glow from the cockpit panel. "I know you're upset. You got a right to be. But a thing like this, it could happen anywhere."

"Right," said Schwarz. "You shoulda seen last summer at the Athens airport. Three dingbats with grenades—"

"Tell us later, Joel—after we've all had a drink and a night's sleep."

"This's going to make a sensational story," Nichols said. "You can't buy this kind of publicity."

"That's another thing." Tucker's voice was nearly conversational now. "I think we better keep this to ourselves. Publicity's liable to encourage some other nut group to take a shot at us."

"You mean these mad bombers read *Variety?* This could be the lift-off we need."

"The answer's no, Nichols. The insurance company gets wind of this and decides the country's unstable, they'll cancel the picture."

The Caravelle rumbled onto the asphalt and over to the terminal where every window in the small cinder block building had been blown out. Dozens of soldiers stood around watching one old man in a djellaba work at the mess with a broom made of twigs tied to a stick. As he swept up splinters of glass, wind carried in sand and sent it swirling across the bare cement.

Climbing off the plane, Jack didn't feel steady on his feet. The staircase trembled in the wind and the aluminum handrail was like a tube of ice. He expected to see his breath, but the air must have been too dry. Even on firm ground he felt unsure of his footing and wanted to sit down.

The terminal was stark and brightly lit. There were concrete benches—more like low shelves—jutting out from the unpainted walls, and a single unattended ticket counter. A sign in French and Arabic indicated the control tower was upstairs, but it didn't appear to be occupied. Then Jack noticed that the walls, as well as the slivers of glass on the floor, were flecked with blood. The wounded had already been carried off.

Tucker came up to Jack and stood with his back to the wind, his beard and hair fanning out in a silvery mandala. "There's supposed to be a reception committee. And cars. I'd like to get out of here quick."

They went over to the ticket counter where Helen had huddled with Barry, Lisa, and her entourage. Sand swarmed over them, needling their skin.

Roberta was irate. "It'll take all night to shampoo her hair. Where the hell are the limos?"

Phil's flat gray eyes swept over the room. "What I want to know is where's that steward? What happened to him?"

No one else appeared to care. They stared ahead blankly, as if

unable to comprehend where they were or what they had survived to get here.

Wind had flattened Helen's loose, pastel dress against her
body, and she was shivering. Jack offered his coat.

"Now you'll freeze," she said.

"No chance. It's colder than this in my studio." As he bundled
the corduroy jacket around her shoulders, he was shaking, but it
wasn't from the cold.

Finally a line of automobiles pulled up to the terminal and
three men got out of the lead car and made an entrance that
might have been arranged according to diplomatic protocol. A
short black man in an army uniform was first, followed at a careful distance by a tall pale American in a blue cord suit, then by a
swarthy young fellow who wore a burnoose over Levi's.

The soldiers braced for a moment, then began helping the old
man sweep up the blood-spattered glass, using their rifle butts
as brooms. The American whispered to the black man, who
marched over to Tucker, one plump hand outstretched. Because
he had tribal cicatrices on his cheeks, his smile seemed exaggerated, painful.

"Welcome, Mr. Garland." He spoke with a faint British accent
and, after shaking Tucker's hand, kissed his own fingers and
touched them to his heart. "Please forgive this trouble caused by
a few *fellaghas*. They have been captured and will be punished."

The American stepped in, a little late. "Minister Benhima, I'd
like to present Tucker Garland. Mr. Garland, this is the Minister
of Culture, Information, and Art. I'm Reid Gorman. From the
Embassy in Moburka."

The Minister flourished his hand, gesturing to the bushy-
haired fellow in the burnoose. "Moha Sefrou. He is with our National Cinema Institute."

"Hey, look," Roberta broke in, "where are those limos we
talked about?"

Benhima pointed through a jagged window space. "The cars
are there."

"Terrif! You mind if we cut this short before all her ends
split?"

Benhima needed an interpreter now, but when nobody volun-
teered, he made a small bow to Roberta. "Not at all."

Protocol completely rearranged, Lisa led the way to the cars with Roberta holding onto her hair as if it were a wig in danger of being blown off. Phil covered their exit. Then Benhima went out with Tucker, followed by Gorman and Barry Travis.

"We're definitely on the B list," Nichols said as he, Helen, Moha, and Jack hurried down the line of Peugeots and Mercedes. The film crew had broken protocol, too, ignored Marvin Tallow's threats, and raced the creative types for the cars, which had coats of grease smeared on their front ends to prevent sand from eating away the paint and chrome.

They piled into a battered Peugeot, one with a sequin-covered, life-size Hand of Fatma dangling from the rear-view mirror. Helen, who had read so many books about the Sahara, said the amulet was to ward off the evil eye.

"Where was Fatma when we needed her?" Nichols asked.

"She was with you, obviously. No one was hurt." Moha was in the front seat facing the three of them in back.

"None of us," Jack said, "but there was a lot of shooting. Somebody must have been hit. Who were those people trying to blow up the plane?"

Moha turned to speak to the driver, who had his turban wrapped around his face. With only a slit left for his eyes, he looked like a mummy propped up behind the wheel. He shoved the Peugeot into gear and sped off after the other cars, sounding his horn as they crossed the vacant expanse around the airport.

"Who attacked the plane?" Jack repeated, wondering about the delay in Marrakech.

"As the Minister told you, just *fellaghas*."

"What are they?"

"Bandits," Moha said.

"You claiming they meant to rob us?" Nichols asked.

Moha didn't answer.

The asphalt ran straight and flat, but the land on both sides was scalloped with sand dunes as pale as snowdrifts. Some of them curved just beneath the telephone wires, and would have swept over the road if bulldozers hadn't pushed them back each day. Feeling and tasting grit in the air, Jack realized he had been wrong. It was never this cold, this uncomfortable, in his studio.

People in billowing djellabas trudged along beside the asphalt and panicked as the cars approached. Like rabbits on a country lane, they darted to the middle, froze in the high beams, then scooted to safety on the other side.

Leaning on the horn, the driver never slowed down.

"They're really not used to cars." Moha might have meant the driver or the pedestrians.

"What are they doing out here?" Helen asked.

"They live back in the dunes. There are many small oases."

Even when there was no one on the road, the driver kept honking. Moha asked him something, and the answer was frayed as it came through the cloth like a voice from a damaged radio speaker.

"He says he blows the horn because then if he has an accident nobody can blame him." Moha was grinning.

Jack had seen faces like his in Spain—the complexion dark, the eyes dark too, the nose straight and sharp, the hair wiry with copper tints when light struck it.

As the Peugeot emerged from the dunes, it sped toward a tall modern building. One side of it was brightly lit, the other dark. Dust had formed a halo on the bright side.

"The Sidi Mansour," Moha said.

"Where's the town?" Helen asked.

"Behind the hotel. You'll see it tomorrow."

The driver accelerated, scattering a few skeletal dogs that had flattened themselves against the road for the meager heat that must have remained there. At the base of the wall around the hotel, three men squatted close to one another.

"Poor bastards," Nichols said. "Look at them huddling to keep warm."

Moha laughed and was still laughing when they passed through a gate and pulled up at the Sidi Mansour. As the four of them raced through the stinging wind, a bellboy in a white ankle-length tunic, red sash, and red fez opened the door at just the right instant so they didn't have to break stride.

But once inside they stopped dead.

"God, will you get a load of this?" Nichols said. "It's like a set for a science fiction movie."

"A famous French architect designed it," Moha said.

"He must have been on LSD."

The lobby had a glistening black tile floor, white plastic tables, orange and red enamel wall panels, and chairs and couches upholstered in purple velours. Nothing looked native to Maliteta or to anywhere else in Africa—especially not the clerk at the reception desk, who wore a pin-striped suit with wide lapels and bell-bottom trousers. Through Moha he informed them their baggage hadn't arrived; the other movie people were waiting in the bar.

Removing his burnoose and tossing it over one shoulder, Moha led them back through the sci-fi lobby to a keyhole arch that gave onto a set for a dramatically different film. The bar was decorated with examples of indigenous handicrafts—bad examples, Moha said. Layers of overlapping carpets muted the voices of the crew members, who had sprawled on leather poufs and gaudy throw pillows. A low shelf or banquette, like the ones at the airport, ran the length of the wall opposite the bar and was cushioned by mats with intricate designs woven into dyed straw.

Tucker, Benhima, Gorman, and Phil sat around a brass tray that was balanced on a trestle of inlaid wood. Lifting a kettle and letting green steaming liquid flow in a long aerated curve, the Minister poured tea.

Tucker waved for them all to come over, but Moha said he'd wait at the bar.

Reid Gorman and Tucker stood up for Helen; Benhima and Phil were busy in conversation. The Minister had his hat off, and his shaved skull was as shiny black as the visor of his cap.

"Drag over a few hassocks and sit down," Tucker said.

"Not me," Jack said. "I just came to say good night."

"The luggage isn't here yet."

"I'll sleep in the nude," Nichols said. "It was good enough for Marilyn Monroe."

"Have guards been posted for the night?" Helen asked.

Gorman frowned, glancing uneasily at Benhima. But he was preoccupied. Phil had taken the Baretta from his shoulder holster and passed it to the Minister of Culture, Information, and Art, who nodded as he hefted the pistol. "Very nice. Still I prefer a larger caliber." He reached for his own revolver.

"If no one minds, I'll skip target practice and get to bed," Helen said.

As she and Nichols recrossed the room, picking their way around the near-supine bodies, Tucker took Jack's elbow and walked him a few steps away from the table. Jack thought he'd get the truth now about the rocket attack. But Tucker said, "You finish the script?"

"Let's talk about it tomorrow. I'm dead on my feet."

"Okay, first thing in the morning."

"You find out any more about what happened at the airport?"

"Nothing to find out."

"We were five hours behind schedule. How'd they know when we'd get here? And why us?"

Tucker grinned. "I told you I had enemies at the studio."

"You'd be singing a different song if they'd hit us."

"Yeah, and I'd be singing a different song if I'd been born without balls. Why worry about it now? Benhima says they caught them and guarantees it won't happen again. Maliteta doesn't have our hangups about *habeas corpus.*"

"It's your party."

"Right." Tucker swatted him on the shoulder. "Get some sleep and enjoy it."

Helen and Nichols were at the bar, she speaking with Moha, he trying to make himself understood to the bartenders. There were three of them, dressed like the bellboy in white tunics, red sashes and fezzes.

"Meet my new friends," Nichols said to Jack. "They're all named Mohammed. There's Big Mo, Little Mo, and No Mo."

Moha stared at the PR man.

"You're Little Mo, aren't you?" Nichols asked one of them.

"*Comment?*"

"Don't play dumb with me. I named you. I damn well know who you are."

"Hey, Nichols, aren't you ready for bed?" Jack asked.

"You gotta be kidding. Almost getting killed was like a straight shot of meth. I won't sleep for a week."

"I've had it," Helen said wearily. "I'm going up."

They left Nichols and went to the reception desk, where Moha fetched their room keys without waking the clerk, who slept with his head on the switchboard.

The keys were attached to huge brass Hands of Fatma, and Moha said, "You should be well protected against the evil eye."

"It's bullets I'm worried about, but this feels heavy enough to stop one." Jack put it into his breast pocket and pressed the button for the elevator.

"Sorry. That doesn't work." Moha showed them to the staircase and said good night.

"You're not staying here?" Helen asked, puzzled.

The boy laughed, just as he had when they drove past the men at the wall. "See you in the morning, *in sh'Allah*."

Since the stair-well lights didn't work either, they stumbled around and bumped into a few walls before finding Jack's room on the fourth floor.

"Guess I've got the penthouse," Helen said.

"I'll walk you up." He went to take her arm, but she seemed to pull back. In the dark it was difficult to tell what she had done, but suddenly she was two steps ahead of him. Irritated a little and determined to show he was being polite, not making a pass, he caught up with her.

The Hand of Fatma clanked against the door. Reaching into the room, Helen switched on a light and shrugged his coat from her shoulders.

"Thanks, Jack." She gave him her firm dry hand. "Good night."

"I've never seen so much handshaking."

"I think it's nice." Kissing her fingers, she touched them to her heart.

Then the door closed and the hall went black and he had to take his time going downstairs. But once he was inside his room and had flicked the lights on he realized he could have found his way around blindfolded. It was as if a Holiday Inn had been crated and transported intact from Interstate, U.S.A., to Tougla, Maliteta. There were two single beds with blue spreads, a chair upholstered in the same material, and a blond wood-grain desk that rang metallically when he rapped it with his knuckle.

Jack put on his jacket and pushed up the thermostat. In the bathroom, water the color of cinnamon spurted from the faucet. He splashed his face, searched in vain for a bar of soap, and left a grimy smudge on the towel. Even under his clothes, his skin was prickly with grit. He wanted to shower, but the room was still too cold.

He checked the thermostat; the heat didn't rush on no matter how high he shoved the register. Swinging his arms, he paced from wall to wall. But this was stupid, he thought, to freeze in the Sahara.

Dialing the reception desk, he woke up the clerk.

"Is the heating system broken?" Jack asked in French.

"Not at all. It works very well."

"Not in my room it doesn't."

"Of course not now. It is turned off at night when people are asleep."

"It's too cold to sleep."

"It will come on during the day, monsieur."

"When it's hot."

"*Oui, monsieur.*"

He considered returning to the bar and numbing himself with scotch. But after a long day with them he needed a break from the movie people, whose high spirits and low humor didn't vary regardless of the hour or the location. By now even the airport attack might have turned into just another joke.

He had never met so many people who seemed to be on stage every waking hour. And the role they were all playing appeared to be a caricature of themselves. At least he hoped it was; he liked to believe if he took the time, if he got closer to them, he would discover where the performance stopped and the real person began. But in his present mood he doubted he'd make the effort. He'd do his job, take the money, and keep his distance.

Pacing again, he wished he had suitcases to unpack, a book or magazine to stare at, anything to divert him. Though exhausted, he was still on edge and knew he wouldn't sleep for a long while. For months he had suffered this anxiety every night—the fear of confronting where he was and what had happened.

Behind burlap drapes, a sliding glass door opened onto a balcony. Jack stepped outside, and what he saw was more disconcertingly familiar than the room. If the hotel was America on the road, then the balcony took him off the main route, back where he'd started. Now that the wind had diminished and the dust had died down, a full moon lit the desert exactly as it did around Odessa, Texas, where he had been raised.

It wasn't the sort of sight that warmed him with nostalgia and he had turned to go in when he heard some commotion below in the garden. The sound of scraping and gobbling carried clearly on the dry air; Jack thought it was a dog pawing in a garbage can. But then a guttural voice shouted in Arabic, and the can clattered onto its side and rattled over concrete.

Two men raced out of the shadows, past the swimming pool. The one in the lead jumped and pulled himself to the top of the wall and fell into darkness. The other stopped, stood watching a few moments, then walked back to the hotel.

Jack went to the phone to call down and find out what was going on. But then remembering his circular conversation with the desk clerk, he dropped the receiver back onto its cradle. Whatever the trouble, he decided, someone else would have to take care of it.

CHAPTER III

Loud caterwauling shook Jack out of a troubled sleep and he lay paralyzed in the dark, shivering, his head thudding from pain. He had had a nightmare that David had fallen from his crib and hurt himself and was sobbing for Sybil or him to come help. But Jack didn't know the way; couldn't move; was useless from the neck down. During the night, as the temperature dropped, he had dragged the spread and blankets off the other bed, and their weight had him pinned on his back, his arms strait-jacketed to his sides.

As the caterwauling continued, he recognized the cry of a muezzin. Or rather the recording of a muezzin. The needle had stuck and a shrill voice kept repeating the same phrase as if in a dream in which past mistakes are replayed with obsessive clarity. Finally someone raked the needle from its dusty groove.

The dense silence could have induced the same panic the noise had. He might have been struck deaf. Or the world, not his hearing, might have disappeared. But then a dull drone started —a fly trapped between the burlap drapes and the glass door to the balcony. Pivoting his head slowly on the pillow he saw gold leaf around the edges of the curtain and thin glowing wires of light that penetrated the loose-woven fabric.

Jack got up and rushed through the cold room, yanked open the drapes, and let in an oblong of orange light. Then he danced beyond the patch of warmth, grabbed his clothes, and scurried back, reminded of winter mornings as a kid when he had huddled over the heating grate to dress for school.

But when he looked out, Maliteta no longer called to mind Odessa. There were no roads, no trailer camps and motor courts, no drive-in restaurants. Just a wind-scoured plain, then the tall dunes tufted with esparto grass.

From the balcony he gazed down at the lush grounds of the Sidi Mansour. Rows of date palms canopied orange, lemon, and almond trees, and along the wall hibiscus and bougainvillea had bloomed. While mist rose from the swimming pool, arabesques of sand swirled over a tennis court.

A man in a burnoose ambled out of the dunes. He stopped at the hotel wall, squatted a few minutes, then scuffed a little sand behind him and set off for town. Now Jack knew why Moha had laughed last night. He almost laughed himself.

When he called down for breakfast, two bellboys dressed like acolytes came up, one carrying a tray of croissants and coffee, the other his suitcases. Jack hadn't changed any traveler's checks, but the boys indicated they'd be happy if he tipped them each a ball-point pen.

After three cups of coffee his headache eased, and he felt curiously tranquil and drowsy and was tempted to go back to bed. But somewhere in the building a cassette recorder burst on as loud as the muezzin's call—Lou Reed was wailing "Satellite of Love"—and Jack went upstairs to Tucker's room.

Marvin Tallow answered the door. "Where the hell you been?"

"Out buying a newspaper."

"This is no joke. We been waiting for you."

"You should have called."

"Couldn't. Tucker's on the phone to the Coast. Come on in and lemme close the door. He can't hear over that racket."

"Why don't you tell them to turn it down?"

"It's Barry Travis. You don't tell a star to do anything. You hint. I hinted already."

Tucker had two adjoining rooms, and Jack could hear him in the other one, speaking in flat, hard tones devoid of his Texas accent. "That's bullshit. Before we got into bed on this deal Peter agreed to two-fifty and a hundred deferred. No, no, nothing that's popped at Paramount has any bearing. Okay, try to get him to take points against net. He doesn't deserve gross."

Tallow and Jack gazed out at the desert, which had started to wriggle with heat at the horizon. Although it was cool indoors, the production manager grabbed a napkin from a breakfast tray, blotting his flushed cheeks. "Tucker wants you to scout around town with this local gofer—Mojoe or whatever the hell his name is."

"Moha?"

"Yeah, the kid with the Brillo-pad hair. Then finish those sketches for the first setups toot sweet."

Tucker called them into the next room where the beds and bureau had been removed and a desk, a filing cabinet, and a photocopy machine had been brought in. Between a refrigerator and a hot plate on which a pot of coffee was perking, a big wooden shooting board leaned against the wall, its purpose to forecast the schedule and reflect day-to-day progress.

Bundled up in a sheepskin parka, Tucker sat with his boots on the desk, shuffling through a stack of photographs. "Morning, bubba."

"Open the windows. It's warmer outside."

"Dust'll get all over the glossies." He turned to Tallow. "Have you cut a deal to have the hotel cater our meals on set?"

"Not yet."

"Not yet? What's more important, Marvin?"

"I gotta get the elevator fixed and do something about the hall lights and make damn sure there's heat at night. You know, nothing ruins morale on location quicker than lousy living conditions. These creative types, they won't do their best work unless you give them first-class treatment."

"Is that true, bubba?"

"Sure. Just think of Van Gogh. He always flew first class."

"Better get busy then, Marvin. We wouldn't want anybody to be the least bit uncomfortable."

When Jack and he were alone, Tucker whispered, "Jee-zus!" and grabbed his beard with both hands as if to yank it out at the roots. "Sometimes this petty bullshit and these assholes I work with are more than I can bear. I should go back to Texas and raise pigs."

He slid the glossies over to Jack. "Here are some snapshots Liebermann took. Glance through them and get an idea where he planned to set up. Then go check the places out. Maybe you can find better ones."

As Jack was flipping through the photographs, Tucker said, "What'd you think of the script?"

He avoided Tucker's eyes, uncertain what to say. "Well, it's the first one I ever read."

"That so? How'd it hit you?"

"Hard as hell to read, aren't they? I mean just the way they're laid out."

"You get the hang of it. What you saw, of course, is the bare bones. Somebody has to pack meat on the skeleton. The first director I worked with used to say a script is a very simple machine. You have to plant a hook early"—Tucker crooked his index finger—"tie a rubber band to it and stretch it and stretch it"—as he drew his other hand away from the imaginary hook, he appeared to strain mightily—"until *bam!* You reach the climax and the rubber band snaps."

"I missed that a little in *Terms of Peace*—that feeling of tension."

"Yes." The word didn't suggest agreement. It was a question, an invitation to continue.

"After the Peace Corps volunteer and the fashion model fall in love, maybe there should be something more complicated, more suspenseful, between the early scenes and the ending— whichever one you decide to go with."

"Yes?" Leaning his meaty shoulders forward, placing his small, soft hands flat on the desk, Tucker wore an expression Jack had often noticed when his students were searching for a handle to a difficult subject. As always, he didn't care to lecture.

"I feel like an ass passing myself off as an expert. I know a lot'll depend on how you film it."

"And on the continuity sketches you do."

He took this as an excuse to turn back to the photographs.

"The actors and I, we're working together," Tucker said. "We should be able to hammer out a lot of the rough spots and tighten up the story line."

"Good."

"Look, bubba, is something bothering you? Get it out front."

Although Tucker wore that same eager, attentive expression, Jack felt he was the student now, the one being quizzed. "I was curious why there were so many scenes of planes landing and taking off."

"Oh, that." He smiled. "That's a deal we cut with Air Maliteta. They agreed to fly the cast and crew and equipment from Marrakech to Tougla for free if we'd include a few minutes of footage showing their planes. You have any idea how much dough we're saving?"

Jack didn't. He also wouldn't admit how much those interludes had reminded him of TV commercials.

"Anything else?" Tucker pressed him. "Throw them hard and straight."

He felt trapped. Much as he wanted to help, he feared the truth would hurt Tucker—and cost him a job he couldn't afford to lose. Whatever he said was bound to be wrong, he thought. But silence had its risks too.

Irritated, Tucker shoved back from the desk and unbuttoned his coat. "Okay, you don't have to say it. As it stands, the script's a piece of shit."

"That's not what I—"

"Doesn't matter. Like I told you, we'll be revising as we go along, and it's gotta be shot and edited. Who the hell knows what it'll look like then? And I won't bullshit you, it's flat better to be working than to be sitting on my ass worrying whether I'll ever get another project."

"I understand," Jack said.

"Do you? I doubt it." Tucker's voice was blunt, pugnacious.

"I know what it's like not to be able to work. And I know what I'm willing to trade for a chance to do what I want."

"Yeah, well, in this business you're free to do what you want twice—at the start and near the finish. But if you screw up your first chance, you gotta eat a mile of shit to get a second one. That's what I'm doing now."

"I know the feeling."

"Maybe you do. Still, I got a problem you don't have. You get the itch to paint, you just need canvas and a couple of brushes. Spend a few bucks and you're set. Even if nobody buys the stuff, never even sees it, you can take some satisfaction doing what you want.

"But me, any director, he can't move until somebody lets him have a million dollars. And to get that kind of money, he's gotta turn a lot of tricks. Okay, maybe Altman or some of these Europeans can keep working without doing a damn thing at the box office, but not your friend Tucker. Believe me, I have the same feeling about shooting film you do about painting, and it eats at me all the time. I read scripts, I bug my agent, I screen old movies and imagine what I'd do with the same material. But I'm fucking helpless until a studio or independent puts up the cash and tells me what movie they'll let me make. This time it's *Terms of Peace*. Who knows why they picked it? Maybe they hope it bombs and they'll get a tax write-off. Don't laugh. It's happened to me before."

"Sorry."

"No use being sorry. That's just the way things are. The point is, I've gotta stay alive, stay in the game. Then maybe someday I'll be able to do what I want." As the defiance ebbed from his voice, he pulled closer to the desk, closer to Jack, appealing to him.

"You see, bubba, I been fooling around with an original screen play. Taking my time, really polishing it. Once I find a way to bankroll it, I plan to step back from this whole business and get shut of all the charlatans and dirtbags in it. Kind of purify myself. Because I want this one to be better than I am. That's what I finally realized. If I hope to do anything worth a damn, I've gotta get clean out of myself and connect with something much bigger. Know what I mean?"

"I think so."

"Sure you do. You're stretching for the same thing, aren't you?"

The direct appeal was there again, and Jack found it difficult to sidestep. As he had admitted, he knew the feeling. "I suppose I am." He gathered the photographs into a folder. "I'll have the opening scene sketches for you soon as I can. And about the script, I—"

"Forget it. Catch you later."

Without windows, the staircase was dark even during the day, and he had to feel his way down the railing to the lobby where

Moha was at the reception desk translating for Tallow, who was bellowing at the hotel manager.

"Ask him what's wrong with the elevator."

"It's broken."

"I know it's broken. Why?"

The manager's response was long and, judging by his gestures, complicated. "He says the elevator hasn't worked since the air conditioner was installed."

"You mean this joint has air conditioning?"

"Yes, but it doesn't work. The pipes and ducts were installed in the elevator shaft."

"Tell him to call the contractor and have it fixed."

"The contractor has been in prison since the last coup."

"Jesus Christ, tell the guy to at least get some goddamn light bulbs for the hallways so we don't all break our necks." Mopping his face with his sleeve, Tallow headed for the bar.

"Somebody better warn Mr. Tallow to calm down," Moha said. "In this weather he'll become sick." Wearing a red checkered cowboy shirt and Levi's, Moha could have passed as a student on any campus in the States. But he spoke with a faint accent and his words, too precisely enunciated, broke into unfamiliar stress patterns.

Jack opened the folder to a photograph of a restaurant. "I'd like to see this place."

"Yes. That's the Chems."

At the hotel door they met Helen Soray and Reid Gorman coming in. He was dressed in a three-piece suit; she wore a black bathing suit with a yellow terry cloth robe over her shoulders. Her short hair was wet, her face was ruddy from exertion, and her long tan legs flexed nicely at the thigh. Next to her color and vibrancy, Gorman appeared to droop like a hothouse asparagus.

"She swam thirty laps," he said. "I counted. She's in marvelous shape."

"You should try it," she told Jack.

"Are you suggesting I'm not in marvelous shape?"

"Not at all. I—"

"I'm afraid the pool isn't very clean," Gorman cut in.

"Cleaner than what comes out of the tap. My bath was orange

last night." Helen scrubbed at her hair with a towel. "Wish I had my horse. I'd love to go out in the dunes."

"I could borrow the Minister's Land Rover," Gorman said.

"See you guys around. I've got to dress for a make-up test."

When she was out of earshot Gorman said, "Terrific woman. Do you suppose what they say about her is true?"

Despite himself, Jack asked, "What do they say?"

Gorman grinned. "I was hoping you'd tell me." Then, spotting Hal Nichols, he crossed the lobby, perhaps thinking the PR man would know.

In the garden workmen stood knee deep in muddy ditches, swinging mattocks, clearing silt and leaves from a web of irrigation canals. When Moha spoke to them, they answered in unison and bowed to Jack.

Although the Sidi Mansour might have been built to the same blueprint as hotels in Miami Beach, it retained a few Arabic flourishes. On the exterior walls of the bottom floor a motif adapted from a native carpet design had been molded into the concrete. But sparrows and starlings had nested in the filigreed recesses, leaving streaks of mud and birdshit. Protective nets had been stretched over the walls and now dozens of birds dangled from it, some still screeching and beating their wings.

"Christ, they should tear that down," Jack said.

Moha seemed embarrassed. "I'll talk to the Minister."

Outside the eastern gate stood a billboard picture of a black man in uniform with tinted glasses and scarred cheeks. A scrawl of Arabic characters appeared to prop up his double chin.

"The President," Moha said.

"What's he have to say?"

"Unity and sacrifice are the first steps to national strength."

"Do folks here buy that ticket?"

"It's hard to know." Moha kept his eyes on the long whips of wind-blown sand that slithered over the asphalt. "Not many people in Tougla can read. And we speak a different dialect from the population south of the Kimoun River."

"I take it the President is from the south?"

"Yes."

"And Minister Benhima?"

The boy gave a small grin. "Are you with the CIA, Mr. Cordell?"

"The name's Jack. I wish I was drawing a steady salary from somewhere, but the CIA hasn't contacted me."

"Keep asking questions and someone will."

"Just taking an interest in local politics."

"Most people here believe it is better to keep their interests to themselves. That way, there is no danger of a misunderstanding." Then, to make sure there hadn't already been one, he said, "I don't mean to be rude. But these questions, they're not for me to answer."

They walked awhile in silence, the heat coming at them from two directions—falling from above, then rebounding off the road. Jack felt his hair baking, the soles of his feet burning.

"You should have worn a hat," Moha said. "The sun will make you sick."

"Don't worry. I won't melt like Marvin Tallow. The weather's about like this where I grew up in Texas."

"Yes, Texas. I've been there on a Greyhound bus. It broke down in a village called Pecos. Very warm."

"When was this?"

"A few years ago. I was on the way to Los Angeles. The government sent me to the University of Southern California. I lived on Hoover Street. A very nice apartment building called the Casa Real. Do you know it?"

"Never been to LA. Never been farther west than El Paso."

"But where do you live?" Moha was puzzled.

"France for the past year. Always in Texas before that."

"Do you find much film work there?"

"I'm not in the movie business, Moha. Tucker's an old friend, and he asked me to fill in as art director. What about you? Find much film work in Maliteta?"

"The government has just started a cinema institute in Moburka. They hope companies from Europe and America will shoot here."

"Any luck?"

"You're the first."

"Kind of unusual, isn't it, a country like Maliteta trying to attract film makers?"

"Not really. For a poor country, it means money. But even rich Moslem countries are investing in movies. They believe it gives them a modern image and encourages tourism."

Next to the road lay a shriveled cow carcass. It looked like a toy animal that had been deflated. The eye sockets were empty, the dusty hide had shrunk over a xylophone of bones. Surprisingly there was no stench.

"A car hit it?" Jack asked.

"It was very dry this winter." The boy was embarrassed again, flustered. "Or maybe it was diseased. Yes, otherwise it would have been eaten. I'll tell the Minister. He'll have it taken away."

"Doesn't bother me."

"Somebody should have buried it weeks ago."

"Don't worry about it. Tell me about going to school in the States."

"Well, the government wanted me to be an engineer. After the first year, I switched to film. I didn't tell anybody at the Education Council, and there was some trouble when I got back. But I told them I could make a bigger contribution through movies. Anybody can build hotels and roads and bridges, but I can show the country to the world and to itself. Now that we're all one people here, that's more important. Don't you agree?"

"Sure."

Jack wondered how old the boy was. He looked to be in his mid-twenties at most, but he sounded younger. These days he seldom heard his own students, even the callowest freshman, speak with Moha's earnestness. That was more the way he and Tucker and their dreamy, naïve classmates might have sounded in the late fifties.

"I'd like to see your films."

Moha squashed a beetle that was scuttling across the road. It made a dry popping sound. "They haven't been released for the public."

"Maybe we could arrange a private screening."

"The Minister has the prints."

"I'm sure he'd let us see them if we asked."

"No, don't do that." For an instant his voice got away from him.

"Hey, I promise not to pass any information about you to the CIA."

That coaxed a smile from Moha, but he said, "Please don't mention this to the Minister."

Tougla was divided into two towns—a small European quarter and a sprawling walled medina. The European quarter had once been a replica of a French provincial city with half a dozen boulevards lined by cafés and shops. Now it looked bombed out, reduced to rubble and dust. Only a few buildings were open for business—a bank, the Syndicat d'Initiative, and a general store decorated with strands of Christmas tree ornaments.

Moha and Jack stayed on the shady side of the street where men in boobas and djellabas walked hand in hand, chewing sunflower seeds, spitting out papery shells. There were no women around.

They passed a Catholic church, its double doors padlocked, all the windows boarded up. The sidewalk out front was an obstacle course of beggars, of the old, the ill, and the malformed. Jack still had no money, and doubted they would be satisfied with a Bic pen as the bellboys had been.

While a brigade of workers with shovels and buckets hauled away sand that had streamed into the city during the night, a tank truck rumbled along behind them, watering newly planted acacia and tamarisk trees. The sight of these men moving through dust-laden light in something like slow motion left Jack slightly dazed.

Moha led him down an alley toward the medina, and once they had gone through a gate, Jack had the impression they were indoors, exploring a huge rambling house. The streets were no wider than hallways, and the ceiling of reeds let in just enough light for him to see old men lounging on low benches.

The hallway became a staircase, and they climbed to a roomlike square with a beehive oven and a communal well that was locked. Women sat leaning against it, braiding camel bridles, the skeins of yarn stretched between their henna-dyed hands and bare toes. Veiled from the bridge of the nose down, they had kohl-rimmed eyelids that gave them the intense gaze of icons.

"Wait," Jack said. "I want to take a closer look. There are scenes we should shoot here."

"The light's bad."

"We could bring in spotlights."

"The Minister won't let you film these places. He thinks they make a bad impression. They don't fit in with a modern image."

"If Tucker wanted a modern image, he'd have stayed home."

"I'm just warning you what the Minister will say. Come, I'll show you where he'll let you shoot."

As they went on through the warren of alleys, past blank walls and passageways that disappeared into darkness, Jack thought it might be difficult to capture the texture of the place on camera. But, God, how he would have loved to paint it. The medina seemed to him a surrealistic canvas brought to life—the illumination eerie, distances distorted, every random glimpse into the houses suggestive of some mystery only a Max Ernst or Di Chirico could decipher.

In a large square surrounded by arcades, vendors sold fly-ridden meat, secondhand clothes, herbs and amulets, and odds and ends of used household equipment. The market, like the medina, looked to Jack as if it might have been designed with an eye for aesthetic effect—for what the movie people called "visual impact and production value." But it didn't require much acuity to see beyond the illusion of abundance. Most grain bins were empty, the spice bowls low. There were hands of bananas, but the fruit was the size of bony fingers. Outside the butcher stall camel heads hung from hooks, sprigs of parsley stuck in their nostrils.

"Do they really eat them?"

"Why not?" Moha said. "You will too at the Sidi Mansour."

"No. Our supplies are flown in from London."

The next stop had a few boxes of freshly picked dates and barrels full of coagulated mash crawling with flies.

"Dates are very nutritious," Moha announced, as if reciting a government report. "A man can live on a handful a day."

"Yeah, those flies look fat and happy."

Finding the entrance to the Restaurant Chems locked, Moha lifted and let fall the knocker—a Hand of Fatma holding a metal ball.

"Strange," he said. "They should be serving lunch."

He tried the knocker again.

Finally the door opened and a man filled it from side to side—the first fat person Jack had seen in Maliteta. The jacket of his gabardine suit couldn't be buttoned, and he proudly thrust his belly forward as though it were a chest. He wore a tarboosh too small for his head, and when he smiled he showed a mouth inlaid with gold. Shaking hands with them, he kissed his swollen fingers, then touched his stomach instead of his heart.

The owner escorted them down a dim corridor, through a second door, and into a courtyard that smelled of jasmine. He kicked off his shoes as if entering a mosque, asked them to do the same, and led them across the glazed tile, past a fountain where goldfish flashed through shimmering water. Green sheaves of banana plants flourished in each corner, and there were hanging baskets of bougainvillea and cages of trilling birds.

Though the dining room bore a vague resemblance to the bar at the Sidi Mansour, Jack didn't need to be told what was better about this place. But the fat man stayed at his elbow, talking at top speed, barely pausing for Moha to translate. The carpets and brass trays were antiques, he said. The tiles were all hand-painted faïence. The cedar-beamed ceiling had been carted piece by piece from the High Atlas and carved into bas-reliefs that matched the wall motif.

"He wants to know how much you'll pay per day," Moha said.

"Tell him that's not my department."

"And he says he'd like to play himself in the movie."

"That isn't up to me either. But let him know how much I like his restaurant. I hope the food's as good as the décor."

As Moha translated, the owner's hopeful smile vanished and he took Jack's elbow, talking even faster, pointing to the stained glass windows that let in jeweled light. Then he smacked a big leather cushion and urged them both to sit down.

"He's asking about money again," Moha said. "I think we better go if you're not ready to bargain."

They retreated to the courtyard, then through the corridor, with Moha offering excuses every step of the way. The man made a last stand at the door, holding Jack, haranguing Moha, who no longer bothered to interpret. Breaking free, they let themselves out.

The square felt twenty degrees warmer and, after the jasmine, the smells were overwhelming.

"Did he mention why he wasn't open for lunch?"

Preoccupied, Moha glanced around. "There." He pointed left. "I think that's the best way back."

"I asked a question."

"We'll eat at the hotel."

"Look, what the hell does it take to get a straight answer from you?"

The boy started to speak, then hesitated, hurt by this bluntness. "He said he's out of food."

They walked steadily and didn't talk. After his flash of anger, followed by confusion, Jack suspected the heat was unhinging him. His eyes ached, his tongue thickened, and his throat grated when he swallowed. Emerging from the shade of the medina, he watched a heat mirage undulate between them and the Sidi Mansour. It receded as they set off.

The air was odorless now and once more, just as that morning, he was conscious of the silence. They moved from the scorching asphalt onto the sand. When the ground seemed to ripple in front of him, Jack squeezed his eyes shut, then took another look. Big, dust-covered bugs scurried ahead of his feet.

At the hotel wall, his sense of smell returned, then his hearing as the muezzin called. The workmen climbed out of the irrigation ditch, crouched down, and touched their foreheads to the ground. Inside, the bellboys and the reception clerk had spread burlap bags and bowed their head to the black tile.

Jack stopped, not wanting to interrupt.

"Can you believe this?" Hal Nichols called across the lobby. Tallow, Schwarz, and a few crew members were with him, watching.

"I'll leave you here," Moha whispered to Jack.

"Where are you going?"

"I have something to do."

"You should have sent me back on my own. At least let me buy you lunch."

"They're doing it in the bar too," Nichols said. "Big Mo, Little Mo, and No Mo are in there praying their brains out."

Before he could thank him, the boy left, and Jack went over to them, whispering, "Can't you hold it down?"

"Sure, they look sweet as choirboys now," Tallow said. "But you know what their buddies are doing by the wall? Lisa Austin was on her balcony sun-bathing and what does she see? A couple of A-rabs taking a crap, that's what she sees. This has gotta cease. You don't subject stars to that kind of aggravation and get a good performance."

"I don't know whether to believe her or not," Schwarz said. "She claimed they waved their trouser worms at her, but they'd have to be hung like horses for her to see from the fifth floor."

When the Malitetans were finished praying, the film crew moved into the bar, and Jack had two quick scotch and sodas— the first to soothe his throat, the second to clear his head. The treatment was fifty per cent effective. He satisfied his thirst but couldn't focus his thoughts, which swam with vivid images of the European quarter and the medina, of how fascinating certain spots were to look at and how awful they must be to live in. He ordered a third drink and carried it into the dining room to lunch.

The headwaiter, dressed in a gravy-stained tuxedo, showed them to a table, and the chorus of wisecracks and complaints droned on like the insects that swarmed over the sugar bowl, the utensils, the serving boy's face. Helen Soray, sitting by herself, smiled at Jack. At least he believed she had, and he was about to break away and join her. But Gorman sidled over and took the second chair.

Nichols jerked a thumb at the headwaiter. "You know, that kid's a dead ringer for Jerry Lewis."

"You're out of your mind," Tallow said. "Jerry Lewis has thirty years on him."

"I'm talking about before, back when he was with Dean Martin." Nichols named a film in which Jerry Lewis had played a daffy, hapless waiter. "Hey, you could be Jerry Lewis' double."

The fellow, who was about Moha's age, smiled uncertainly, showing two chipped front teeth.

"Don't you speak English?" Nichols asked.

"I speak very well English. And French. Two summers I

worked in Marseilles in a restaurant where we have American groups."

"You ever get tired of that, just call me and I'll set you up as Jerry Lewis' stand-in."

"I would like to go to America."

"Don't blame you a bit. So would I," Schwarz said. "How about bringing us a bottle of wine, pronto?"

From where Jack sat, he saw the fellow's smile dissolve as he turned and snarled in Arabic at one of the serving boys. When he swung back to the table, his broken-tooth grin reappeared.

After lunch, the climb to the fourth floor was almost as awful as the sun-drugged hike from Tougla to the hotel. Now that it wasn't needed, the heat had rushed on, and Jack's room was an oven. Opening the door to the balcony, he took up his sketch pad and tried to start the restaurant scene, but soon had to put down his pencil.

His hands were shaking, his breathing was shallow and erratic. The heat, the drinks, and the heavy lunch had left him feeling queasy. Yet he knew he was suffering more from what could only be called culture shock. He couldn't decide whether the symptoms were worse when he concentrated on the drawings or when he stared out at the desert.

CHAPTER IV

During the night he was awakened by a skirmish at the garbage cans, and it sounded as though both sides had brought reinforcements. There were metallic clashes, curses and screams, followed by a foot race to the wall. Then silence except for the wind.

When he woke again, he discovered he had forgotten to close the drapes. An orange glare, utterly without warmth, suffused the room. It was pointless to shut them now and try to go back to sleep. Upstairs everybody was awake. Jack heard phones ringing and voices raised in the unmistakable cadences of long-distance speech—sentences crisp and complete, punctuation emphatic.

One thing you could say about these movie people, they stayed in contact. For days in Cannes he had watched them sending and receiving telegrams, placing and accepting international calls, leaving and picking up messages. Of course they could afford to communicate; if they didn't have the money, EPC did. But Jack knew there were other differences between them and him. Having convinced himself he was better off for every letter he didn't answer, for every emotional demand he didn't respond to, he no longer saw the purpose in being in touch.

Swarms of flies showed up an instant after his breakfast tray. Hoping to keep them off him, Jack was setting a dish of jam on the balcony when he noticed the Malitetans gravitating toward the west gate of the Sidi Mansour. Men in djellabas and boobas strolled out of the sand dunes; others in European clothes came from Tougla.

More than a dozen already stood at the wall, careful not to set foot on the hotel grounds. But the new people jostled the crowd from behind and gradually nudged it into the garden, up the sidewalk, halfway to the door. There they stopped and jockeyed for positions, men in European clothes elbowing their way to the front, flinging to the rear the dwarfs and hunchbacks, one fellow on crutches, and two in makeshift wheel chairs that looked more like wheelbarrows.

When Marvin Tallow and the director of photography, Donald Wattle, stepped out of the hotel, the crowd surged forward, engulfing them, hollering in French, Arabic, and mangled English. Somebody grabbed Tallow's shirt sleeve and he pulled back, leaving the man a fistful of yellow cotton. Wattle flailed his arms, fighting to hold his head above the rip tide of close-packed bodies. Every few seconds someone was sent reeling and, finding himself on the fringes with the hunchbacks and cripples, he burrowed back to the center.

Tallow and Wattle were struggling toward the Sidi Mansour, dragging people with them, when Benhima and a soldier sprinted out. Using his fists, the soldier cleared a path for the Minister of Culture, Information, and Art, who fumbled his pistol from its holster and fired twice in the air. Panicking, the crowd broke for the gate, but Benhima fired again and brought them up short.

While Tallow and Wattle stumbled into the lobby, Jack left the balcony and ran downstairs.

"Did you see them? Did you fucking see what they did?" Tallow screamed at Moha and Nichols.

Wattle was bent over, hands on his knees, muttering, "Teddible, teddible." An Englishman with a sparse blond mustache and a purplish complexion, he had a stripe of zinc oxide on his nose. "If Tucker wants misties, he can bloody well hire them himself."

"They're excited," Moha said. "They want jobs, that's all."

"Yeah, well, one of them got so excited he gave me a hickey." Tallow showed the red welt on his neck.

Spotting Jack, Nichols said, "Those guys who missed us at the airport came back for a second chance."

"You think it's so fucking funny, you go out there," Tallow snapped.

"You should have let them come one at a time to your office," Moha said. Then to Jack, "We put out a call for extras. They just want jobs."

"But they'll take blood," Nichols said.

"Two dollars a day is a lot to them," Moha said. "They don't make two hundred a year."

Wattle kept muttering, "Teddible, teddible."

After Benhima had driven the crowd beyond the wall and lectured them for a few minutes, he holstered his pistol, left the soldier standing guard, and returned to the lobby. "You can go out now."

"Damned if I will," Wattle said.

"You're safe. I told them what will happen to the first man who touches you. I'll come with you."

Moha and Jack went too.

Although the crowd had scattered and regrouped, people had maintained roughly the same places. A phalanx of men in cheap European suits and scuffed shoes stood up front. Confident their clothing gave them a great advantage, they smiled and struck poses as though already on camera.

But Wattle and Tallow pushed past them to the ones dressed in boobas and djellabas, sandals and babouches. A light meter in one hand and various lenses in the other, Wattle had regained his composure and worked briskly, wearing the sort of imperturbable expression Jack had noticed on a doctor at a three-car collision. As he moved among them, peering through his lenses, he might have been examining their ravaged eyes and teeth and faces. But of course his only concern was how they would come across on the screen. One or two out of every dozen he sent over to Tallow, who drew up a list of their names with Moha's help.

Wattle even took a perfunctory stroll through the fringes of the crowd where the men were misshapen, mutilated, and wrapped in rags. But he didn't use his lenses now, since to stare into their eyes—they were bloodshot, crossed, blanked out by trachoma, or missing altogether—was to risk having your stomach turned.

"I think we've got enough," Wattle said.

One hand on his holster, sweat sluicing down his scars, Benhima dismissed those who hadn't been hired. A few in European clothes began grumbling, but the Minister shouted and they scurried off.

A man on crutches paused beside Jack and whispered something. Because one side of his jaw was missing, he had trouble forming words, but Jack knew what he wanted.

"Tell him I don't have anything to do with hiring," he said to Moha.

As the boy translated, Jack reached for his wallet, then recalled that he still hadn't changed any traveler's checks.

"Tell him I'm sorry."

"He says he understands," Moha said as the man limped away.

Back in his room, reviewing the sketches he had done yesterday, Jack wasn't sure he understood. When he took the job, he believed he had computed its potential gains and losses, the personal compromises. Now he knew there were trade-offs he hadn't counted on.

Touching up the drawings, trying to inject character into the smooth features of the actors, he thought that, after all the portrait commissions he had done, it was as if he had seen faces for the first time. In Maliteta, people didn't *wear* expressions; they were carved into their flesh. An American or European might disguise his feelings one minute, then reveal them for effect the next. But here the rotting teeth, mashed noses, and ruined eyes couldn't be hidden—and could hide nothing. Everything was hideously clear.

He found he couldn't work, thinking of those men.

Her own hair dry and spiky as a tuft of weeds, Roberta, the hairdresser, answered the door to Lisa Austin's room. "Yeah?"

"I'd like to do a few sketches of Lisa," Jack said. "Just to make sure I know how she sits and stands and carries herself."

"Wait here. I'll ask."

She shut the door on him, and he heard what might have been silk being torn.

Roberta came back. "She says okay."

"So I told Phil to switch the bed around so my head's to the north," Lisa said, "and so, you know, the polar energy flows straight through me."

"Anything else flowing through you these days?" Barry Travis asked.

A pan of molten wax between her knees, Lisa sat spraddle-legged on the floor, wearing a T-shirt and what was either the bottom half of a bikini or a pair of red underpants. Dipping what looked like a tongue depressor into the wax, she slathered it over her thigh, starting at the leg band of her briefs and spreading down. Then she pressed a strip of cloth to the wax, bit her lower lip, and ripped away the cloth. It sounded like adhesive and left a red mark.

"That must hurt like hell." Barry sat opposite her, leaning against the wall, fiddling with the ivory cock ring he wore on a gold chain.

"The price you pay." She glanced at Jack. "I don't have to put on make-up, do I?"

He told her she didn't.

"Just a bra," Barry said, "so you don't bounce."

"Screw you." She tore off another strip of waxed cloth.

When Jack pulled over a chair and opened the sketch pad, both Lisa and Barry sat up straighter, and their faces tightened.

"Just go on talking. Ignore me."

But Lisa picked up a magnifying mirror, shook her hair into place, and held her face this way and that.

"This side's good," she said of the left profile. "The other side, there's something wrong with my nose."

"Hey, Phil, come help me," Roberta called.

He stepped in from the balcony, his jacket off, his holster looking like an orthopedic brace for his shoulders. Lisa was smoothing another strip of cloth over her waxed thigh and when she bit her lip Phil bit his too. But when she ripped the cloth away, he was watching her breasts, not the red stripe on her leg.

"Phil, I'm waiting," Roberta said.

Shoulder harness creaking, he followed her into the adjoining room.

"Why the bodyguard?" Barry asked.

"It's in my contract."

"Because you're working in Maliteta?"

"No, I had one on my last picture too. It was in Oregon."

"You been getting threats?"

"Nothing like that. What it is, you see, after a couple of my films really took off, my agent said it was time to make a few demands. Now I get a personal hairdresser and a bodyguard on top of expenses."

"Maybe I should ask for something." Barry ran the cock ring back and forth on its chain. "I've got a car and driver twenty-four hours a day."

"Me too."

"But there's nowhere to go," he said. "It'd be a groove to have my dune buggy, but by the time they crated it up and shipped it here, we'd be back in the States."

"Too bad. You should have thought of that before."

"How the hell was I to know what this hole would be like? Have you been into town?"

"Haven't left the hotel. I love hotels. I feel at home. Sometimes I go a whole film and never leave the hotel except for the set."

"How about you?" Barry asked Jack.

"I took a walk through it yesterday."

"A real zero, isn't it?"

"A lot of it was interesting, especially back in the medina."

"I wouldn't go there again on a bet. The whole place stinks like the monkey house at the zoo. And the people, my God, they look like they'd slit your throat for a quarter."

When he saw Jack was sketching him, Barry sucked in his cheeks, but his face had the contours of a snowman. A few curved lines sufficed for his profile.

"In town," Lisa said, "were they selling stuff?"

"Nothing you'd want."

"There has to be native jewelry, rugs, that kind of thing."

"Maybe, but how much of that crap can you buy? What I been wondering is how I'm going to get rid of a thousand dollars' worth of *gourdes* every week. Tucker told me we can't take any of our expense money out of the country. And have you looked at it? The bills are so filthy, I wouldn't even snort coke through them."

Roberta returned from the other room with a hypodermic needle. "Lunchtime, baby."

"Oh, Christ, lemme out of here." Barry scrambled to his feet. "Man, I could never be a junkie. Can't stand needles." He turned to a window.

"It hardly hurts at all." Lisa stood up. "You oughta try it. It's the best way to lose weight."

"What is it?" Jack asked.

"Horse piss," Barry said.

"A hormonal extract," Roberta said.

"And the hormones are from horse piss."

"Wherever they're from, what it does for you, it makes you lose weight right where you need to, right where you take the shot." Lisa lowered one side of her briefs, exposing a pink butterfly tattooed to her left buttock.

Roberta shook her head. "Every time I see that, I get sick. It's so trashy."

"Don't be silly. Lyle Tuttle has tattooed everybody in Hollywood. Even Cher has one."

"I don't give a damn. It's tacky and it's trashy." She jabbed the needle into the butterfly, then called Phil who brought in the lunch—a wedge of steak, a salad, and a glass of red wine.

"Christ Almighty," Roberta said, "how many times do I have to tell you—white wine! Always white. Red stains her caps."

While Phil hurried to fetch the white, Jack shut his sketch pad.

"Going?" Lisa asked.

"Yeah. Thanks. I've seen enough."

Still troubled by the thought of those men fighting for jobs, he knocked on Helen Soray's door, and when there was no answer, he left the sketch pad in his room and went down to the lobby to change traveler's checks. Then he drifted toward the dining room. Several crew members brushed by on the way from the bar, and he was considering taking his chances with room service when someone stopped beside him.

"Going in?" It was Helen. She removed her sunglasses and stuffed them into a shoulder bag.

"Haven't made up my mind."

She frowned. "It's so loud."

"I was looking for you," he said. "I'd like to do a few sketches."

"I've been hiding."

"From what?"

"Everybody. Especially that guy from the Embassy."

Jack glanced at the table where Nichols sat. He had grabbed the headwaiter and was introducing him to Gorman, probably going through his Jerry Lewis routine.

"Why does every man in America think he's a comedian?" she asked. "Why don't they go back to imitating Clark Gable or Cary Grant?" She put a hand on his arm. "Let's eat somewhere else."

"The restaurant in town is closed."

"We'll have a picnic."

Stepping over to a sideboard, she picked up a basket of fruit and put in a baguette of bread and a slab of gruyère cheese. "My driver'll take us to one of the oases."

"Let me get my sketch pad."

"No, I don't feel like posing." She started across the lobby, then hesitated. "Sure you want to do this?"

"Yeah. Let's go."

Helen's driver, Ibrahim, had sun-scorched Semitic features and one eye milky from trachoma. When he heard where they wanted to go, he narrowed his good eye and said they should tell Minister Benhima, who would assign a soldier to escort them.

"To hell with that," she said. "I'm not going to have a whole army ruining my picnic."

The road to town writhed with heat and the tires hissed as if on wet asphalt. Pushing the Renault up to seventy-five, Ibrahim spotted a pedestrian half a mile ahead and jammed his hand against the horn.

"Please stop that," Helen said.

He let up on the horn, looking puzzled, hurt. But then he began lecturing like a tour guide about Tougla's former importance on the caravan route to Timbuktu. Jack tore a hunk of bread from the baguette and handed it to him along with a wedge of cheese. That cut the lecture short.

"All my books said the Sahara was a place of 'profound silence,'" she whispered. "I should have remembered who I'd be here with."

"I'm keeping as quiet as I can," Jack said.

"Not you. It's really not Ibrahim either. It's the movie people. They're driving me nuts. Don't they bother you?"

"Not much."

"Oh, they must. All their jabbering is such a bore."

"Well, I admit I don't like a lot of what they say. But I've put up with worse things in my life."

"Name one."

"For five years I taught a summer course in colonial American art and frontier furniture to high school teachers who needed extra credits."

Helen laughed. "Jesus, you poor guy."

"Believe me, I'd much rather be around Barry and Lisa."

"You like Lisa's looks?"

"Nice eyes."

"I just bet that's what you noticed first. They're full of silicone, you know. I met her masseur, and he told me. In confidence, of course."

"She's not my type, anyhow."

"Come on. She's got the perfect nymphet look, the kind that appeals to the latent pedophiliac in every American male."

"Not me."

She tucked one long leg up under her. "Okay, what's your type?"

If honest, he would have admitted he prized leanness over everything, and in faces, as in paintings, he admired asymmetry, sharp angles, interesting plays of shadow. Helen, for instance. But a warning tone had begun to hum in his inner ear, like those guitar strings that start to vibrate of their own accord when a note to which they have been tuned is sounded on another instrument.

"I've always liked redheads," he said.

"Odd." She bit into the cheese. "A hell of a picnic—barreling along like this."

"We went any slower, the flies would catch up."

Barely decelerating, the driver thumped off the road, detouring around Tougla over ground that was as firm and flat as asphalt.

"How do you know Tucker?" Helen asked.

"From Texas. We were at the University together. Lived in the same dorm freshman year and hit it off from then on."

"Hard to imagine. You two don't seem to have much in common."

"Sure we do. At least back then we did. You see, we were both poor country boys, so we had a lot of talking to do about all the things we couldn't afford. And we argued which of us came from the raunchier, low-rent family."

"Who won?"

"I did, hands down. Although Tucker would probably still dispute that. Then we spent hours fantasizing about what we'd do after college when he was a famous director and I was a famous artist, and we were both rich as Lamar Hunt. I guess he won that one."

The driver bore down on two buzzards pecking at something in the sand. At the last second they flapped aloft and hung there just long enough for the Renault to pass beneath them.

"Afraid I'm making our friendship sound pretty dreary," Jack said. "It wasn't. Tucker had a hell of a sense of humor. He owned this old pickup and he'd go trucking around Austin looking like any other shit-kicker, except on the gun rack in the rear window he had a furled umbrella and a flute. And big as he is, he was the first Texan I ever met who announced in public he hated football."

Helen brushed the bread crumbs from her slacks. "Well, whatever else you can say about him, he doesn't fit the old cliché about directors being weasly, embittered guys who were too short to be actors."

"No, there's nothing small about Tucker."

"So after being your college buddy, he went Hollywood?"

"No, to Yale Drama School first."

"And let me guess. He said he switched from stage to film because the medium presented more challenges and he could reach a wider audience."

He smiled. "You're plain vicious, aren't you?"

"If I am, it's because I've been around too many directors. What did you do after college?"

"Went to grad school, then started teaching."

"What about your painting?"

"I can't make a living off that. Not with the stuff I do. You gotta remember an art exhibit in Texas is likely to be something Sertoma holds for charity and the catalogue always describes big canvases as 'sofa size.'"

"So you're doing this." She shook her head. "I've known a lot of writers and artists who tried TV or film work thinking they'd get ahead of the game, but it usually ended the same way. It took up all their time and killed their talent."

"I doubt it'll have any effect on mine."

"Oh? You know something F. Scott Fitzgerald didn't?"

"I wouldn't go that far. But I used to have this argument with Tucker, and back then I was on your side. Warning him about selling out. Badgering him about 'going Hollywood.' Reminding him how movies corrupted this genius or that. What he never pointed out—maybe he was too polite—was that 'going Hollywood' couldn't possibly be worse than 'going University of Nebraska.' Or going broke."

"You don't know this business."

"I know other businesses; I know myself. You can't corrupt anybody who doesn't want to be."

She raised her eyebrows. "Oh, so that's why you're here—you want to be corrupted?"

He attempted to make his voice as light as hers. "I'm way past that. I don't know whether I have any talent left or had any to start with. But if it's gone, I did it to myself and I'm through worrying about it."

"You say that like you feel relieved."

He paused, wondering whether she meant to provoke him with her questions. Or maybe his answers were the provocation. Whichever, he saw no reason to give way. "The fact is, I don't feel anything any more. That's the pleasant surprise."

Again she brushed at her lap. "Seems to me we have our roles reversed. I'm the insider. I should be defending movies. And I'm not completely against them. What makes me mad is how much better they could be. Remember back in the sixties how everybody was saying film was the art form of the future? All the Picassos and Mailers of the new generation were going to be working with hand-held cameras. Well, is *The Sting* or *Star Wars* what we were waiting for? Is that the best we can expect? Every time I see the money and energy that go into a project like this one I think it's as if the Egyptians had taken what they knew about geometry and built a McDonald's stand instead of the pyramids."

"Yes, but be honest. Don't you love their French fries?"

Smiling, she shook her head. "You're hopeless. Tucker should fire Nichols and let you do publicity."

The driver followed a dirt track into the dunes where fences of braided palm fronds attempted to hold back the desert. But the sand went where it wanted, and the archipelago of sunken oases survived only because farmers dug them out each morning, shoveling sand into wicker baskets, then hauling it off on donkey back. Some of the excavated gardens were so deep the tops of the palm trees were level with the land Jack and Helen drove over.

Coming to a herd of emaciated camels, Ibrahim nudged the Renault in among them and cut the engine. "Camel parking lot," he said and, delighted by his joke, threw his head back in laughter, revealing the black stumps of his molars.

Helen and Jack scarcely heard him. They were watching a gang of children clamber over a pile of bones as big as a jungle gym.

Ibrahim said, "Camels good for eating." Then, noticing how little meat there was on the live ones, he added, "Many get old and die, but the skins are still good for making tents."

When the three of them got out of the car, the kids rushed over, yelling, *"Fluss, fluss,"* and *"Donne-moi l'argent."* The boys in baggy cotton shorts had their heads shaved except for a topknot, and their scalps were encrusted with scabs. The girls wore tattered dresses made from grain sacks with the American seal stenciled on one side and on the other: *This Is a Gift from the United States of America. It Is Not for Sale.*

Letting them get close, Ibrahim slapped one boy's head and chased them all away.

Jack grabbed him. "Don't do that."

"Bad children. Beggars."

"Don't hurt them."

"The Minister doesn't want you to be bothered."

Helen walked over to the children, who were wary now.

"They're not bothering anybody," Jack said. "Wait for us in the car."

"But I am your guide."

"I'll tell Mr. Benhima that you've been an excellent guide." He steered him toward the Renault.

Surrounding Helen, the kids whined for money, waving their cupped palms. She motioned for them to be quiet, and when that didn't work, she leaned down and made faces at them, pantomiming a succession of exaggerated emotions. Passing a hand over her face, she wiped away anger and replaced it with a clownish expression. While they laughed, she changed the clown mask to sadness, then to a sobbing baby face. They laughed at that too and continued to laugh as she twisted her mouth and squinted, a not altogether convincing witch.

"This is awful," she said to Jack. "They look like they haven't eaten in weeks. Do we have anything to give them? The basket of fruit?"

"There's not enough to go around. I'm afraid they'd fight."

She searched her handbag. "I've got a lot of change."

"So do I. But wait till we're where the driver can't see."

They moved to the edge of an oasis and, gazing down into its dense foliage, Jack was suddenly dizzy. After the bleached dunes, this greenery was too intense, almost painful to the eye, and standing above the treetops made him feel he was floating.

Digging in their heels, they descended, setting loose little avalanches of sand. But the kids had no fear, and several boys flung themselves headlong and rolled to the bottom where the ground had cracked and curled at the edges like a ceramic slab left too long in the oven.

Going into the palm grove, they might have been entering an enormous tent. The light was apple green, the soil loamy and dark. Banana, almond, and fig trees grew in the shade, and below them were plots of grain and beans. Parallel to the paths, the irrigation ditches described one intricate grid within another —an arabesque of water and earth that seemed to repeat the same mazelike pattern as the streets in the medina.

As they walked through the oasis, the kids cried out in broken French for Jack's watch, Helen's handbag, their shoes, their shirts, their rings. But they were grateful to get a fistful of coins minted from a metal as light as balsa wood. Several of them ran off then, as though afraid the money would be taken back. The rest stayed, perhaps hoping for more or that Helen would put on another performance.

"God, it's beautiful," she said. "But do you think what's growing here is enough to feed these kids?"

"Moha told me dates are the main thing. A grown man can live on a few of them a day."

"Yeah, I've read that." She glanced doubtfully at the orange, unripened clusters.

When they reached the raised lip of a well, she said, "I'd love to have a drink."

"I wouldn't, if I were you."

They sat on a fallen palm trunk, and the kids crouched in front of them, quiet now. The heavy air hummed with flies, fearless ones that landed on their eyelids and mouths. No amount of swatting could chase them away for good. The kids didn't bother trying, and several had a sticky film on their pupils. Like the driver, they would eventually develop trachoma.

Jack had seen enough—too much—and was about to suggest they leave when Helen said, "I've got a bottle of Visine. You think it'll help?"

"You can't come back every day and clean their eyes."

"The hell with that. I'm here now."

She found the plastic vial in her shoulder bag, leaned back, and squeezed a drop into each eye. Then she laughed and ran through her repertoire of happy expressions, motioning for the kids to scoot closer and line up.

A little girl was first, curious, yet frightened. Helen gently tilted her head, shooed away the flies, and applied the drops. Though they stung, the girl laughed and hurried to the end of the line for a second turn.

Then Jack noticed more kids coming up the path—the ones who had run off earlier with their money. They were leading a woman who had a baby clinging to her shriveled breast. Powdered with grit, she had a gold ring through her left nostril and her hair was swept back from her forehead and wound into plaits. With flesh drooping from her bones in loose folds, she looked far too old to be the baby's mother.

But the baby too looked old, its skin hanging from stick-thin arms and legs, and stretched taut over a swollen belly. What Jack had thought was a birthmark on its shoulder was an open sore covered with flies.

Helen stood up. "What's wrong with them?"

"I don't know. Maybe malnutrition."

"Starvation, you mean."

Wailing, the woman didn't understand Jack when he asked in French what she wanted. He gave her money—his hand had gone into his pocket almost automatically, just as it had so often in the past two days—yet she kept repeating the same string of phrases. He pointed to his mouth; she shook her head. It wasn't food she wanted. An older boy told him in garbled French that she was asking for aspirin.

"That baby should be in a hospital," Helen said. "So should she. Tell her to come with us in the car."

But he had to depend on the same boy to translate and couldn't be sure how much the fellow understood or how much he managed to get through to the woman, who was still moaning, one hand out, opening and closing. Jack motioned for her to follow him up the path. She didn't move. He tried to take her by the elbow. She pulled back and wouldn't let him touch her. Through it all, the baby never cried, never stirred. The lone sign of life was a faint sucking sound of dry lips working at the fallen breast.

"She understands," Jack said. "I'm sure she does, but she's scared. The boy says she keeps asking for aspirin."

"This is crazy. I always carry aspirin." Rummaging in her bag, Helen found a tortoise-shell comb, change purse, compact, key ring, and a box of breath mints.

The woman's hand snaked out for the breath mints. Helen pulled back, shaking her head. The woman made a second lunge.

"Let her have them," he said.

"She'll give them to the baby." Tears were pooling in her eyes.

"I don't think they'll hurt."

He gave the mints to the woman, and she fled into the oasis. A few kids went with her; the others stayed, still waiting to have their eyes washed with Visine.

Helen zipped her bag. "Let's go."

On the climb out of the palm grove, sand swirled around them, burning their bare skin like cinders, grating in their eyes and mouths. Helen slipped to her knees, and Jack helped her up and kept his arm around her the rest of the way.

The kids thought it was a game and were laughing again, taking pratfalls. But at the crest of the dune Ibrahim saw something was wrong and sideslipped down to meet them. "I told you, bad children." He slapped at them.

"For God's sake, make him stop," Helen said.

Jack shouted, "It's all right. They didn't do anything."

The man was bewildered. "I am helping."

"Just take us to the hotel."

The children raced along beside the car, yelling and laughing and banging at the side panels, until Ibrahim hit the accelerator, boiling up dust and gravel in their faces.

Tucker stood alone in front of the Sidi Mansour staring at the birds tangled in the net. As Jack and Helen came up the walk, he said, "Can you believe this?"

"I can believe anything," Jack said.

Helen shrugged his arm from her shoulder and brushed by Tucker.

"What's with her?"

He waited until she was in the lobby. "We were out at an oasis and saw—"

"Before I forget," Tucker broke in, "don't go wandering off again without leaving word. I got enough to worry about without wondering where my supporting star has disappeared to."

"You mean because of what happened at the airport?"

"No, bubba. Nothing like that. It's just on a location like this it's hard to keep track of everybody."

Jack gazed over Tucker's shoulder at the dead and dying birds. "Yeah, it's a hell of a place to make a movie."

"I admit that's not too appetizing. I'll tell them to tear it down."

"It's not just that."

"Okay, okay." Tucker's voice was ragged with irritation. "I know, it's freezing in the morning and roasting in the afternoon. The food's crummy and the service is worse. There's no light on the stairs and half the crew is down with the trots. But what do you expect me to do? It's the best hotel in this part of the country."

"I'm not talking about the hotel. We saw a woman with a baby that was nothing but bones."

Tucker plucked at his shirt front. He wasn't sweating; the air was too dry. "I'm sorry. I don't mean to sound like a shit-heel. But it's no secret this place has problems—no different than a lot of places in Africa. I can't stop what I'm doing till everybody in Maliteta has what he needs or we'd be here forever."

Jack ran a hand through his hair and came away with grit on his fingers. "At least mention it to Benhima. Maybe he can do something. The woman wouldn't come with me."

"Sure, I'll do that. But don't you agree we're already helping by giving people jobs?"

"I guess so."

"There's no guessing about it, bubba. We're dropping over two million dollars into Maliteta."

"Hope it gets to the people we saw."

"Some of it's bound to filter down." He slung an arm around Jack's shoulder and walked him toward the Sidi Mansour. "How about those sketches?"

"I'll have them to you before dinner."

"Good." They entered the lobby. "One thing you should know, we're shooting the restaurant scene here instead of the Chems."

Jack stopped short. "You'll lose the atmosphere. This dining room is no different than a Howard Johnson's."

"We're going to set up in the bar."

"Still, the other place is much better."

"Marvin went over the budget with Schwarz and we'll save a bundle of dough."

"I see."

"It's not just the money. This way we won't have to haul the crew and cast and equipment to town. It'd be a bitch getting in and out of those alleys."

"Plus the hotel has food," Jack said. "Hard to do a restaurant scene without that."

Tucker's arm slid off his shoulder. "Right." If he heard the sarcasm in Jack's voice, he gave no sign of it.

At sundown the heat clicked off and the temperature in the hotel fell ten degrees in a matter of minutes. During dinner the wind flung gravel against the windows, and the curtains swayed in the draft that seethed in around the loose casements. Complaining of the cold and the rotten food, everybody drank too much, ate too fast, and hustled to their rooms to pull on another layer of clothing. Later, when they gathered on the third floor in a suite that had been arranged as a projection studio, they were dressed like alpine explorers. A few even wore scarves and gloves.

Word had gone around that Tucker would be screening his first movie tonight. Nobody was ordered to be there, but all the creative types showed up, and most of the crew members too. "It's a courtesy thing," Jack heard several people say.

He came not out of a sense of courtesy or loyalty. He simply wanted to see *Traveling Light* a second time and gauge how much Tucker had changed and whether he himself had changed more. Maybe Tucker's motives for showing the film were as personal as Jack's for wanting to see it—although he imagined Tucker also had professional reasons for reviewing his early work before starting something new.

Just before the lights went off, Tucker arrived with Benhima and Gorman, Helen, Barry, Lisa and her entourage. But while the others sat in the front row, Helen took a chair between Moha and Jack. "How was dinner?" she asked.

"Freezing. But you'd have survived in that outfit."

She had on a white cable knit sweater and blue jeans tucked into suede boots.

"Have you seen *Traveling Light* before?" Moha asked her.

"No, never have."

"You'll like it." Then he added what no one else in the room would have admitted aloud, "It's his best."

Jack agreed with Moha. From the opening frames he remembered all that was wrong with the movie. Filmed in grainy black and white, its focus wavered and the sound track was sometimes garbled. In an interview Tucker had said he was hindered as much by inexperience as by a low budget and tight schedule. But he had compensated by staying close to what he knew. Without the confidence or cash to indulge himself, he had shot in quick takes that captured what was necessary and nothing more.

Set in the countryside around Palestine, Texas, the story dealt with a boy just back from the Marine Corps. Because he wasn't confronted by a baffling range of choices or by affluent parents anxious to have him fulfill their ambitions, reviewers had seen *Traveling Light* as a reversal of *The Graduate,* a grittier vision of American youth.

The boy worked in a gas station and struggled to fit into the town social life that centered on a honky-tonk where men who raised pit bulls gathered every evening to argue the merits of their fighting dogs. During the course of a year he trained his own dog, promptly overmatched it, saw it mauled, and then had to shoot it. In the end he was back in the honky-tonk, one of the men now, but aware for the first time that he had to get out.

Whatever its technical flaws, Jack thought *Traveling Light* caught the look of Texas, not the usual Hollywood parody. The characters spoke with poignant conviction and the script seemed not so much written and performed as starkly recorded.

After the last frame, the lights flickered on and there was a moment of silence. Then in the back of the room Hal Nichols started clapping. A few others took up the applause. But Tucker pitched to his feet, turned, and silenced the PR man with a stare.

Excusing himself from the Minister and Gorman, he stepped over to Helen, Moha, and Jack. His eyes were narrowed against the fluorescent glare, his bearded chin jutted forward. Jack recognized the expression. It was the way Tucker often looked when he was upset and struggling not to show it. Whether his reaction to *Traveling Light* was personal or professional, he obviously didn't care for what he had seen.

"Your story boards, they're fine, bubba. Too good really. I don't need that much detail. Just lay out the action and lemme have a few angles to shoot from."

"Sure. You know, I liked *Traveling Light* even better this time."

Tucker gave an impatient shrug, shaking off not just the compliment but the whole subject. "Afraid you'll have to wake up before breakfast tomorrow. Couldn't find enough European extras around town, so we'll be using whoever we can spare from the crew. Wear your undertaker's outfit and be down at the make-up room by six."

Though Tucker's face was still a frozen mask, Jack thought it was worth taking another chance to break through to him. "I mean it, I enjoyed the movie."

"So did I," Helen said.

"Yes," Moha said. "Someday you should make another one just like it."

"What the hell do you want to do, gimme more gray hair?" Though he forced a grin, Tucker's voice had jagged edges. "That's the last thing I need."

"Why?" Moha seemed to expect the sort of earnest discussion of film he must have had in college.

"Because I'm not a kid any more. Because nobody's going to give me the money to jerk my own chain again. Because it wasn't all that goddamn good to start with." Shoving ahead of people, Tucker bulled his way up the aisle.

Moha pulled his hands under his burnoose and fixed his eyes on the blank projection screen. Embarrassed for the boy, Jack wished he could have withdrawn into himself. The room went quiet an instant; then the crew members, who had turned to look, shuffled toward the door.

"Don't let it bother you," Jack said. "He's been touchy all day."

"Everybody likes to think the last thing they did was best," Helen said.

"I only wanted him to know how much I enjoyed his movie. We studied it in film class."

"Is that right? Jack tells me you went to school in the States."

"Yes."

"Isn't that sort of unusual? For somebody from Maliteta to go to an American college?" She labored mightily to keep the conversation alive.

Moha glanced around the almost empty room. "When the French were here, they sent a few boys to Paris each year. It was a way of showing that opportunities existed in the colonies. And it helped control young people. If a boy was threatening to make trouble, they didn't need to throw him in jail. They put him in school in Paris, and usually he came back and took a job with the administration. After liberation the government sent students to America instead. They said it asserted our independence."

"I'm kind of surprised you came back," Jack said.

"This is my home."

"But if you want to be a director, wouldn't it have been better to stay in Los Angeles?"

"Maybe in some ways. But I know this place and these people, and there are films I'd like to make here. Someday I may get the chance." He smiled faintly. "But as Mr. Garland said, first someone has to let you have money. In Maliteta that means the government."

"How do you go about getting it?"

"By doing a good job on this movie. By proving I am trustworthy and would never shame the country." He stood up, glancing toward the door where Benhima appeared to be waiting for him. "I must go now."

When they were alone, Helen let a few moments pass before saying, "Do you think there's something wrong?"

"What do you mean?" he asked, although he feared he knew.

"I have a feeling something's wrong here."

"Look, it's no secret Maliteta has a lot of problems—just like every country in this part of the world." It was what Tucker had said that afternoon, yet although Jack tossed it out casually, he realized how anxious he was to believe it.

"I guess you're right," she said. "You read about places like this all the time, and see them on TV. We're just not used to being on the spot."

Jack walked her up to the fifth floor, down the dark hall, her boot heels resounding on the tile. She unlocked the door, switched on the light, and offered her hand just as she had the first night. But after they had shaken, she kissed her fingers and touched them to his cheek instead of her heart.

"I learned something about you today," she said.

"Oh?"

"In the car you claimed you didn't feel anything any more. But you're wrong. I saw it on your face when Ibrahim was bullying those kids. Then when that woman showed up with her baby. And just now when you were talking to Moha."

"I don't know whether to be happy about that or not."

"Be happy," she said, and shut the door.

In his room he tried to block out a few rough sketches for the next scene, but couldn't concentrate. He found himself thinking of Helen and then about the woman and her baby, and that reminded him of David, who from infancy had been sturdy, alert, and energetic. Every evening after dinner as they rough-housed on the living-room rug, Jack had marveled at how perfectly formed his son was. Life hadn't had a chance to mar him or wear him down, and Jack had wanted to keep him that way as long as he could, not in the vain hope of shielding him forever from sadness and pain, but to protect him from the kind of calamity that would leave him too scarred to live normally again.

Then one night in France after putting David to bed, he and Sybil had lain awake arguing. It could have been about anything —money, homesickness, sex—but after hours of monotonous bickering it had flared into a savage fight that might have lasted until morning if Jack hadn't heard something in the hallway. He told Sybil to shut up, and she heard it too. He hadn't been frightened, just annoyed at the interruption, and he switched on a light and ripped open the bedroom door as if to tell the burglar to be quiet and let them finish.

In the hall David was huddled on the floor, his teeth chattering. He must have fallen from the crib and been coming to climb into their bed when he heard them yelling. It couldn't have been the first time, but when Jack went to pick him up he cringed, scuttling away, sobbing. Sybil had to calm him; he wouldn't let Jack touch him.

It was then he knew that, if he hoped to protect David, the

best place for him was far away. A few days later he put him on a plane to the States with Sybil.

Ever since then distance had seemed the solution to all his problems. He had kept everything and everybody at arm's length. He had tried not to think—or rather to think only of himself. He had agreed to take this job partly because it looked as if it would put him beyond reach a while longer. But it wasn't working out that way. Helen hadn't been wrong; things were getting to him. And what bothered him most was that, no matter what he saw outside, he wound up in here working on these ridiculous sketches.

Somebody rapped at the door, and Jack answered it before there was a second knock.

Tucker held up a bottle of Johnnie Walker Red. "Thought you might like a nightcap." He strode over to a chair, but stayed on his feet. "I know that was kind of abrupt, the way we parted company after the screening. I want to apologize."

"You don't owe me an apology. Moha's a different matter."

"I thought you maybe could tell him I'm sorry. Didn't mean anything by it. You don't know what it does to me to watch one of my movies. Shrivels me right up. I wouldn't look at the fucking things if I wasn't afraid of repeating myself."

"Tell that to Moha."

Tucker nibbled at his mustache. "Got a glass?"

When Jack brought the toothbrush glass from the bathroom, Tucker sat down and poured him a triple shot. "That should get you started. I'll drink from the bottle." He took a long pull at it, then stared into space.

"Hey, why the long face? I meant what I said." Jack sat on the bed. "The movie was goddamn good. Everybody liked it."

"I know what's good about it, bubba. And I know I can do better—even though I haven't so far."

"You will."

"Will I? I wonder. Like I told you the other day, I'm scrambling for a second chance, but sometimes it seems harder than coming back from the dead."

"I always knew you had a high opinion of yourself, but I never expected to hear you give yourself better billing than Jesus H. Christ."

That got a grin out of Tucker. He took another drink. "Couple years ago I did a documentary about a major league baseball team. Know what they say when a player gets released or sent down to the minors? They say he died. That's the best definition of failure . . . death."

"You're overdoing it just a little, don't you think? Or am I missing something? Is this a wake? Where's the body?"

"Sorry to be in such a black-ass mood. But all day trouble's been piling up like flapjacks. First it was Nichols."

"What'd he do?"

"He doesn't have to do a damn thing except walk into the same room with me and breathe. He reminds me of one of those big old cockroaches we have back home. What was it Darrell Royal said? It ain't so much the garbage they gobble up or carry off that makes them godawful. It's all the good things they fall into and fuck up."

"Why'd you hire him?"

"Didn't. Somebody at the studio stuck me with him. To keep an eye on me, I suspect. Or to make trouble and screw me up."

"I see why you're upset."

"Hell, that's not the half of it. Before the screening tonight I was with Barry jawboning about his concept of the script when I suddenly realized what the problem was. The son of a bitch hasn't read it."

"You're not serious."

"Yeah, I am. Oh, he's read his part and memorized his lines and cues. But he's just skipped around in the rest of it. Remember that one stretch of eight pages that doesn't have any dialogue? He doesn't have any idea what happens there."

"Jesus!"

"My sentiments exactly." Tucker raised his eyes to the ceiling and lifted his hands. "Sweet Lord Jesus, save me."

"How did Barry explain it?"

"Claims he tried to read it, but it was too long. He's like a lot of them—a functional illiterate. What it is, bubba, we always thought of ourselves as ignorant Texas goat ropers, but now we're around real *analfabéticos*. Like it's an oral culture, man. The written word doesn't mean diddly-shit. That's why there aren't more good scripts. Hell, maybe somebody's writing them, but who'd read them? Who'd understand them if he did read them?

Jack couldn't help laughing.

"It ain't funny." But Tucker was laughing too, delighted to have got Jack going. "Tell you how bad it is. We're dealing with brain-damaged geeks. We're talking about a business that sold shark fetuses in jars of formaldehyde to promote a film. We . . ." He was laughing too hard to finish.

While Jack sipped his whiskey and Tucker resumed his ranting, he felt on familiar ground and was surprised at how quickly old attitudes and conventions cropped up between them. Most of their talk, it occurred to him, had always been jokes, playful scoldings, and jibes. Yet Jack felt his old affection return for his friend, who had always been big enough to admit a mistake and to make fun of himself. He thought no matter what erratic course such a man might run, ultimately you could trust him.

Tucker pushed himself from the chair, moving toward Jack, "How about a refill?"

"No, thanks. I have to be up at five, I better get some sleep."

"Guess I should too." Capping the bottle, he stretched and noisily yawned. "See you in the morning, bubba. I'll have that talk with Moha first thing."

CHAPTER V

Jack was in the make-up room when the muezzin wailed at sunrise. Dabbing powder at his face, one girl said he had excellent skin tones while another girl combed back his coarse hair and said he should have it styled or start wearing a dog license.

Then he went down to the bar where grips had been working with the set dresser since 4 A.M. A snake's nest of wires coiled around the cameras and sound equipment, and booms and carbon-burning arc lights swung from overhead scaffolds. The grips called the big lamps Brutes, the small ones Pups.

At seven o'clock Moha led in the troop of Malitetan extras and instructed them not to smoke, chew gum, or spit. At Donald Wattle's insistence, he also collected their sunglasses, wrist watches, and plastic sandals, which didn't fit the director of photography's image of the Sahara. Wattle didn't give a damn whether every man in the country wore them. He had staunch notions about the look he was after. Anything else was "teddible."

Along with the men, half a dozen women had been hired. At least Jack assumed they were women. Since they were draped from head to heel in shapeless black cloth, it was impossible to tell. Only the pointed toes of their babouches even indicated which direction they were facing. They sat in a tight circle separated from the men, who sprawled full length on the floor, pulled up the hoods of their djellabas, and, in spite of all the noise, slept.

Jack wished he could have slept, but a second assistant had sentenced him to a table with Hal Nichols and Reid Gorman, who smelled of the sweet, milky ointment he used to protect his sensitive skin.

"What's the chance of getting this president of theirs to fly up and meet Tucker and the stars?" Nichols asked.

"Very little," Gorman said. "He prefers to stay put and look after . . . uh, his interests."

"Come on, it'd be good press for him. Lots of pictures."

Gorman smiled, his sparse eyebrows arching. "I think PR is low on his list of priorities."

Wearing a bellboy's outfit instead of his gravy-stained tuxedo, the headwaiter hurried over, whispering indignantly to Nichols, "Everyone in the kitchen is laughing at me."

"Well, you told me you wanted to be in the movie."

"Not as a bellboy. I worked hard to become a headwaiter."

"Forget that. This is your chance for a new career. How I figure it, your future's in movies. I mean with a face like yours."

When Tucker arrived with the principals, Jack thought they were ready to start. But Tucker wandered through the crowd, a coffee mug in hand, and might have been another mildly curious onlooker. It was the first assistant who shouted and swore and shoved at people.

Everybody, it seemed, even the actors, had brought cameras. As they discussed lenses and lighting and duty-free shops where you could buy Nikons and Leicas for next to nothing, they snapped pictures of the extras, of Benhima and Jerry Lewis, of the set and especially of each other—standing, whenever possible, next to Lisa, who lounged on a pile of throw pillows. Roberta, mouth bristling with bobby pins, hovered over her, still working at her hair.

Only Helen stayed to herself and read. Dressed in a severely tailored pants suit, she was supposed to play an agent, but to Jack's eye she looked more like a high-fashion model than Lisa, who appeared itchily uncomfortable in her costume.

At last Barry Travis and a supporting actor were seated at a table and, while Wattle eyed them through his lenses, Tucker stood behind Barry, massaging his shoulders like a fight manager. Then, moving off camera, he nodded to his assistant, who shouted, "Silence!" The French interpreter yelled, "*Silence!*" and the Malitetan interpreter sounded as if he had spat. "*Skoot!*"

A boom swung over Barry's head. "The desert is in my blood. I'll never leave it," he vowed.

When he clapped his hands, an immense black man entered, stage right, carrying a platter covered by an orange ceramic cone. Although he wore one of the bellboy outfits, he was a former linebacker for the Los Angeles Rams and outweighed any Malitetan in the room by seventy-five pounds. Setting the platter on the table, he lifted the ceramic lid, releasing a dense cloud of steam from a mound of couscous.

"Cut," Tucker said. "Looks like we're shooting in the Continental Baths. Let it cool off."

Minutes later Barry said, "In this country you have to learn to eat with your hands." Sinking his fingers deep into the semolina, he made a fist and popped a ball of couscous into his mouth.

Tucker called, "Cut," and a crew member rushed over with a plastic bag into which Barry spat the gummy wad of food. Because of his weight problem he had been forbidden to swallow.

Then they shot the sequence again and again and again. Tucker wanted it from every angle and asked for so many close-ups and reaction shots, Jack lost count. He measured the passage of time by the growing pile of couscous in the plastic bag, and although he wasn't hungry, he looked forward to lunch as a break in the monotony, a chance to move around and stamp some life back into his feet. But at noon the AD ordered them to stay in their places while waiters served them. The meal, of course, was couscous, and it looked no better than what Barry had chewed up and spit out.

Marvin Tallow came over, arguing with a French gaffer who looked as if he might mash his lunch plate into the production manager's face.

"Hey, Jack," Tallow called. "Tell this guy what I'm saying."

"I speak English, I speak English." The gaffer was incensed.

"He maybe speaks it, but he sure as hell doesn't understand it. Tell him that's a hot meal what he's holding there."

"*C'est un déjeuner chaud.*"

"*C'est pas chaud. C'est froid,*" the gaffer insisted.

"He claims it's cold," Jack said.

"He's full of shit."

The Frenchman offered Jack a bite of his couscous.

"Go ahead, try it," said Tallow. "That's hot, isn't it?"

"It's kind of lukewarm."

"You see, not hot." The gaffer was triumphant.

"You got any complaints," Tallow said, "call your union rep and tell him to send a thermometer."

The Frenchman stomped off muttering, "*Sale con.*"

"What is this?" Jack asked.

"The frogs, it's in their contract they get a hot lunch or we gotta pay them time and a half. There's a little trouble with the steam tables and the French right away claim the food's cold. Chrissake, it must be a hundred and five in here. They can eat my weenie and call it a hot lunch."

The afternoon, Jack feared, would be more of the same, but things got worse. The boom smacked Barry in the head and he called the sound man a cocksucker. When Lisa blew the same line for the fourth time, Tucker raised his voice for the first time. "What are you, coked up again?"

Then a Malitetan extra had a coughing fit and ruined a take. They set up again and, as if on cue, the man coughed again, interrupting Lisa with deep, phlegmy croaks.

The AD hollered at Moha, "Get him the fuck out of here."

Moha glanced from the assistant to Tucker as he offered the man a bottle of water. "He'll be all right in a minute." But the extra was still hawking to clear his throat.

"We're wasting time," the AD said.

"He needs this job."

"How long did we hire him for?" Tucker's voice sounded concerned, soft compared to his strident assistant's.

"Three days."

"Explain we have to let him go, but we'll pay him just the same. Tell him we're sorry."

While they set up once more, Tucker circled the room, sipping his coffee, struggling to regain his concentration. When Marvin

Tallow intercepted him, he waved the production manager away, but Marvin insisted and tapped the crystal of his watch. It was six o'clock.

Nichols whispered, "That's all, folks. Marvin's telling him the numbers. They do another take, it'll cost overtime for the frogs."

Nichols was already moving toward the door when the AD said, "All right, we'll knock off till tomorrow. Call sheets'll be in your rooms by ten."

Jack stood by the table, a prickly pain stabbing from his ankles to his hips. Helen had gone to get her book and handbag, and he was waiting for her. But then he noticed Gorman was waiting too, flexing his white bony fingers as if they had fallen asleep. Jack crossed the room on wobbly legs to make sure he got to her first.

"Sit with me at dinner?" he said, and it sounded like something he might have asked a girl in high school.

"I couldn't eat. Not tonight."

"Then have a drink."

"With all these people it'll be a madhouse." They could hear the crew clamoring in the lobby where a temporary bar had been set up.

"I'll have a bottle sent to my room."

"It'll cost a fortune."

"At this point I'd pay a fortune for a drink."

"I think I would too. Have them send it to my room. The wardrobe girl will be stopping by for my costume."

As they picked their way through the cameras, wires, and fuse boxes, shouting broke out at the table where Barry had been sitting. Benhima had caught an extra sneaking off with the bag of half-chewed couscous and he held the man by the hood of his djellaba, shaking him back and forth so that he seemed to agree with whatever the Minister said. Moha tried to intercede but appeared reluctant to touch Benhima.

"Hey, like we could care less," Tallow kept saying.

"He was stealing," Benhima said.

"We'd have thrown it out anyway."

"That doesn't matter. He must be punished."

Jack had paused, wondering whether to send somebody for Tucker.

"Are you coming?" Helen called. Slowly he followed her into the lobby, over to the staircase. In the bar they were still yelling.

After the raw light, stale air, and racket of the set, Helen's room was quiet and cool. In the souk she had bought hand-loomed blankets to replace the drab bedspreads, and prayer rugs in bright, primary colors to cover the floor. On the walls gleamed tribal amulets and a pair of brass trays.

To Jack, who had always thought himself in transit, even in Texas in the house where he had lived for ten years, it never would have occurred to put his personal mark on anything except a canvas. But he was delighted to see what Helen had done.

Kicking off her shoes, she sat on one of the single beds, leaning against the headboard. "If I wrinkle this costume the wardrobe girl's going to give me hell." But she didn't make a move to change.

"You were good today."

"Oh, you probably say that to all the girls."

"I mean it. It was like watching a professional trapeze artist work with amateurs. I was afraid they'd drag you down with them. But you were too strong for that."

"Barry's all right," she said. "Sure, he's overweight and this role doesn't give him much to work with. But he can act."

He wandered over to the bureau. On top, between a sand rose and a vase of flowers, was a framed snapshot of two little boys in baseball uniforms. "Your sons?"

"A couple of years ago. They're twice as big now."

"Nice-looking boys. Too bad they couldn't come with you."

"They're in school."

When a bellboy brought the whiskey and a bowl of ice, Jack caught himself about to give an absurdly large tip. He knew what a self-congratulatory gesture it was, an obvious attempt to salve his conscience. He started to slip half the money back in his pocket, but then decided, what the hell, even if he couldn't help the others, even if it wasn't so easy to let himself off the hook, he might as well give this boy something to celebrate.

Jack handed Helen her drink; she took a quick, deep swallow. "Thanks. I was just thinking, I've done nothing around you but bitch. I'm not usually this bad."

"You've been fine." Dragging a hassock over near the bed, he sat and leaned against the wall, conscious of not mentioning that one of the things he liked best about her was that she didn't share the mindless cheer and optimism of the others in the company.

"Anyway, I don't want to talk about myself any more. Yesterday you were telling me how you and Tucker had these terrifically intense debates about who came from the worse family. How poor were you?"

"Piss poor. Both of us. And proud of it."

"Proud? Why?"

"Well, you see, we'd convinced ourselves we were up from slavery. Regular Longhorn Horatio Algers. The competition was to prove which one of us had come further—and would go further. Tucker would brag, 'There never was a book in our house I didn't bring there.' But I'd top him: 'My parents didn't even read the newspaper.' Then he'd claim, 'I never had a pair of new shoes before I went to the university. I wore my brother's hand-me-downs.' And I'd go him one better. 'I didn't have a brother. I'm wearing my father's castoffs now.' By this time he'd be groping. 'We never had napkins at the supper table. We passed around the dish towel.' I'd tell him that was nothing. 'In our house we didn't bother with niceties like wiping our mouths.'"

"How long before you ran out of ammunition?"

"We kept at it the whole fall semester of freshman year. Then we started embellishing, and the stories slopped over into this really rancid self-pity. I mean at first we seemed to think we were destined to be famous *artistes* because poverty had shaped our exquisite sensibilities. But there was always this other assumption—one we never admitted out loud—that we *deserved* to be famous, that somebody owed it to us on account of our poor stunted childhoods."

Helen was laughing. "Sorry," she said, "but you make it sound so funny."

"The thing that's funny is we were so serious. We figured ourselves as the Sylvia Plaths of the Lone Star State. Our suffering was more than the first step toward art. It *was* art. And suicide, that was the big pay-off, the Nobel Prize of the second rate. We weren't up to that."

"You say you always won the competition?"

"Indeed I did. I told such sad-assed maudlin stories Tucker was in tears half the time. The other half, he was torn up laughing."

"What was the prize winner?"

"You don't want to hear it."

"Yes, I do." Drawing up her legs, she wrapped her arms around her knees.

He glanced at her thighs sheathed in the tight material of her slacks. Then he looked into his glass and wondered whether he could be drunk already.

"I'm waiting," she said.

"Okay, here it comes. The uncontested championship tale of woe. Keep the Kleenex handy." He downed a long swallow of scotch. "When I was eleven or twelve, somewhere in there, I wanted to join the Boy Scouts, a thing my father thought was damn fruity and he said so straight off. He called them the Bung-Hole Buddies and told me to wait and go into the Marines. But I went ahead and joined, and because I didn't have the money to buy a uniform, I made one."

"You sewed it?"

"God, no! What I did was bad enough. I had a cousin in Abilene who'd been a Scout, and he gave me one of his old shirts and I sort of improvised around it. I never could afford an overseas cap or Scout shoes, but my boots were brown, and I bought a big yellow hankie to wear as a neckerchief. What I was proudest of, though, I had a crow's foot, a regular claw, instead of a bolo to fasten that hankie."

"A claw?" Helen wrinkled her nose.

"Yessir. I found a crow dead on the roadside and cut off its talon, leaving just enough of the tendon so I could pull the thing tight around my neckerchief."

"You must have been the envy of the neighborhood."

"Not exactly. Most guys kidded me for not having a real uniform, and I was afraid Mr. Bradford, the Scoutmaster, would call me down for it. But he didn't say anything, not until there was this state-wide Scout Jamboree in Austin. We drove on over from Odessa and met up with all the other troops and we were supposed to march up Congress Avenue to the Capitol and pass in review in front of the governor. It sounds silly, I know, but that was a thrilling thought to me and I'd been looking forward to it for weeks.

"Well, Mr. Bradford, he parked his station wagon down near some warehouses next to the river and told us to fall out and get into formation. But after he called roll he ordered me back into the wagon. Then he marched the troop to the end of the block, talked to them a minute, and double-timed it back and slid onto the seat beside me and put his arm around me and leaned his face down close to mine."

"Oh no," Helen said.

"It wasn't what you think. He looked me in the eye and asked if I had any idea what kind of neighborhood this was where we'd parked. I shook my head that I didn't. 'A nigger neighborhood,' he said. 'Niggers and Meskins.' And if we weren't careful, some nigger or greaser was sure to happen along and swipe all our camping equipment. 'Somebody has to volunteer to stand guard,' he said. 'It's a tough assignment, a dangerous one, and it calls for a tough man.'

"He waited for me to speak up, but I didn't say a word. I knew what was coming and I about broke down and cried. 'I'm asking you to stay behind with the car,' Mr. Bradford said. 'Sometimes one Scout has to sacrifice for the good of the whole troop. Can I count on you?' I still didn't answer. But he gave me a smile and a squeeze and said, 'You're a good old boy, Jack. Don't you go taking too many chances. Keep the doors locked. If they surround you, blow the horn till help comes.' Then he left and led the troop up Congress Avenue to the Capitol."

"And you say you knew what he was doing?"

"Sure. What the hell, there were big guys, fifteen, sixteen years old in the troop. Why would he pick me? No, I knew it was because I didn't have a uniform. Looking like I did with that crow claw, he didn't want me marching with the other boys. Years later I thought maybe there was a chance he believed he was doing me a favor, saving me from making an ass of myself in front of the governor and everybody. But I didn't see it that way back then."

"What did you do?"

"Cried, I guess." Jack laughed. "I told Tucker I threw away

my shirt and neckerchief and hitchhiked home. But that was bullshit. That's what I wish I had done. I sat there all day, too dumb and disappointed to know what else to do. After a while I saw there wasn't any sense crying, but I still felt plenty sorry for myself and wished someone would try to steal our stuff and that I'd fight him off and be the hero and they'd chip in and buy me a uniform as a reward. Then, the later it got, I decided, no, I'd help the guy rip us off. It would serve Mr. Bradford right. But it's funny how things work out. Even though I quit the Scouts the minute we got back to Odessa, I never hated Mr. Bradford or the other fellows. I hated my parents for being so fucking poor."

"That's awful," Helen said.

"Yeah, it is. I didn't realize how awful until I told my mother what happened; she broke down and bawled. It was the first time I ever saw her do that."

"What did she say."

"She begged me not to tell my father. She said how much it would hurt him. And there was another reason. She knew her man. She was afraid he'd kill Mr. Bradford."

"Jesus," she said.

"I told you it was an award winner."

Jack finished his drink and insisted on freshening Helen's before he poured himself another. "You'd think something like that —or all the crap Tucker went through as a kid—would have turned us into radicals or communists. But that's Texas for you. If you're born rich, you're sure to be a gold-plated capitalist. And if you're born poor, you're likely to be an even more fanatical one. Kind of makes you wonder."

"The only thing it makes me wonder is how anybody could treat a little boy that way."

"Hey, there's nothing to be mad about. What I told you is the secret of my career, the great driving force that made me what I am today."

"It really eats at you, doesn't it? Those things you were talking about yesterday—success and failure and all this competition with Tucker? Don't tell me again you don't feel anything. I know that's not true."

Laying a hand on her bare ankle, he spoke in a voice full of self-mockery. "If I do have any feeling, it's just regret that I didn't have the imagination or daring to fail on a grand scale."

"You're hiding behind these jokes."

"Not at all. Be honest now. Wouldn't you rather be in the Sahara with the kind of man you've read about in your books—the kind who's pushed out against his limits so hard and deranged his senses so long, he's finally fallen over the edge into . . . I don't know, revelation, ecstasy, transformation! An artist driven mad by the need to paint, one willing to sacrifice anything for his vision." Jack shrugged. "Instead you're having drinks with a cartoonist who's mildly disappointed that he hasn't fulfilled his adolescent daydreams."

"You're more than mildly disappointed. I don't care how funny you make it all sound."

"Good. I'm glad you're taking me seriously. Because I speak for the American artist, and we're as capable of despair and alienation as anybody from Paris or Prague. But we refuse to let that prevent us from having a swell time at parties."

Helen laughed, and her drink splashed over the lip of the glass, down the front of the pants suit. "Oh, damn, there it goes." She hopped up, brushing at her lap. "I'd better change. But don't go away. I want to hear more about the plight of the American artist."

"The plight of the American artist is the natural paltriness of his plight. So he hounds himself into a mental and physical breakdown trying to invent one. Some very gifted people—and I include myself among them—have failed simply because they were never able to find a plight that fit."

Touching his shoulder, she stepped past him and into the bathroom.

Jack knew the scotch had hit him now, but he poured himself another and mixed Helen a new drink. Although he had drunk a lot in the last few months, he had never felt this buoyant or been as willing to believe that his life—all his troubles—were terribly funny.

Helen returned in a pale blue caftan which, because of the dryness of the air, clung to her in spots. She had not washed off the make-up, which emphasized the curving line of her mouth, the hugeness of her eyes, and her high cheekbones. Jack was still on the hassock, and when she came nearer, the light caftan, crackling with static electricity, brushed his cheek. Raising his arms, he encircled her thighs, pressing his face against her. He felt her tense, then relax, and after an instant she slipped a warm hand under the collar of his shirt.

"Look," she said, "I was going to ask—"

Someone knocked at the door.

"That's the wardrobe girl," she said. "I'll get it."

Breaking free of his arms, she fetched the pants suit and handed the hanger to the girl without mentioning the spilled drink. When she came back she stood a short distance from Jack.

"What I was about to ask, are you planning to stay?" Then before he could answer, "Because if you are, I'm going to take a shower."

Watching her eyes, he wanted to be sure. "Yes, I'd like a shower too."

"Be right back."

He heard the hissing spray and suddenly wasn't at all sure. There was no doubt about her question, but he felt he had other things to be uncertain of.

She returned with her dark hair slightly damp, her face scrubbed, the caftan clinging now to wet patches on her skin. "Hope I left you enough hot water."

As they passed without touching, it occurred to him they could have showered together, except that that somehow required an intimacy which exceeded sex.

The mirror was steamed, and he was grateful he didn't have to watch himself strip off the black corduroy suit and hang it on a hook beside the door. He stayed under the shower a long time, then slowly dried off and wrapped the towel around his mid-section—not at his waistline, a little higher where it hid the slight looseness of his stomach muscles. But this subterfuge struck him as foolish, demeaning. Dropping the towel, he returned to the other room hiding nothing.

Helen had tossed the caftan over a chair, one sleeve dangling like a pennant. In bed, the covers drawn up to her chin, she slid over, making space for Jack, and the moment she touched him, he was aroused. He was tempted to joke and tell her it had been a long time and this wouldn't inconvenience her for more than a few seconds. But then her mouth covered his, and she pressed the cool length of herself against him, and he felt the frail articulation of her shoulder bones, the smooth column of her spine. His palms moved over her taut bottom, down to the backs of her thighs, between them.

She whispered she wanted to be on top and, raising herself upright, straddled him, rocking in a slow ellipse. He started to tell her to stop; he couldn't last that way. But before he could speak, she leaned forward, her breasts barely brushing his skin. Then she let her full weight down on him, her lips moving at his throat and face. When her mouth tightened, she moaned; he didn't so much hear it as feel it in his own chest.

As Helen lay in the crook of his arm, Jack ran his fingers from her shoulder to her wrist and gripped her hand. "Know what I like best about you?"

"My hands."

"They're not bad. But what I like are your bones. Everywhere I touch, they feel so elegant and fine."

"That's a compliment? You make me sound like a skeleton."

He squeezed her. "No, there's flesh too. But I'm glad to know what's underneath."

"You think you know that?"

"Sure. It's an architectural principle. Form follows function; exterior indicates interior. You're stripped down, finely structured, solid."

"Now I sound like a Bauhaus building."

"Okay, how would you describe your body?"

She glanced at her waist which, though flat and firm, bore a faint tracery of stretch marks. "I'd say it looked lived in." Then, apparently embarrassed, she rolled onto her side. "What do you think of Lisa Austin's basic blueprint?"

"I don't have any tactile experience, but I get the impression of a plastic frame liberally padded with styrofoam."

"That's mean."

"Hold it. You're the one who told me about the silicone."

"I shouldn't have. I've been around her a lot in the last few days and learned she's not so bad. I know she's obsessed with herself, but you have to remember she was a model for ten years. When you're treated like a piece of meat that long, it's hard to think of yourself as human any more. She told me she's lonely."

"Ah, the cruel cost of success."

"You don't think it's true?"

"I'm sure it is. I'm just not convinced obscurity is any cheaper or less lonely."

She propped herself on an elbow. "Are you married?"

"Hey, who put you up to these questions? Somebody's lawyer?"

"I take it back. I knew you were. Tucker told us."

"*Us?*"

She sensed the change in his voice and spoke faster. "Naturally everybody was curious. So he explained who you are. Nothing bad. Believe me, he likes you. And you have to understand, movie people are practically weaned on interviews and gossip columns. They expect to get down to personal details right away. But it doesn't mean much to them."

"It does to me."

"What I'm saying is they probably don't remember a thing Tucker told them. They were too busy waiting to talk about themselves. Haven't you heard them describe their broken homes and casebook childhoods and sex hangups? It's almost as if they expect you to applaud. And everything's wrapped in these shiny ribbons of jargon they've picked up in therapy or from reading self-help books."

"What exactly did Tucker have to say?"

"That you have a lot of talent."

"I'm not interested in that. What about my marriage? He called Sybil before he left the States, and I'd like to know what story she's spreading around."

"He just said she never understood what you were trying to do, never believed in your talent."

Jack laughed. "Why should she have? I told her I was going to be a great painter. For ten years I kept telling her that."

"Ten years isn't long for an artist."

"How long should she have waited? The rest of her life? I don't know about where you're from, but in Texas the statute of limitations on marriage has changed."

"Okay, so she gave up. That's no reason for you to give up on yourself."

"I haven't. I'll go on painting, if that's what you mean. But it'll be different from now on."

"How?"

"I'm not dragging anybody else along with me."

"She really did hurt you, didn't she?"

He sat up and, seeing goose flesh on her flanks, tugged the cover over her. "Look, it's too easy blaming Sybil. I hurt her a lot too. She took it as long as she could. Earlier I was joking about not being the kind of artist who's willing to drive himself crazy for his work. Well, what I did was worse. I damn near drove her crazy, and our boy."

Helen pulled him down beside her and shared the blanket. "Cover up. You'll catch cold."

"All I know about you," he said, "is you have two kids. There must be a husband around somewhere."

"Used to be. He's dead."

"I'm sorry."

"No use being sorry now. It happened more than seven years ago."

"Was he an actor?"

"God, no! A lawyer. I'd never marry any kind of entertainer. I've seen too many of them get the jitters before they go on and scream at their wives, 'Where the hell's my hot comb? How could you forget it again?'"

"That must have been rough on you, raising the kids alone."

"Probably rougher on them. Still, we did all right. Sometimes I do wish I could move out of New York up to my farm in Vermont. I'd like to spend more time with the boys and read and work with my horses. But . . ."

"Why don't you?"

"There are a few small complications. Like the kids being in school."

"Aren't there schools up there?"

"I suppose so. Who knows whether they're any good? And there's this slight hitch that I have to work."

"It's not like you put in eight hours at a desk every day."

"No, but I have to be where they can reach me. You have no

idea how much of their lives actors and actresses spend waiting for the phone to ring."

"And of course there are no phones in Vermont."

"You don't understand. Unless you're Barbra Streisand, what you can't risk doing is going beyond the limited memories and imaginations of producers and casting directors. And you shouldn't ever underestimate the extent to which impatience controls everything in the industry. If I moved to Vermont they might forget who I am. Or decide I had died. Even if somebody remembered me, they wouldn't know the Vermont area code and couldn't waste time looking it up."

"Nobody's that impatient."

"I see you need a language lesson, a whole new dictionary of Hollywood definitions. Out there 'impatience' doesn't mean childishness or a lack of self-control. It's the ultimate badge of success, the Rolls-Royce of the emotions. The demand for instant gratification proves you've arrived. If you have to put up with delays and compromises, if you have to wait for service or food or sex, then you know you're a loser. So everybody projects this image of utter impatience. Only a confessed failure would bother to learn the Vermont area code and dial three extra digits."

"So you're stuck in New York?"

"Absolutely trapped."

There was a knock at the door.

"That's the call sheet," she said, snuggling down next to him, "It's too cold to get out of bed."

"I'll get it."

"No, I'd better."

Grabbing the caftan, Helen stood up, lifted her arms, and let the light blue cotton flow down her body.

When she returned she told him they both had a six o'clock call, then stripped off the caftan. Jack rose to meet her, enfolding her in his arms.

"A demand for immediate gratification?" she asked. "You must be feeling very successful tonight."

"Yes, but I'm willing to take my time."

Raising herself on tiptoes, she rubbed against him, a cat caressing herself. Then she lifted one leg, looping it around him, and suddenly he was inside her, and she was off the ground altogether, hugging him with arms and legs. Swaying, they stood that way a few moments before Jack set her down gently on the bed and they lay there together a long time in the chill room with only body heat to warm them.

Finally he said, "I'd better go."

"No, stay. It'll help me sleep."

She pulled the covers over them and switched off the lamp, but neither of them slept and, as they talked, Jack found himself straining to hear something in the darkness beyond her voice. At first he couldn't figure what it was. But then when she rolled onto her side, and he wrapped his arms around her from behind, one hand on her belly, the other on her breasts, he realized he was waiting for the clamor that came each night from the garbage cans.

CHAPTER VI

In the following days Jack's language lesson continued and he learned what could be said and what couldn't, what certain things were called and which ones had no names. He had known "sweetheart," "darling," and "baby" meant "friend"—or maybe just not "enemy" at the moment. Now he learned what lovers called one another. They didn't call each other anything. At least Helen and he didn't.

They avoided melodramatic declarations—the large words which too often masked small emotions, or none—and after fumbling into the past several times, they let it be and voiced no assumptions about the future. Even in bed their vocabulary was pared down, and they wasted no time devising a private argot to euphemize their desires. Much as they talked before and afterward, they seldom said more than, "No, not that," or "Yes, that," as they made love.

Jack remembered the way his students talked about sex and rare relationships that lasted. Earlier they had spoken of "chemistry" between men and women. Then came "electricity" . . . which had evolved by a process as mysterious as alchemy into a purer current called "vibes." Now there had been a regression to a more rudimentary physics. His students told him of lucky couples who just happened to fit. That might be all it was with Helen and him. That might be all anyone had the right to ask for.

Not that he took things for granted or had lost his capacity for wonder. But while he recognized the implausibility of having Helen with him at night, this seemed no more improbable than what he saw and did during the day. Some mornings he woke early and was bewildered when he heard charwomen in the hall chattering in Arabic. Then he went down to breakfast, listened to Nichols, Tallow, or Schwarz, and didn't understand them either. Though he did it repeatedly, he still found it disorienting to go from the hotel into Tougla. Or to return from the desert to the manicured oasis of the garden. Or to produce continuity sketches which were discarded whenever Barry, Lisa, or Donald Wattle claimed to have a better concept. As far as Jack could tell, they had come to Maliteta to make a movie that had little to do with the original story, not much more with the script, and nothing at all with the place. But every week, he got his expense money in cash, and a check for fifteen hundred dollars was deposited in his bank account. For that, he told himself, he could learn to ignore what he didn't care to think about.

After lunch on the fourth day of shooting, Tucker did a last take in the bar, then gave the crew and cast the afternoon off. Although already behind schedule, he couldn't go on to the next scene; he still hadn't decided where to set it.

Moha suggested they drive north to scout locations in a place called Picture Rocks. Borrowing the script girl's Polaroid, Tucker asked Jack to come along, then sent for his car. But Benhima insisted they needed a jeep, not a taxi, and he ordered a soldier to drive them in his personal Land Rover.

"I hope you like the Picture Rocks," Benhima said. "They are very old. You will see, my people were giants before the colonialists starved them."

Moha rode up front with the soldier, a scowling, ill-tempered man who clearly didn't care to drive into the desert at this time of day. Jack and Tucker were in back and, as they followed the paved road toward Tougla, Tucker pointed ahead to Barry Travis, jogging in a green rubberized sweat suit. "Tell the driver to blow the horn," he said to Moha.

The soldier honked and Barry shied like a scared colt, stumbling off the macadam onto the sand. Although rapidly pumping his arms, he was barely moving his legs. As the Land Rover sped by, Tucker hollered for him to pick up the pace.

The soldier muttered something to Moha.

"He doesn't understand why Barry is running," Moha said. "He asked, 'Is he afraid or is he crazy?' Here it's so hot nobody except children run."

"Explain he's exercising."

"In his dialect there's no word for 'exercise.' There's 'work' and there's 'play.'"

"Say he's working to lose weight."

"He wouldn't understand that either. In Maliteta only rich people are fat and they're proud of it."

"What the hell," Tucker said, "go ahead and tell him Barry's crazy. It's about time people knew the truth."

"I'd better not. He'll take the story to Benhima, and you'll have to explain again. I'll say Barry's playing."

They circled Tougla, traveling north past a whitewashed dome the size of a house, the shape of a salt lick. Moha said a *marabout,* or holy man, was buried there. Then they snaked into the sand dunes on a swerving strip of asphalt deserted except for a few children who rushed out to sell sand roses. Some of the rocks were too huge to be lifted overhead; the kids balanced them on their shoulders, staggering under the weight.

Where the dunes ended, the paved road stopped too and a couple of soldiers left a thatched lean-to and signaled with submachine guns for the Land Rover to pull over. While one soldier spoke to the driver, the other stared in at Tucker and Jack. He had flies, like punctuation marks, at either end of his mouth.

"What's up?" Tucker asked.

"Just a check point," said Moha.

"Are they looking for anything particular?"

"They know it's the Minister's car. This won't take long."

When the soldiers waved them through, they bumped across the *hammada,* an immense sheet of rock where the light was incandescent, the landscape without depth. The sun surrounded them and for a moment it seemed to Jack they were floating on the mercurial surface of a heat mirage. But then his eyes adjusted enough for him to see that there was nothing to see—no people, no boulders, no vegetation except scattered clumps of weed that had sprouted in cracks.

Miles later, the sun glinted on metal or glass, and Jack squinted several moments before recognizing massive steel pylons rippling in the heat. Shiny lengths of cable linked them together and hummed in the wind, a low moan like an untuned radio. At the base of the pylons people had stretched scraps of canvas and animal hides from the lowest struts and huddled there in the shade. Goats and camels nosed around in the gravel, nibbling at wiry plants and trash.

"What the hell is this?" Tucker asked.

"The power line from Moburka."

"No, these people, what are they doing here?"

"They're Bedouins."

Several men waved and shouted, but then, seeing the Land Rover wasn't going to stop, they crouched back in the shade.

"You mean they live here?"

"They live wherever they are." Moha had swung sideways in the seat, watching the driver as well as Jack and Tucker. "They move around to find grazing land."

"Jesus, did they come to the wrong place," Tucker said.

A camel clomped toward them, its hump nearly flat, its hide pocked with running sores. A dead raven with wide iridescent wings had been fastened by cord to the camel's neck.

"It's to keep other birds from pecking at the sores," Moha said. "The live ones stay away from the dead ones."

"Jeezus," Tucker repeated, clawing at his beard.

Following a washboard track away from the power lines, they crossed a broken stony field that set the fenders ringing. Several miles ahead an outcropping of rock burst from the desert floor in the vague shape of a volcano. It couldn't have been much higher than two hundred feet, but it looked mountainous looming above the monotony of the *hammada* and it showed a spectrum of ocher tints that appeared to change as the Land Rover approached.

Sandstorms had buffed the rocks smooth in some spots and carved them into narrow, winding corridors in others. The soldier drove around to a ravine, pulled into it, and killed the engine. Then he stayed behind while Moha, Tucker, and Jack went ahead on foot to a fifty-gallon oil drum that had been sawed in half to serve as a watering trough. Now it held six inches of bleached sand.

Beyond it, the gorge got narrower and they had to walk single file, swiveling sideways from time to time. Their voices echoed all around them, and when they were silent, Jack heard their breathing amplified against the high faint whistle of wind through splintered stone. The air grew progressively cooler, then the ravine widened and sloped toward a large pond. Reflecting without fault the paintings on the arched walls around it, the water resembled a polished marble floor.

Moha said the spring-fed pool was called a *guelta* and herdsmen sometimes came here to carry water through the winding corridor to their animals. The pictures were prehistoric. Nobody knew who had done them, but a French archaeologist claimed . . .

Stunned by the colors, Jack and Tucker barely listened. Snapping shots with the Polaroid, Tucker prowled the edge of the water, looking for better light. After photographing the murals themselves, he focused on their mirror image in the pool, then found an angle from which to shoot both.

Jack, too, moved from point to point, studying the paintings from different angles. He supposed they were the work of dozens, perhaps hundreds, of artists over a period of centuries. Finding a source of pigment right here at their feet in the lumps of ocher scattered around the *guelta,* they had created a desert daydreamer's vision of paradise. There were leafy trees and lush fields of grain with rivers running through them. Naked hunters ten feet tall, their bodies striped with bright geometrical designs, stalked elephants and hippos; women watched over fat grazing cattle, roasted slabs of meat on spits, made love to the warriors, had babies.

Moha said this area of Africa had once been fertile; the pictures showed how it looked thousands of years ago.

"You mean back when Benhima's people were giants?" Tucker asked.

The boy smiled. "Yes, and elephants were the size of sheep."

Despite the problems with scale and perspective, Jack noticed in the best murals a sophisticated attention to detail. Stylization

must have come later when the climate changed and the vegetation died off. As the desert advanced, the skills of the artists had
deteriorated. Or maybe the urge to paint died before the ability.
Whichever, in the end they had simply etched stick figures on
the walls.

But Jack believed these desperate scratchings were, in their
way, as accurate as the earlier paintings. Under hellish conditions this was what it meant to be human; it meant being
diminished, having pinhole eyes, nostrils, and ears, and a mouth
that might have been fashioned by an inverted fingernail. No
skeleton had much more individuality than any other.

When Tucker ran out of film he stood beside Jack, shuffling
the Polaroid snapshots. "Look at these goddamn pictures."

"I'm looking."

"Is there another way in here?" he asked Moha.

"No, just the ravine."

Tucker glanced at the high, jagged wall of rocks. "No hope of
hauling equipment over that. If only I had a helicopter. Christ, I
gotta find a way of bringing in lights and cameras. Maybe we'll
widen that corridor."

"No, they won't let you change anything," Moha said. "You
could use hand-held cameras."

"Yeah, I have a couple of Eclairs. But there's a hell of a lot of
shadow."

"The sun's over there in the morning. You could set up Pups
for afternoon shooting."

"Wish you had your sketch pad, bubba. You could start block-
ing out the scene."

"I'd feel foolish working here. Kind of like doodling in the Sis-
tine Chapel."

Tucker slipped the snapshots into the pocket of his bush
jacket. "Then let's get back to the hotel."

The soldier was slumped over the steering wheel, asleep, and
Moha had to shake him awake. Backing out of the ravine, they
clattered across the field of rubble and slag and had gone less
than a mile when they spotted a man in a fluttering blue *gandurah* sprinting toward them. Moha spoke to the driver, who

muttered and kept on going. Moha raised his voice sharply; the soldier steered for the man.

"Something's wrong," he said. "I told you, nobody in Maliteta runs."

The Land Rover hit a chuckhole, scraping the differential, and the soldier started muttering again.

"It is a tradition of the Sahara to help anybody in trouble," Moha said. "You never know when you'll need help yourself."

Although the man in blue saw them coming, he didn't slow down. Barefoot, he bounded over the scorched stones, his loose *gandurah* luffing in the wind. Part of his turban had been wound around the lower half of his face, leaving only his eyes and the bridge of his nose visible. Half a dozen pouches flapped from leather thongs around his neck, and he had a sword in an ornate sheath hanging by a red and gold braid rope.

"Why's he in that getup?" Tucker asked.

"He's from one of the Berber tribes."

"That's not what the people under the pylons were wearing."

"A different tribe."

"Terrific-looking guy. Wish I had saved some film."

When the Land Rover rocked to a halt Moha climbed out. The man drew himself up and strode forward slowly now, as if making an entrance. Much taller than Moha, he offered his hand, and they pressed their palms together, let them slide apart, and closed them into fists just as their fingers lost touch. After they had done this half a dozen times, he put one hand on his hip, the other on the hilt of his sword, and stared at the Land Rover as he spoke to Moha. He had stubbed his toes and his nails were split and bleeding, but he took no notice of them.

"This is what I was hoping for," Tucker said, exuberant about the rock paintings and now this Berber who appeared to be striking poses. "Some people at the studio kept screaming it'd be cheaper to shoot in the States, but you'd never get this kind of production value."

Moha returned to the Land Rover looking troubled. "His camel is sick. Over behind the Picture Rocks. Everything he owns is there. He wants us to give him a ride."

"Where to?"

"A camp five or six miles north." Moha stared in that direction instead of at Tucker.

"Tell him to climb aboard. I'd like to talk to the head man at the camp about hiring some extras."

"I don't think they would be interested. They're very proud."

"You're kidding. You see those guys at the hotel the other day? They were fighting for jobs."

"I told you, this is a different tribe."

"Let's cycle on over there anyway. I believe I can change their minds."

"The problem is"—when Moha turned to face Tucker, he looked more troubled than before—"the government has laws about their working. You'd better speak to the Minister first."

"Before we give the guy a lift?"

"Yes."

"What the hell, a minute ago you said the rule around here is to help folks. Now you're telling us to bug out."

"The place he's going to, it's not a tribal camp. It's a relief station run by the army. The Minister will be upset if you see it."

"Why?" Jack asked.

"Nobody's supposed to know about it. Of course everybody in Tougla does. But they'd be angry if foreigners found out."

"Found out what?" Jack asked, experiencing a deep uneasiness.

"Some people say there's a drought in the north. Not in Maliteta," he hastened to add. "But much farther north they've had no rain for years and the Berbers and other nomads have been moving south looking for water and grazing land. The government has forbidden them to cross the Kimoun River. Those who make it this far are held in camps. Kind of refugee camps."

"And that's where this guy wants to go?" Tucker said.

The boy nodded. The wind had blown his bushy hair forward, and he brushed it back.

"Well then, don't you agree we better help? I mean if his camel's hurt, how else is he going to get there?"

"I just know there'll be trouble if I take you."

"Trouble with Benhima?"

"Yes, the driver is sure to tell him."

"You let me worry about that. Now go tell the fellow we'll be glad to carry him." When Moha left, Tucker said, "Sounds like a hell of a situation."

Jack didn't know how to answer. It was what he had expected, had feared—a hell of a situation.

Moha returned to the front seat; Tucker and Jack slid over to make room for the man in back. But he studied the door handle a moment, then couldn't open it. When Jack shoved it wide, he clambered in, sat stiffly, and gazed straight ahead. He hadn't closed the door.

"You see how proud and stubborn they are?" Moha slammed it. "He has probably never been in a car before, but he wouldn't admit it."

As the Berber spoke in a high-pitched voice that scarcely stirred the *litham* over his mouth, the driver doubled back toward the Picture Rocks.

"He says he's from the north," Moha said. "His group set off five weeks ago, but his goats and cows died and his camel weakened and couldn't keep up. He hopes to meet his people at the camp. He must be weak too or he wouldn't have left the desert."

"You think he's hungry?" Tucker asked.

"I can't ask. It would be a great insult to do that and not offer him something to eat."

As they came near the ravine, the Berber signaled for the driver to go around to the other side. Then, lifting a hand under his *litham*, he picked at his nose, bringing out a small crushed leaf, and dropped it to the floor.

"The leaf smells good," Moha said. "They roll them and stuff them up their nostrils. It's better than smelling a camel all day and breathing dust."

"Is that why he wears the veil? To cut down the dust?"

"Nobody knows. Even the Berbers have different explanations for that and why their women are unveiled. Some say it's because the men used to be smugglers and bandits. They ruled this area of the Sahara and treated the other tribes as slaves."

Tucker said, "Now that's what I call one sick camel."

It was laid out as if on a butcher's block, the carcass cut into six ragged sections—head, neck, forelegs, rib cage, hind legs, and rear quarters. Blood had oozed into the sand, and beyond this circle of glittering red was a saddle that looked something like a cobbler's bench. Made of wood bound in leather, it had a high, cross-shaped pommel decorated with brass studs and splashes of paint.

The air hummed with flies and reeked of offal and raw sun-braised meat. A vulture waddled away from the camel, an eyeball in its beak and, after a ponderous, loping start, managed to get off the ground.

"Tell him to grab his stuff," Tucker said, "and let's move on out of here."

"He wants to take the camel."

"He's out of his mind. How?"

"There's a luggage rack on the roof."

"I don't believe Benhima would appreciate us bringing back his jeep stinking like a slaughterhouse."

For the first time the Berber spoke with the sort of urgency which must have sent him sprinting after them over the spiked *hammada*.

"He says he can't let the meat rot. People at the camp need food."

"What was he planning to do before we came along?"

Sensing Tucker held the power, the man turned to him. Sweat trickled down his forehead, dark-tinted with dye from his turban.

"He was going to carry as much as he could," Moha said, "Then come back with friends and get whatever the vultures and wild dogs hadn't dragged off. When he saw us, he knew it was the hand of Allah."

"Okay, for Chrissake, tell him to heave it up on top. Then let's roll before these flies eat us alive."

"It's heavy," Moha said. "He'll need help."

"The driver'll lend him a hand."

But when Moha spoke to him, the soldier shouted and slapped the steering wheel.

"He's afraid he'll ruin his uniform. He says he's the Minister's personal aide, not a slave to this Berber."

"He's worried about that chintzy fucking uniform?" Tucker grabbed his bush jacket. "This coat cost me two hundred bucks. If he thinks I'm going to—"

"The hell with this." Jack shoved the door open. "I'll help."

Moha and the man climbed out with him, and as they sized up the job their feet sank in warm, bloody sand. Moha hadn't been wrong. Even hacked into pieces the carcass was heavy and slippery; it took two of them to lift the head alone. The sickle-shaped neck weighed as much as a mahogany log and it bent this way and that as the three of them groaned and hoisted it onto the roof. The rear quarters were heavier yet and it was hard to find a spot to grab hold of that wasn't covered with engorged ticks.

After watching them struggle a few moments, Tucker stripped off his jacket, rolled his shirt sleeves, and got out, his grin a mixture of apology and irritation.

"Been a long time since I wrestled with the ass end of an animal. But I don't reckon it's any worse than a lot of things I've done lately." He threw his weight behind it.

When they finished, they were gummy with blood up to their elbows, and the flies attacked in a feeding frenzy.

They followed the Berber's example, scrubbing themselves with sand. What this didn't scrape off, it covered with a thin gritty crust. There was nothing they could do about the stains on their shirts and trousers.

After the man stowed his saddle and belongings behind the seat, they set off across the plain where bright splinters of light shot at them from mica flecks in the rubble. Soon sections of the carcass were sliding around on the rack, bones scraping enamel. Blood streamed from the roof over the windows. Grumbling, the soldier switched on the windshield wipers.

"He says the Minister will be angry."

His hair and beard matted, his face smudged with grime, Tucker had been pushed too far. "I'm fed up with hearing what Benhima's liable to do. Tell him to keep his mouth shut and drive."

At first Jack thought it was dust—thick columns the color of the dry blood on his pants. Then he saw it was smoke from hundreds of dung fires throughout the camp. The driver swerved around clumps of bones nearly as big as the Land Rover. They were the bleached remains of cattle, goats, and camels. But the sight of them was unnerving since they were scattered among graves marked by piles of stone and covered with thorn branches to keep off scavengers.

Reed huts and animal-hide tents had been pitched in no particular order. Nothing rose higher than a man's waist, and no one was on his feet. Everybody, even the few animals, looked as if they had been knocked flat and barely had the strength to crawl to a shady spot. While the men lay under lean-tos the size of umbrellas, women huddled in the tents with children nesting around them. Many of the kids were naked and, like the baby Jack had seen in the oasis, they had distended bellies, eyes that seemed to stand out on stalks, and orange kinky hair.

Without being told, the soldier drove to a corner of the camp where several army trucks were parked beside an enormous khaki tent. A black officer strolled out wearing a red beret and baggy fatigues. Moving around to Moha's side, he rapped the blood-streaked window.

Moha rolled it down. The officer had tribal cicatrices, but they hadn't healed right; instead of neatly sliced furrows, there was a welt of scar tissue on each cheek. As Moha spoke, the officer gazed past him at Jack, Tucker, and the Berber. Then he broke in with the same tone Jerry Lewis used on the serving boys.

"It's what I warned you," Moha said. "He won't let us out of the car."

"Tell him we're from the film," Tucker said. "Benhima sent us."

"Nobody sent us. There could be worse trouble if I lie."

"Did you tell him I'm here to hire extras? I'm here to help."

The boy hesitated.

"Go ahead."

As Moha translated, a gust of wind carried a ripe stench to Jack's nostrils. It was from the decomposing camel, open latrines, filth and sickness. Several veiled men gathered a careful distance behind the officer and gazed into the Land Rover. Or perhaps at the meat. They were dressed like the man sitting beside Jack, except that they weren't wearing swords.

The officer laughed, pleating the scar tissue on his cheeks.

"He says they're too lazy to hold jobs. They always had blacks do the work for them."

Tucker spaced his words, struggling to hold his temper. "Ask how I get permission to visit the camp."

"He'll tell you to ask in Tougla."

"That's what we'll do then. He will let this fellow stay, won't he?"

The officer said yes, the man and the camel meat should remain there. Shouting to the men who had been watching, he stepped aside while they unloaded the gristly joints and lugged them into the tent. Then he ordered the driver to leave.

They swung around and rode along the perimeter of the camp, staring into the warren of huts and tents. There was little noise and less movement. The tribesmen turned their heads away and that was all. Perhaps it was in anger or embarrassment at their helplessness. Or maybe just to avoid the grit dug up by the Land Rover.

In the jeep no one turned aside, not even when the smell hit them again. Jack held his breath, but the air had a taste, a thick cheesy texture. He saw bodies laid out, covered with white cloth.

"How many in this camp?" he asked.

"A few thousand. East and west of here there are other camps. In some ways," Moha said, "it's not any better for them than staying in the desert."

Tucker scratched at his arms, flaking off the crust of sand and blood. "What's stopping them from moving into town?"

"It's not their home. They wouldn't be welcome."

"That doesn't make any sense."

"It does if you understand the tribal divisions in this country. Other people always feared and hated them. And you have to remember what it means to live the way nomads do. They don't want to be in town. They don't want to give up their customs. In the old days they would have migrated south of the Kimoun River and waited until the weather changed."

"Why won't the government let them go there now?"

Moha glanced at the soldier.

"You'll have to ask someone else."

"Who? Benhima?"

"Yes, the Minister might know."

"Would he tell us if he did?" Jack asked.

"He would tell you something."

"I get the feeling *you're* not telling us everything."

"I don't know *everything*."

"Well, damnit," Tucker said, "tell us what you do know."

"I've already told a lot."

"I realize that," Jack said. "And I think I'm getting the picture. Is there a famine in Maliteta?"

"Farther north—"

"I'm talking about here."

"There are rumors."

He waited for Moha to go on and, when he didn't, Jack said, "But the government denies the rumors and doesn't do anything."

"It set up refugee camps," Tucker said.

"But don't you see? They're barely keeping them alive."

"You don't know that."

"I know what I saw. You saw it too. You think those people looked healthy? How about the ones under the sheets? We're making a movie right in the middle of a famine."

"You're guessing, bubba."

"And what are you doing?"

"I'm not shooting off my mouth till I talk to Benhima and find out the truth."

"You're assuming he'll tell you the truth?"

"I don't figure it's any smarter to assume we already know it."

The sun went down while they were in the dunes. One minute the sky was drained of color, the next it blossomed with shades of carmine and purple. Then just as suddenly it was black. Children rushed out of the darkness, still trying to sell sand roses, looking in their flapping djellabas like giant moths attracted to the headlights. Blinking his high beams, the driver blew the horn, but the kids stayed in the middle of the road, waving the stones, leaping aside at the last second. Nothing Moha said could make the soldier slow down.

In Tougla lanterns and braziers had been lit, and in front of the shops along Avenue de la Libération a few forty-watt bulbs threw pools of dull yellow on the sidewalk. At the end of the road the Sidi Mansour blazed like a Christmas tree and sand whirled around it, piling up in drifts on the window ledges.

They found Benhima in the bar where the set had been dismantled. He sat on the banquette with Schwartz, Tallow, and

Nichols, all of whom had spent the afternoon by the pool and were badly sunburned.

"Did you like the Picture Rocks?" Benhima asked.

"Yes, very much," Tucker said.

"Sit. Have something to drink."

"Not right now, thanks."

"Looks like you tangled with a bear," Schwarz said. "Is that blood?"

"I'd like to talk to you," Tucker told Benhima, who was also staring at their stained pants and shirts.

"You must be tired, Mr. Garland. Once you've showered and rested, we'll have mint tea."

"I'd rather talk now, if you don't mind. Could you come up to my room?"

"We'll go to mine. It's closer."

The Minister's room was on the ground floor, just off the lobby, and was like all the others except that it had an armed guard at the door, an automatic rifle next to the night table, and a two-way radio on the desk. He motioned them to one single bed while he sat opposite them on the other. Because of the upward sweep of his scars, he always looked as if he was about to smile or had just stopped, but Jack noticed something register on his face—perhaps simple surprise—when he realized Moha and he were staying with Tucker.

"I am pleased you liked the Picture Rocks," he said. "Now when you film them, the whole world will see our landmarks and tourist attractions."

"Yeah," Tucker said. Then paused. "Out at the rocks. We ran into this Berber. And he asked us to carry him to a camp."

"Oh?" Benhima's eyes swung over to the boy.

"Moha warned us the camp was off limits," Jack said. "But the man was in trouble and we had to help."

"Quite right."

"We wanted you to know it was our fault. Not Moha's."

"There can be no fault in helping a stranger in the desert." He rubbed a hand on his uniform trousers, buffing his big white fingernails.

"These Berbers"—Tucker still spoke haltingly—"they're very colorful. You know, very exotic to an American. They'd come across great on camera. I was thinking, well, I'd like to have them in the movie."

"Moha should have told you these people will not work."

"If we can change their minds, do I have your permission to hire them as extras?"

Jack was puzzled. This seemed a strangely oblique way of proceeding. But he tried to remain patient.

Benhima flourished his hands, the palms a tender-looking shrimp pink. "I'm afraid this isn't my affair. You'll have to ask the Minister of Labor. But I believe he will tell you most Berber tribes don't have papers."

"Work permits?"

"Identity papers. For years they have wandered from country to country, violating borders, not bothering about visas. This causes many problems. Our policy is to encourage them to settle and become Malitetan citizens."

"I see your—"

"But they refuse to register with the local prefect or pay taxes and serve in the army."

"I see your point. But I thought the government might like to have them make a little money. Under the circumstances."

"Circumstances?"

"Well, with them living in relief camps, it's gotta be a drain on the country."

"We can care for our own people," Benhima said flatly.

"I don't doubt that. It just seemed to me, if they had jobs, they could pay their own way."

"Save the jobs for Malitetan citizens, Mr. Garland." Then he smiled. It wasn't just the angle of his scars that made Jack think he had. "You know, in Moburka we never understood why you decided to make your movie in the north. In the south we have water and trees and jungle and elephants. What do you have here? Only sand and camels. And the people . . . well, you have met them now."

"We didn't actually meet them," Jack said, unable to keep quiet any longer. "The soldiers wouldn't let us out of the car. But from what we saw, they looked hungry."

The Minister lazily moved his eyes to Jack. "I told you, we can care for our people."

"But the Berbers aren't your people. You just said they don't have papers. There are international agencies that could take care of them, while the government looks after its own citizens."

"Our policy is to deal with our own problems."

"Of course, but in the case of a famine—"

"There is no famine. Who told you that?"

"Nobody had to tell us. People are fighting for what's in the hotel garbage cans and those tribes are forced to live in camps."

"Nobody *forces* them." Benhima bristled. "They come on their own."

"He means maybe conditions force them," Tucker said.

"You cannot expect the President to control the climate. There has been a shortage of rain and some cases of crop failure. North of our border. That's all."

Jack waited for Tucker to say more, and when he said nothing, Jack asked, "Why don't the Berbers go south to all that water and jungle you just told us about?"

Benhima was buffing his nails again. "These desert tribes, they could be terrorists from Libya or Algeria. They might even be the ones who tried to blow up your plane. They are very primitive, very stupid violent people. It is best for them to stay in the camps. For one thing this prevents them from spreading disease."

He was tempted to ask, Is hunger contagious? But Benhima rattled on, "Our country needs unity and security. We have tried to win the loyalty of all the tribes. But how can we help these Berbers if they are too ignorant to help themselves? If they insist on wearing masks and swords and living in the desert? Excuse me for saying so. I know Moha is from this region and he is a modern young man and educated. But as for the rest of these people, what are we to do?"

"Feed them," Jack said.

Benhima stared at him.

"What Jack means," Tucker started.

"I said what I meant."

"What Jack means is, if the problem ever gets too big, you can always call on us."

"We are a young country, Mr. Garland. But we have wise

leaders. Strong leaders. Since liberation we have not allowed any foreign interference. We never will."

Tucker pushed himself to his feet, and Jack thought at last they had come to a showdown, the point where the sparring stopped. But Tucker said, "We understand the government's position. I hope you understand ours. We brought this up because we're grateful for what you've done for us and we'd like to return the favor."

"I'll tell the President of your gratitude." The Minister shook Tucker's hand, kissed his fingers, and touched his heart. He didn't bother with Moha and Jack.

They walked in silence through the hallway, then paused in the lobby, which smelled of food. The crew and cast were leaving the bar for the dining room.

"Well, we tried," Tucker said.

"Now what?" Jack asked.

"Now nothing. It's their country."

Moha was watching them, and Jack knew it made no sense to involve him more than they already had. "Thanks for showing us around. If there's trouble with Benhima, let us know."

"Yeah," Tucker said. "Want one of the drivers to run you home?"

"I'll walk."

When he left, Jack said, "Let's go upstairs. We've got to talk."

"Chrissake, bubba, can't it wait? I'm hungry, I have a headache, I smell like camel shit, and I'm dying to take a shower."

"No, now."

He started up the dark staircase, and after an instant Tucker followed, saying, "That Moha, he's a nice kid. Smart too. You notice him at the rocks? He knows his film making."

"Yeah, well, we just put that nice kid in a hell of a fix."

"Benhima wouldn't dare do anything with us around."

"What about when we're not here?"

By the time they reached the room they were both shivering. Tucker peeled off his bush jacket and pulled on his sheepskin parka, muttering, "This miserable fucking place." He flopped onto the swivel chair behind the desk. "Want a sweater?"

"No." Jack sat in front of the desk, hugging himself for

warmth, still trying to figure out why Tucker hadn't been more forceful with Benhima, why he seemed to ignore the full consequences of what they'd seen. "Look, don't you think we better decide what to do?"

"There's nothing to do. People refuse your help, you can't cram it down their throats."

"It wasn't 'people' who refused. It was Benhima."

"He's the man that matters around here."

"You could go over his head."

"What am I supposed to do, pick up the phone and say, put me through to the President? And think about what Benhima said. You really believe he was offering a personal opinion? Hell, no. The party line on this famine is it doesn't exist and that's that."

"Okay. But couldn't we go public? Or threaten to?"

Shutting his eyes, Tucker sucked in his breath. "Bubba," the nickname slipped out as he wearily sighed, "we're in their country making a movie with their permission and co-operation and you want me to start threatening? You talk like you've lost your marbles, like you've been listening to too many campus Che Guevaras." His eyes opened. "Let's look at this logically for a minute. If there was a serious problem, don't you think they'd accept help? They'd ask for it."

"Not if they wanted to force all the nomads into camps. Or wipe them out. That's what it sounded like to me; they're settling a score."

"Assuming that's the case, why hasn't anybody else noticed?"

"Who's to notice? Tougla isn't exactly swarming with tourists."

"I don't know. Somebody from one of the embassies. That guy Gorman, for example. If he saw or heard something, he'd tell the right people, and if things were really as bad as they look, the Embassy would pressure the Malitetans into declaring an emergency."

"They could lie to an ambassador just as easily as they lied to us. They could turn down American help just like they turned down ours."

"You're right, bubba!" Tucker made one of his explosive movements, smacking the desk top. "You're absolutely right. So figure it out yourself. If the U.S. of A. doesn't have the clout to come in

here and tell these folks how to run their country, what chance
do we have?"

"A pretty good one. Have Nichols send out a few articles on
the drought and famine instead of Barry's diet. Send snapshots
of that camp to newspapers and magazines. What the hell, do a
film clip and lay it off to some TV network. In a couple of weeks
there'd be so much heat on Maliteta, they'd have to ask for
help."

"Maybe. Maybe not. One thing's sure. They'd bounce us out
on our asses."

"Look, Tucker, I don't want that to happen any more than you
do. You know how much I need the money. I'll be honest, I suspected something like this from the first day. But I didn't want
to believe it. I told myself that's the way things are in this part of
the world and there's nothing I could do about it. But if it's a
matter of standing by and letting a lot of people starve to
death—"

"Don't be so goddamn naïve. You make it sound like we're
starving them. What are we supposed to do? I'm a film director,
not Jesus Christ. I didn't make this world. I just live in it like everybody else."

"You live in Bel Air. You don't live like everybody else."

"Don't break my balls for that. You live on the Riviera. You've
got a job, a house, a car, you don't look like you missed any
meals lately. It isn't so easy to be pure and poverty-stricken, is
it?"

Stung, Jack stayed quiet while Tucker bulldozed on. "We're liable to start screaming about this famine and find out nobody
cares. We'll get our asses kicked out and nothing here'll have
changed. In case you haven't noticed, bubba, life's unfair, it's
cruel, it's outrageous. The reason a jerk-off like Barry's fat and
these Berbers are starving is because Barry's bankable and
they're not. I don't like it any better than you. I am human, you
know. But I'm not going to bust my chops over something I can't
change. Now if that makes me a no-good son of a bitch in your
opinion, that's too bad. And if you don't want to work with me,
well, that's tough shit too."

Jack kept quiet a while longer, knowing it would do no good
to fight Tucker and be fired. That would end his chances in more

ways than he cared to remember. Then he tried to speak calmly, with no hint of accusation. "You talk like I'm blaming you. I'm not. I just think you're holding more cards than you realize. The other day you mentioned the film's pumping two million dollars into Maliteta. That gives you a lot of leverage. You threaten to leave and they'd damn well have to listen."

Tipping back the swivel chair, Tucker gazed at the ceiling. He too had calmed down, but his voice was full of condescension. "I can see it's about time you had a little economics lesson and learned how business and art and probably even that jerkwater college of yours work. And I'm just the guy to give this lecture because in the last few years I've had the equivalent of a Harvard education in capital investment, amortization, tax shelters, cross collateralization, rolling breaks, and percentages of the gross as opposed to the net. I already told you a few of the reasons for filming here. The one I didn't mention was the deal."

"What deal?"

"The deal with the Malitetan government. I won't go into all the details. You wouldn't understand. I don't understand some of them myself. But basically it's a package the studio put together with a French corporation that had currency blocked here. We did a trade-off, buying up their blocked *gourdes* at a terrific exchange rate. Of course we needed the government's approval and to get that we had to cut them in for a piece of the action. They own a third of the movie. So if we threaten them, we're really threatening ourselves. We can't transfer the *gourdes* out of Maliteta and nobody'll buy them back. Even if we decided to leave and take our losses, the Malitetans might try to squeeze out their percentage by impounding all the cameras and film and stuff. Hell, for all I know, they'd impound us."

Tucker swung back and forth in the swivel chair. "So we're locked in. I got about as much leeway as a bug in a bottle. All I can promise is once we have our equipment and people out of the country we'll . . . we'll maybe hold a benefit or something for those tribes."

"That'll be months from now. It may be too late. And how are you going to get the money to them unless the government lets you? Which it won't."

"For all I know, it's too late now. But that's the best I can offer."

"It's not like you to give up this way."

"Sure it is. I've had a lot of practice lately."

"No, you're a battler. Always have been. I don't buy this world-weary role from you."

"It's no role. I *am* tired. I know exactly how much juice I got left and I'm not going to shoot my wad trying to be some kind of hero. You sounded the same way that first day at the Carlton. We're both too old to pretend we don't have to pay a price for what we want."

"You're making other people pay the price for you."

"There's no connection. If the money wasn't going into this movie, it'd go into something worse. If I was shooting in Arizona they'd still be hungry here." He climbed to his feet. "Tell you something else, bubba. I got a suspicion even if I did what you want, you'd find another way to zap me. It's like you been licking your lips at every chance."

"What are you talking about?"

"I'm talking about the way you been on my ass ever since we got down here. Seems to me you're trying to pay me back."

"For what?"

"You tell me. Maybe because I was out of touch for a few years. Maybe because I gave you a job and you think you're too good for it. Maybe you think you're too good for me. All I know is you don't like the script and you don't like the location and you don't like the way I do things."

"Wait a minute." Jack stood up; now he was as steamed as Tucker. "I didn't say anything about the script."

"So I noticed. I drew my own conclusion. You want to quit, go ahead. It'll be a bitch working without sketches, but I'd rather do that than have you grinding at me all the time."

"For Chrissake, give me a little credit. If I was out to hurt you, I could fly to the States and blow the whistle on what's happening here."

"Right. You could." Taking off the parka, he unbuttoned his grimy shirt and unbuckled his pants. "Do it if it'll make you feel better."

"You don't think I'd stand a chance, do you?"

"Who knows? Maybe some network or wire service would take your word and send a team down. And if the government let them in, and if they managed to reach a camp and sneak in with a camera and out of the country with the film, and if the situation here looked gruesome enough and there was nothing sexier to put on the tube that night . . . Well, like I said, who knows?" His broad upper torso broke into goose bumps. "Just tell me what you decide."

"Yeah, I'll do that."

"Meanwhile, if you're staying on the payroll while you're making up your mind, start on that scene at the rocks."

"The way you're talking, it's like you're working overtime to convince me you're a prick. Maybe you're trying to convince yourself. But you don't fool me. You're a better man than that."

"You're right. I'm a regular fucking prince." Tucker was naked now, his big body shivering, and he grabbed the loose roll of flesh at his waist. "But gravity, bubba, it even gets to the royal family."

Bundled in her robe, the covers pulled up to her waist, Helen was in bed, propped up by pillows, eating dinner from a tray.

"You look beat," she said, and moved over, making room for him.

"I'd better not get near you. I stink."

"I'll call room service and have them send up your dinner."

"I'm not hungry."

"A drink?"

"I'll shower first."

"Anything wrong?"

"Talk to you when I'm finished."

Waiting for the water to get hot, Jack took off his clothes and threw them into the corner. The stench of the camp had worked its way into the weave of the material. He feared it had sunk deep into his pores too and that when he perspired it would come dribbling out, so that weeks or even months from now he'd wake in a sweat, and the memories would rush over him.

He rinsed his hands and touched his face. There was dust everywhere—on his eyelids, in his ears, tracing the web of wrinkles around his mouth. When the spray was steaming, he ducked

under it and stayed there until he was afraid he had scalded his
shoulders. Then he reversed the spigots and soon the water was
so icy it made his teeth ache. Shivering in great spasms, he held
himself under the freezing shower a long time. Obviously there
was no water shortage here. Had the hotel hoarded it, letting
some people go thirsty so others could keep clean? Tucker would
have claimed it couldn't be that simple; the mere act of eating
didn't make you a cannibal. But Jack felt otherwise.

For days he had ignored what he suspected was going on. He
had tried to seal Helen and himself in a fortress of self-absorp-
tion that would protect them from everything outside. Now he
knew the fortress was a sand castle; all around him walls were
crumbling.

Putting on clean clothes, he returned to the other room. The
food tray was on the bureau; Helen's robe and nightgown hung
from the back of the chair; the covers were up around her bare
shoulders. Seeing he was dressed, she said, "What is it?"

"You were right. There's something wrong here."

He came and sat beside her, and as he described the Bedouins
clustered around the electrical pylons and the Berber who had
only his dead camel left and the people at the camp, Jack tried
to make Helen see what he had. But he lacked confidence in his
words and wouldn't have had much more in pictures. He was
sure she had seen snapshots and film clips of famines, just as he
had, yet he realized now how misleading they were.

A photographer followed aesthetic principles, centering the
subject, intensifying the colors, cropping the frame. But there
had been no balance or symmetry at the camp, no shaping vision
to impose order on people who had lost control of their bodies
and their lives. And no photo could capture that stench of
vomit, dysentery, and death.

As he continued talking, he held her hand, tightening his grip
for emphasis whenever he feared he wasn't making his point.

Finally Helen said, "I see what you're driving at. But I can't
do it."

"I'm not driving at anything."

"Sure you are. You're saying I should walk out on Tucker. Or
threaten to so he'll do something."

"No, I wasn't suggesting that." In fact, he was hoping she would suggest it.

"Then it's my guilty conscience, I guess. I didn't do this to Maliteta." She flung her head as if the room, this ludicrous simulacrum of an American hotel, were the problem. "But now that I know what's happening, I feel responsible."

"I do too."

"But it wouldn't work. He'd call my bluff and I couldn't carry through. I have a contract. If I break it, I'd never get another job."

"The way you've talked about movies, the way the whole business eats at you, would it matter that much?"

"Well, I wouldn't miss a lot of the people and the silliness. But . . ." She slipped her hand from his and glanced around, distracted. "But I kind of depend on movies. I can do one or two a year and make enough to wait for the right stage parts."

"You get paid for being in plays too, don't you?"

"Not as much. Not nearly. And I don't work very often. For one thing, there aren't many good roles for women. For another, I like to fit things in around the boys' schedule. And you know what it costs to live in New York."

"As a matter of fact, I don't."

"It's damned expensive. I own my apartment, but they're always raising the maintenance, and the kids are in private schools and it'll cost more when they go to college. The place in Vermont might seem like a self-indulgence, but I owe it to the boys to . . ." She raked a hand through her short hair. "Hell, I don't want to hide behind them. It's me. Once you've reached a certain point and have what you want, it's hard to go backward. If I didn't do films from time to time . . . I don't know, I'd feel trapped."

"Trapped?"

"I'd have to start all over, making rounds, being seen certain places, taking parts I hate, going on tour, maybe doing commercials. That's if I was lucky. If I wasn't . . ." She shrugged. "Do I sound like a selfish bitch?"

"No. You sound human. Nobody wants to go backward. Everybody wants to be happy."

Holding the sheet to her chest, she slid closer to him. "It's no crime being happy."

"I know. It's just that it seems wrong to be happy by myself."

"You're not by yourself."

He touched the back of her neck. "I mean the two of us being happy while all those people . . ." When he felt the cords in her neck tighten, he lowered his hand to the bare smooth warmth of her spine so she couldn't pull away. "What I'm saying is it's like that lifeboat argument you always hear. All the experts claim there's only so much room, so much money, so much food. If we let everybody aboard the lifeboat, it'll sink. But people like us, we're not in some dinky rowboat. It's a luxury ocean liner, and when I realize how many are left behind, I'm tempted to jump ship and take my chances with the rest of them."

She looked at him. "Are you quitting?"

He took a moment to consider, although as he saw it there wasn't much choice. "No. It wouldn't do any good. It wouldn't change things here. I'd just lose the job and any chance of getting out of debt."

He didn't like to think what he would have done if he was sure his quitting would change things. Money wasn't the only reason he was here. There had been the escape from that dim freezing room and his botched canvases. To lose the job would be bad enough, but now to leave Helen and go back to France alone . . .

"I don't like to sound glib," she said, "but maybe things aren't as bad as they seem."

"You wouldn't say that if you saw the camp."

"I mean maybe there's some other way to help. Why not give money to those tribes? Then they can buy food. I've got thousands of *gourdes* and nothing to spend them on."

"The government wouldn't let us."

"Does it have to know? There must be a way to do it secretly. Why not ask Moha?"

Jack didn't answer. The idea didn't seem worth discussing.

Curling onto her side, she laid her head in his lap, turning her face where he couldn't see it. His hand flowed from her hip down to her waist and up to her shoulders, goose flesh trailing his finger tips. She shivered, but he didn't cover her, and she didn't ask him to.

She was exposed to him in a way she hadn't been before. For an instant, as they talked, Jack had felt he didn't know her. But now they were down to bare facts. Much as she might complain about the script, the frivolous people, the foibles of the business, she had a career, commitments. "Trapped," she had said. "Locked in," Tucker had called it. It didn't make Jack care for her less. It just . . . just what? Just left him feeling helpless and angry.

Maybe Tucker would have explained this by claiming Jack was locked in too. Trapped by his recognition that things were drastically wrong and he could do nothing about them. Nothing except carp. Nothing except make hollow gestures. But Tucker was mistaken if he thought Jack was grinding at him. He was grinding at himself, certain something should be done, wondering what it was.

Helen moved, pressing insistently against him. Even through his clothes he felt the warmth of her breathing. Then the warmth was his own as she touched him.

"Look, I don't think . . ." he started.

She took him in her hand, pressed his heat to the coolness of her cheek, then moved over him with her mouth.

Finally Jack leaned down, kissing her belly, both her thighs, then between them.

Afterward, when the room was dark and he had moved from Helen's bed to his own, they heard the noise—the loud clash of galvanized tin.

She sat up. "What's that?"

"Garbage cans."

"Yes." She settled back, saying, "At the farm there's a raccoon that gets into the garbage. But this sounds like a dog."

Jack didn't correct her. He knew that would only keep them awake longer and leave him feeling worse.

Book Two

CHAPTER VII

When the crew and cast departed early for the Picture Rocks, Jack remained at the hotel, feeling like someone who had returned from a long trip or recovered from an illness and found that nothing had changed. He believed he had changed, along with his understanding of the situation, yet here he was doing what he had done before, behaving as if nothing had happened.

Last night as he quarreled with Tucker the choices had seemed clear-cut; this morning as the sun rose and the sky took on the dull sheen of scoured aluminum, the clarity disappeared. He carried his breakfast tray onto the balcony and sat eating buttered croissants, sipping strong coffee, and staring at the desert. It was, he thought, a bit like looking at one of those puzzles for children—a picture in which the shapes of birds and animals and people were disguised in the landscape. But narrowing his eyes against the glare, Jack followed the undulations of the dunes and discovered no pattern. Or, as Tucker had said, there was no connection; nothing related. On this location, life seemed to be lived on parallel lines.

Still, he thought there might be a pattern to events. Liebermann had resigned; somebody had attacked the airport. Maybe both were attempts to call attention to the famine. Maybe in America Liebermann was doing . . . What? Without pictures, without proof, there was nothing to do.

After breakfast he went down to the fourth floor to the room he used now as an office. He had finished a few rough sketches when Moha stopped by and dragged a chair over to the desk. The boy was wearing a T-shirt with an ad for *Jaws* on the front —a gaping mouth full of bloody teeth. Although he, like the shark, had his implacable eyes fixed on Jack, there was no menace in them. He appeared content to sit there silently, waiting.

But Jack felt acutely uncomfortable. "Well, I tried." As soon as he said it, he remembered this had been Tucker's lame comment after speaking to Benhima. "I know how you feel. I feel the same way myself. Something has to be done. But . . . but it's not easy."

"I didn't think it would be," Moha said.

"What I'm trying to say is we're visitors here. Guests of the government. And it'd be hard to—"

"Is Mr. Garland afraid of offending people?"

Moha was usually so deferential, Jack had trouble believing he was capable of sarcasm. "What he's afraid of is getting his ass kicked out of the country. There's a deal between the studio and the government, and it doesn't leave Tucker much room to maneuver. He's locked in."

"You make him sound like a prisoner." There was no mistake now about the sarcasm.

"In a way he is—if he wants to finish the movie and protect the studio's investment."

"But a man like him, a famous director, he can do whatever he pleases. Why does he care about the government?"

"It's the studio he cares about. And Tucker's not as famous or powerful as you think. I know it's silly compared to the problems here, but he's in trouble. He's worried about his career." When Moha smiled, Jack's temper flared. "Look, you lived in the States. What the hell, you studied the movie business. You probably understand this end of it better than I do."

"Oh, I understand, all right. It reminds me of everybody in California talking about their troubles and how they were going to find themselves. They'd drop out and go live in the mountains or on the beach and say they were getting themselves together. I remember explaining that in Tougla nobody talked about their troubles. They were too busy working. And they couldn't waste time finding themselves when they were so worried about finding food. And how could they drop out? There was nowhere to go except into the desert."

Jack shut his sketch pad and carefully arranged the pencils next to it. Although annoyed at being forced to explain himself— annoyed even more by the boy's small, knowing grin—he didn't want to hurt him. "I'd like to help, but . . ."

"But you're a prisoner too."

"No more or less than anyone else. I haven't given up hope. Helen had an idea. We both get a lot of expense money each week. We're willing to give it to the people in the camps."

"The American way," Moha said.

"Damn right! Of course it can't compare with the Malitetan way. And it's not the perfect solution. But with money they could buy food and medicine and maybe better treatment from the soldiers."

Moha shook his head. "Impossible. The Minister would never permit it."

"The hell with him. Don't tell him. Bribe the guards. Or smuggle it in."

"Very difficult. And dangerous. If we were caught—"

Jack saw his opportunity and pounced. "I didn't think it'd be easy."

As Moha's own words flew back in his face, Jack felt sorry for him. It had been so easy to set him up. He himself had no great confidence in the idea of giving money and he had suggested it mostly to prove a point—everybody had limits. One way or another, they were all locked in.

Believing the boy understood this now, Jack tried to let him off with no more embarrassment. "Maybe we'll think of something else, something safer."

"There are some men I could talk to. It'll take time to find out if I can trust them. How long will it take you to get the money?"

"It's ready whenever you are. But, listen, I don't want to put you on the spot."

"Excuse me, how much money?"

"About three thousand dollars right now. There'll be more every week. Better think it over though."

He appeared to be doing just that as he rubbed his arms,

which were covered from elbows to wrists with dark curly hair.
"You're serious then?"

On the defensive again, Jack wondered whether he should
back off. But he thought maybe there was a safe way to arrange
it. "You look into it and let me know."

"Good." Moha stood up. "We will have to work quickly before
things become worse at the camps." Then he gripped Jack's hand
and repeated, "Good."

It was during the filming at the rocks that everybody began to
talk about escape. Each day, after hours in the desert flayed by
sand and fried by the sun, they returned to the Sidi Mansour and
sat shivering in the bar discussing "the scenario." It was a joke,
but one which they laughed at less and less as they got down to
details. Someone had a Michelin map of Africa, and they decided to steal a Land Rover, drive north, and cross the border
into Algeria.

But after adding up the miles and computing that it would
take two weeks to reach Algiers by car, they said they'd better
hijack a plane. That way they'd get to Nice in eight hours.

It was only when the first batch of film went off and they
learned there wouldn't be another flight for a week that their
faith in "the scenario" weakened. Still spooked and self-pitying
as soldiers in a combat zone, they spoke less about escape and
more about the relief plane that would be dropping supplies.
They were waiting for mail, for back issues of magazines and
newspapers, for cosmetics and cassettes they had ordered
through the production company's London office.

And as they waited the time recorded by clocks and calendars
seemed a lie. The only true measure was the depth of their bore-
dom, the growing length of their silences, the abruptness of their
anger. The French continued to complain about cold lunches;
the Americans complained about the French. After several fist
fights broke out on the tennis court, Tucker put it off limits.

Nobody, as far as Jack could tell, took any interest in where
they were or what went on around them. And much as they complained about the long workdays, they appeared to prefer them
to Sunday when there was nothing except drink or sex or gossip
to float them from one meal to the next.

He too had trouble killing time and holding his temper. Some mornings he woke tense, seized by an inexplicable premonition of menace, and was sure something was about to happen. Other days he doubted anything ever would or had.

Helen urged him to visit the set more often, but he said he was afraid of arguing with Tucker and getting fired. What he didn't admit was that he was avoiding Moha.

When he heard Reid Gorman was flying back to Moburka at the end of the week, Jack lingered outside the dining room to make certain Benhima wasn't around. Then he suggested Gorman and he have lunch.

Gorman nodded gravely. "Yes, I was hoping we'd get a chance to talk."

The headwaiter—Jack had learned his name was Fatih—led them to a place next to half a dozen wardrobe girls. But Jack asked for the corner table across the room.

Gorman promptly unscrewed the cap from the salt shaker, sprinkled some onto his palm, and licked it up. "I'm out of tablets," he explained. "When I don't take them, I find I wilt in the afternoon."

"Guess you're glad to be going back to Moburka?"

He nodded again, giving off the milky scent of his protective skin cream.

"What's it like?" Jack asked.

"Like Tougla, only bigger and with black faces and jungle instead of brown ones and desert. Maliteta's a hardship post no matter where they stick you."

"How's the food in the south?"

"We shop at the commissary."

Fatih returned for their orders, and they both asked for onion soup, *escalope de veau,* salad, and a bottle of white wine.

Peeling the cellophane from a pack of bread sticks, Gorman noisily chomped one. "Is it true Hal Nichols is taking Jerry Lewis to the States?"

"I haven't talked to Nichols lately."

"They tell me he promised to hire him as a house boy. I'll be glad to help arrange a visa."

A serving boy brought the soup—small bowls clotted with croutons and gruyère cheese. Gorman spooned up a mouthful.

Jack sipped his wine. "The reason I asked about the food in Moburka, everybody here is tired of eating at the hotel. It'd be nice to try a different place, but the owner of the Chems said he ran out of food."

Gorman patted his mouth with a napkin. "The Minister mentioned you and Tucker had had a talk with him."

"Then I don't have to work up to this. You know about the famine."

"I don't know anything of the kind." A bit of color came to his cheeks. "I just know Benhima was very upset."

"Don't blame him. I'd be upset too if people in my country were starving."

"You better get your facts straight before you make charges like that."

"I know what I saw."

"You saw a relief camp."

"I didn't notice any relief. People there were sick. Some of them were dead and laid out. And the kids all had bulging eyes and that orange hair."

"Kwashiorkor." Gorman tilted the bowl for the last crouton.

"You've been there?"

"No. Nobody at the Embassy has been receiving engraved invitations to the camps."

"Then you can't imagine what it's like."

"Oh, I think I can. I was in Ethiopia for two years. A pretty grim place. If my information was accurate, a few hundred thousand people died in the drought there. That's the trouble though. In these countries you never get accurate information. Only rumors."

While one boy cleared off the soup bowls, another brought plates for the entrée.

"I'm not talking about rumors," Jack said. "Right here at the hotel guys are eating out of the garbage cans. It all adds up."

"Adds up to what?" he asked mildly, motioning for more sauce on his veal.

"A drought. A famine."

"Not necessarily. Take the question of drought. Before you can be sure, you have to find out how much rainfall there's been during a particular period. And what's the normal rainfall? What's the water table? The soil composition? Is it agricultural or grazing land? Have you looked into any of this?"

"Chrissake, Gorman, you don't need to know—"

"Yes, you do. It's a complex subject. To simplify it is counterproductive."

"So is going hungry."

"What I'm trying to say is declaring a famine is a drastic step. First you have to define your terms and figure out how many calories a day an average man needs. Then you make allowances for different physiques and occupations. And there are adjustments for women and children and babies. It's not a case of spotting a couple of malnourished kids and jumping to conclusions."

"You sound like the French arguing whether the lunch is hot."

"I'm sorry you're getting upset, Jack." He put down his knife and fork. "This your first trip to Africa?"

"Yes."

"Ever been to Asia or the Middle East?"

"No."

"So you're seeing this sort of thing for the first time? Well, it's not a pretty sight, I grant you. Even in good years these people don't really get enough of the right foods. The question then is how much worse this dry spell has made things."

"No, the question is whether they're dying."

"Of course they're dying. Life expectancy in the Sahel is less than forty years. So the crucial question is how many more of them are dying now and how much younger? That's hard to determine."

The sauce on Jack's meat had congealed; he shoved the plate aside. He hadn't expected Gorman to agree with him—not at first, anyway—and he'd been prepared to argue. What he hadn't counted on was this measured detachment which simultaneously claimed expertise and powerlessness.

"Okay," Jack said. "But while you're waiting for all the facts and figures, I think something should be done."

"Something is being done. You saw the relief camp."

"You know it's not a relief camp. It's just a place to dump those tribes."

Gorman glanced at him from under pale lashes. "If I were you, I wouldn't spread that around."

"Are you denying it?"

"I don't know anything about it. Neither do you."

"I know the government isn't giving them enough to eat. I know it won't let them move south to better grazing land."

"You're simplifying again. Look at it from their point of view. If you let thousands of Berbers migrate south, you don't solve the problem. You just switch it from one place to another. Before long they'd ruin that area too."

"If Maliteta can't handle the problem, why doesn't it ask for help?"

"You're the one assuming they can't handle it."

"From what I've seen they don't give a damn about handling it."

"Well"—he signaled the boy for the salad—"there is some question whether any underdeveloped country can afford to put up with these nomadic tribes. They may be fascinating to anthropologists, but they're a pain in the ass to everybody else."

"Is that the official Embassy position?"

Gorman grinned, not about to be baited. "Let's hope they'd express it more diplomatically."

"I'm curious. What is the Embassy doing about this?"

"Same thing we're doing. Talking. There's not much else to do until Maliteta asks for advice."

"Oh, come on, Gorman. America's always got some kind of leverage."

"Look, anybody asks for help, we deliver." He salted and peppered his salad. "But we stick our noses in here, we're liable to get the delegation expelled. Not that Maliteta itself is all that important. But we're firming up our image in Africa, and you don't do that by telling a country how to run its internal affairs.

"Now I'm glad we had this opportunity to talk, Jack. As soon as the Minister complained, I knew we'd have to hammer out an understanding. I'm warning you—and it's a friendly warning—

stop meddling in things that don't concern you or the Embassy'll put you on a plane out of here."

"Did you give Tucker the same warning?"

"That wasn't necessary. He understands our position. Do you?"

Jack didn't answer.

"What I suggest . . ." He leaned back, smiling. "I suggest you concentrate on Helen Soray. She'll keep your hands full."

"I've got a suggestion for you. Don't say another word about Helen or I'll knock your scrawny ass all over this hotel. After that, it'll be my pleasure to be deported."

Jack shoved away from the table.

Gorman was consulting the dessert menu.

CHAPTER VIII

Days later, when Jack rode out to the airport, it was like traveling the length of a fluorescent tube. The sky was cloudless, high, incandescent. One could call it empty, but the real emptiness was underneath it. That desert sky diminished everything.

Arriving at the airport, he was reminded of a trailer camp. Trucks, taxis, Land Rovers, and trailers were parked in rows at the edge of the runway. There were no planes in sight.

Jack's driver pulled in behind the longest trailer, the one marked Meal Mobile. A ramp led in one end, past a cafeteria counter, and out the other end where many of the French and Americans had stripped to the waist and were sun-tanning as they ate. The Malitetan extras had crawled under the Meal Mobile to escape the heat.

Although hungry, Jack didn't have time for lunch. Donald Wattle had stopped in the middle of a scene and refused to go on; he claimed the entire thing had to be rethought and reshot. Jack had been called in for an emergency conference, and he hurried into the terminal to sit with Tucker, Moha, and Tallow, and listen to the director of photography's tirade.

"It's so bloody flat."

"The dialogue?" Tucker asked.

"That's your department. Your problem. I'm talking about the look. You put your eye to the camera and there's nothing there."

"Barry and Lisa are there."

"Like sticks of furniture in a warehouse. It's not a question of acting. It's the setting. There are no eye-grabbers! You have two people walking along the tarmac—which is black and dead—and behind them you've got the desert—which is white and dead. There's no back action, no planes landing and taking off, not a thing on the runway."

"This is costing money for you to *kvetch* about what can't be changed," said Tallow. "A flight comes once a week, refuels, and leaves. Are we supposed to wait around for the next one?"

Wattle wasn't listening. "Then they walk in here." He pirouetted, pointing to the unpainted cinder block walls, the shelf-like benches, the buzzing lights overhead. "Who'll believe it's an air terminal? There's no color, no restaurant, no bar, not even a bloody magazine rack."

"This is what airports in the Sahara are like," Moha said.

"I don't care bugger-all about that. Nobody else knows it and they'll blame the director of photography. It's very simple. When you shoot an airport scene it should look like an airport."

"I thought the point of filming on location was to be authentic."

"My good fellow, that may be what they teach at USC, but there's no sense being authentic if it's ugly. The way we're headed, this movie is going to have the look of something a graduate student shot in his basement with a Bolex."

"Any suggestions?" Tucker asked, fuming. "I'd like to get something in the can today."

"Let's at least put signs, pictures, *something!* on these walls. And as for the extras, when they're dragging around in those dreary djellabas, we might as well be shooting sacks of potatoes. Why not choreograph the scene and show them meeting friends, doing that handshaking lark? You think you could arrange that?"

Moha nodded, his face set in the neutral expression Jack knew so well.

"Please pound it into their thick skulls not to look at the camera."

"Yeah." Jack smacked the boy's knee. "Wouldn't want to ruin the illusion of reality Donald's building."

Tallow laughed. Tucker concentrated on the floor. Wattle went right on talking. "Another thing, we ought to shoot day for night. It's a love scene. We'll wet down the tarmac. Nothing makes for a more intimate atmosphere than a rainy night."

"It hasn't rained here for years," Jack said.

"I could care less what you learned from the weather report. I just want that tarmac to gleam."

"Why?"

"You shoot day for night, bubba, you can dim the sunlight with a filter. But that doesn't get rid of the shadows. If you wet the asphalt, the shadows look like reflections in the puddles."

"Where the hell are you going to get that much water? It'll take thousands of gallons."

Tucker turned to Wattle, open to persuasion from either side. Jack had never known him to be so indecisive.

"I saw a tank truck sprinkling the trees in town," Wattle said. "That'll do the job."

"Still Jack has a point," Moha said. "This will waste a lot of water."

"They were dousing those bloody little trees with it."

"Tell you what," Tucker said. "Explain the situation to Benhima and ask if there's any to spare."

Moha was fretting with a belt loop on his Levi's. "The Minister won't know how much water there is, but he'll want to help and he may—"

"Tell him to be frank. We can live with whatever he decides."

The boy went off to phone the Sidi Mansour.

"What are you working on now, bubba?"

"The scene in the medina. The one where Barry brings Lisa to his house."

"You have a location?"

"Not yet. I'm going to look at one this afternoon with Fatih."

"Fat who?" Tallow asked.

"The headwaiter. Jerry Lewis. He's showing me his house."

"Okay, keep in mind what Donald's been talking about. We need a lot more visual excitement."

"Why don't we flood the house and have Lisa and Barry swim through the scene?"

Before heading back to the hotel, Jack stopped in one of the air-conditioned trailers to speak to Helen. But Lisa Austin was there, for once without Roberta and Phil, and it was obvious something was wrong. She sat at one end of a rust-colored couch, her arms folded just under her unyielding breasts. Helen was at the opposite end grimacing at Jack, who couldn't decipher her meaning.

"Sorry to interrupt," he said. "I'll see you tonight."

"Stay," Lisa said. "It doesn't make any difference. I'm sure you already know."

"Know what?"

"The crew's been talking," Helen said. "Lisa's a little upset."

"A little, hell! I've never been this low. I'm so depressed I can't eat, I can't sleep. I'd just like to know who started the rumor."

"What rumor?" Jack was seized by an unreasonable hope that news of the famine had spread.

"Everybody's saying I'm tripling with Roberta and Phil. I bet Barry started it. He's jealous he doesn't have a bodyguard."

"I wouldn't let it bother me," Helen said.

"Don't you see the insult? If I want sex I'll have it. But I don't care if I hadn't been laid in a year, I think better of myself than to get it on with anybody on my payroll. Do people really think I have to pay for it?"

When the door opened, a gust of scorching air rushed through the trailer, and Tucker came in. "What's this? An encounter group?"

"No," Lisa snapped, "we're warming up for a three-way fuck."

"Great! Let's make it a four-decker sandwich." He flopped down on the couch, slipping an arm around her.

She pulled away. "I'm not in the mood for your jokes."

"Who's joking? You know how I feel about you." He was grinning at Jack.

"Yeah, I know how you feel. You don't feel anything for me."

"Come here. What are you talking about?" This time when he brought her close she didn't pull back.

"You mean you don't mind being near me?"

"Mind it? I love it."

"Then why are you keeping the camera a mile away?"

"We did three close-ups this morning."

"You call them close-ups?"

"What do you want me to do? Shoot right up your nose?"

"You have a very weird definition of a close-up."

Jack headed for the door.

"Leaving?" Helen said. "Thought you enjoyed language lessons?"

Lisa and Tucker quit bickering and glanced at him.

"Guess I've lost my interest in semantics."

"Where are you going?" Lisa asked.

"Into town to scout a location."

"I'm coming with you."

"Hey, what the hell," Tucker said, "we have work to do."

"Shoot around me. It's what you're doing anyway." She grabbed her purse and went outside to wait for Jack.

On the ride to the hotel Lisa let a minute or two pass before saying, "Look, if this is a bother, you can just drop me. I'll go to my room and take a bath."

"It's no bother. But I'm going into the medina. Will you be comfortable in that?"

"Sure. It's light and cool."

That wasn't what Jack meant. She wore a gauzy summerweight dress with nothing underneath.

"None of this would have happened," she said, "if Tucker wasn't being such a bastard. I see him all the time in LA, you know."

"I didn't know."

"What the hell, I lived with him once. But ever since we got here he's acted like I have a disease. I might as well have. Except for Helen, I haven't talked to anybody in days."

"I'm sorry."

"Don't be. It's nice of you to take me with you."

Smoking a Marlboro and leafing through an issue of *Jours de France*, Fatih was waiting in the lobby of the Sidi Mansour. Except for his acting début when he had dressed like a bellboy, this was the first time Jack had seen him out of his tuxedo. Yet he still seemed to be in a costume of sorts.

He had on stacked-heel boots and trousers so tight he couldn't fit anything into the pockets. He carried his spare change and cigarettes in a little leather purse that dangled from his wrist.

Several sizes too small, his knit pullover didn't quite meet the waistband of his pants and an inch of bare midriff showed.

When he learned Lisa was coming with them, Fatih nervously stabbed the cigarette into an ash tray. "I am happy to show you my home. But please, it is nothing like your Hollywood apartments."

"That's fine," Jack said. "We need a typical medina house."

"Mine is not typical perhaps, but you will like it."

He walked them out to the car and squeezed into the back seat with them. On the road to town they passed the tank truck heading in the direction of the airport.

"I knew a minor thing like a drought wouldn't keep Benhima from wasting a few thousand gallons of water."

"Is there really a drought?" Lisa asked.

"What do you think?" Jack asked Fatih.

"The weather does not interest me. When the hot months come, I will be gone."

"You don't call this hot?"

"It is spring. The air is still fresh. And it can be hot in other countries too, can't it? I have many souvenirs of the heat in Europe."

Lisa squinted. "What sort of souvenirs?"

"Of days when I had to change my shirt three times and nights when it was too *humide* to sleep."

Jack realized he meant memories.

When they reached Tougla's main square, Fatih told the driver to wait for them, then led Jack and Lisa onto the sidewalk and stopped. In the motionless air the tamarisk and acacia trees resembled stabiles made of scorched foil. Fatih glanced around as if he had lost his bearings.

"You must see the Sahara museum," he said.

"Not now."

"But it is right here in the Syndicat d'Initiative."

"Another time," Jack said.

In his boots Fatih clomped up Avenue de la Libération, his purse swinging on his wrist, just as Lisa's did on hers. From a café that exhaled the odor of stale urine, someone shouted, and he stopped to answer.

"A friend wants us to take a glass of tea with him," he said.

"Look, I'm sorry, but I have to finish those sketches by this evening."

"I'll tell him we are on business for the film and are *très, très pressés.*"

Yet as they walked along streets where they could have driven, Fatih took his time, and Jack suspected he was ashamed to show Lisa his house. But when he paused again to speak to friends, repeating his histrionic explanation of how busy he was with the movie, Jack realized he simply wanted to prolong his moment of importance.

At the edge of the European quarter, he set off across a field away from the medina.

"Wait," Jack called. "Where are you going?"

"My house." He was moving briskly now, shoving through a gang of boys playing soccer with a goat's bladder.

"But the scene, it's in the medina."

"This is better. You will see."

Lightheaded from the heat, Jack didn't argue. Lisa and he followed at a distance, detouring around an empty corral fenced by cactus and thornbushes. Then they came into a courtyard where several women sat on the shady side fashioning water bags from used inner tubes. Fatih didn't speak to them or to the old man who had been in the doorway but backed out, bowing, as the three of them entered.

The house, a single room with a smooth dirt floor, reminded Jack of a mud dauber's nest. He knew Donald Wattle would never shoot here. No eyegrabbers. Not unless you counted the pictures Fatih had clipped from magazines and pasted to the walls—snapshots of Muhammad Ali, rock stars, and the French national soccer team, a pink Ford Mustang, a McDonald's double cheeseburger, and an ad for Supphose which could have appealed only to a man raised in a culture where a woman's legs are never seen.

Motioning Lisa to a sofa—actually the back seat of an automobile—and Jack to a beach chair made of aluminum tubing and green nylon rope, Fatih asked if they would take tea. Since they saw nowhere in the house to fetch water and no way to heat it, they said they wouldn't put him to any trouble.

"But you must drink something." He lifted the carved lid of a cedar chest and rearranged some clothing, brought out a bottle of Perrier and displayed the label as if it were a vintage wine.

"Shall I open it?"

Thirsty as he was, Jack could see the boy was reluctant to waste the mineral water on them. "No, I'm fine."

Fatih placed the bottle in the chest and returned with a menu from the restaurant in Marseilles where he worked summers. "I cannot tell you how much I shall miss it. Even when I go to California, I suppose I shall always feel myself to be an exile from France."

"You like France so much," Lisa said, "why not move there instead of California?"

"Oh, it is a beautiful country and I have many happy souvenirs of it, but it is a place of the past. America has more opportunity, more money."

"Won't you miss Maliteta?" Lisa asked. "Your family, your friends?"

"Will you miss it when you leave?"

"It's not my home."

"It's not mine either. Not any more."

Sitting primly with her purse on her knees, her dress wrinkled and smudged, her hair blown to tangles by the drive, Lisa looked lost in this mud hut, and her voice sounded slightly forlorn. "Los Angeles is a big town. You might be lonely there on your own."

"No, I have many friends. Americans I met in Marseilles and at the Sidi Mansour." Dropping the menu into the chest, he picked up a hairbrush and dusted off his trousers. "And Hal Nichols will be there." He spat on his left knee, scrubbing at a stubborn spot.

"Hal may not be able to do all he promised."

Fatih stopped scrubbing. "He said he'd find me a job."

"What if you don't like the job he gets you? It costs a lot to live in America."

"I'm saving. And I'll make money when they do the movie in my house. Mr. Schwarz said he would pay."

"Yes," Jack said, "if they decide to shoot here. But I wouldn't count on it. I wouldn't count on anything."

"What are you saying?"

"I'm saying don't quit your job at the Sidi Mansour. Don't tell that restaurant in Marseilles you won't be back."

"Aren't you going to make a movie of my house?"

"That's up to Mr. Garland. I just do the drawings. But I don't want you to be disappointed."

"You asked to see it. What's wrong with it?"

"Nothing. It's a nice house. But the scene is set in the medina."

"This is better. It's new and doesn't smell bad."

"But it's small," Lisa said. "Remember when we shot the restaurant scene, how many cameras and lights and people there were? There may not be enough room."

Fatih glanced around. "I will move my things into the court-yard."

"We can't use an empty house," Jack said.

"Tell me quick, what should I do?" His anger had taken on an edge of desperation.

"Like Jack said, it's not up to us."

"That's right. You are not the bosses. Mr. Garland is. Do your drawings," he ordered Jack, "and show them to him."

He knew it was futile, but there was no other way to calm Fatih or salve his own conscience. So he did a few quick sketches while the boy leaned over his shoulder, insisting on ab-solute accuracy, pointing to objects he had missed—a sliver of mirror on the bureau, a cracked porcelain bowl, a tortoise-shell ash tray—as if these would convince Tucker to film here.

Before they left, Fatih asked for one of the drawings and tacked it up with the pictures of Muhammad Ali and the rock stars.

They were coming around the corral when they bumped into a man in a buttonless wool topcoat, undershorts, and tennis shoes. He tried to show them what was in the straw basket he carried.

"Don't bother with him," Fatih said. "He's crazy."

The fellow was making moist gargling sounds with a tongue that looked too large for his mouth.

"What's he saying?" Lisa asked.

"He wants you to look at his baby gazelle. Just push him away."

"Wait. I'd like to see it."

The man set the basket on the ground, and Lisa crouched for

a closer look. The animal had the markings of a newborn fawn and the mild, blinking, long-lashed face of a lamb. When Lisa touched it behind the ears, it shook its head, then calmed down as she stroked its flanks.

"Where'd he find it?"

"In the desert," Fatih said. "We must go. I have to be at the hotel to prepare for dinner."

"What'll he do with it?"

"Eat it."

"You're kidding," she wailed.

"Not at all. What else should he do with it?"

"I thought he'd raise it as a pet."

"This fool knows nothing of pets. I told you, he is an idiot. Here they believe that means holy. That's the kind of country we have. And you ask why I want to leave?"

"We better go," Jack said.

"I want to buy it."

"Don't joke. He won't understand."

"I'm not joking," Lisa said. "I'll have the carpenters build a pen in the garden."

"But what about when we leave?"

"I'll take it with me. I own ten acres out in the valley. It'll have plenty of room."

"You're talking crazy."

"You heard Fatih. That means holy. Ask him how much."

"You can't pay for a worthless animal," Fatih said.

Lisa stood up, opened her purse, and pulled out a fistful of *gourdes*. "Ask him how much or I'll give him all this."

"Do you know how much that is?" Jack asked.

"Who cares? It's all play money anyway."

"You'll give him that while I may get nothing for the movie to be made in my house? This is not fair."

The fellow in the topcoat flicked his malarial eyes from one of them to the other like someone watching a ping-pong match.

"Take it yourself then." Lisa slapped the wad of bills into Fatih's hand. "Pay him what he wants and keep the change. But I'm keeping this baby." Picking up the basket, she strode across the dusty field, sunlight silhouetting her body in the gauzy dress.

When Fatih peeled off five dollars' worth of *gourdes,* Jack said, "Give him more than that. Now take the same for yourself and let me have the rest."

"No! She told me to keep it."

"She's upset. I'll give her the money when she calms down."

"Now this crazy one has as much as I do."

"It was his gazelle."

The fellow stuffed the bills into his topcoat and trudged away from town toward nothing Jack could see.

"But I showed you my house, I offered tea, I helped—"

Jack hurried to catch up with Lisa.

While the rest of them waited in the bar, Tucker went upstairs to screen the first batch of rushes. A second assistant had passed the word that Tucker wanted no one else to see them except Wattle and the principals.

Lisa Austin insisted, however, on bringing Roberta to make sure her hair was right, and since her contract called for around-the-clock protection, Phil came too.

Barry Travis was equally adamant about not going. He stayed in the bar drinking Coors and munching dry roasted cashews which had arrived on the same flight as the rushes. "I know what's on Tucker's mind. I see how fat I am, he thinks I'll stick to my diet. But what the hell is there to do in this dump except eat?"

"What I'd like to know," Nichols said, "is what's on Lisa's mind. I mean nobody, not even a dingbat like her, buys a pet gazelle. Jerry Lewis told me she paid a hundred bucks for it."

"She paid ten," Jack said. "Then she gave ten to Fatih."

"All that nose candy has eaten away her brain," Barry said. "I predict she'll wind up on stage in Tijuana doing an animal act with this gazelle."

"No, you wait, one of these fuckers'll steal it." Marvin Tallow's complexion had turned the color of raw meat, just as it did each evening after his fourth drink. "The bastards would swipe the nickels off a dead nigger's eyeballs. Last week we lost half a dozen first aid kits. Today we're missing a pair of walkie-talkies. Now I ask you, what the shit is anybody here going to do with walkie-talkies?"

"I bet somebody's trying to get a message back to the real

world. My agent claimed he called twenty times one day," Barry said, "and the international operator kept saying, 'Sorry. Maliteta doesn't answer.' You ask me, the whole country's off the hook."

Jack left the bar for the lobby, stood by a window, and stared into darkness. Keeping his eyes straight ahead, his back turned to everybody, he feared that someone would wander over and strike up a—no, not a conversation. As far as he could tell the concept didn't exist among these people. Strike up the usual monologue of wisecracks, gossip, and anecdotes about other films, other locations, other actors.

At first this litany of bitching and backbiting had touched him as no more than vague background noise, what the sound men referred to as "acoustic cologne." But gradually it had become as oppressive as the bleak soughing of the wind, the churring of insects, the nightly scrimmage at the garbage cans. For years Jack had believed nobody could be more self-absorbed than his fellow academics. Now he knew better and half hoped some of the stories about the easy availability of sex in Hollywood were true. If they couldn't communicate through language, if even their eyes seldom made contact—most of them had a habit of staring over your shoulder while they babbled in your face— then maybe flesh laid to bare flesh would force them to acknowledge that someone else was alive and the ear wasn't the body's most attractive organ.

Later, in their room after the rushes, Helen sat at the edge of the bed unzipping her boots. Jack was mixing her a drink and feeling better now that they were alone. He knew she was about to undress and that he would watch and then they would make love. The watching had become as important to him as the love-making, for he was at the stage where he was noticing new things about her—the lean sculptured muscles of her back, the smooth, close-grained skin of her thighs, two dimples, like thumbprints, at the base of her spine, the way she held her head poised, chin lifted slightly, when she was tired, as she was now.

He handed her the glass. She sipped at it, thanked him, and set it on the night table.

"How were the rushes?" he asked.

"You looked terrific in the restaurant scene. Sort of like Jack Nicholson only with more hair and less weight."

"What about the rest of it?"

"Maybe we'll get lucky and they won't release it."

"That bad? What was Tucker's reaction?"

Unbuckling her blue jeans, she stood up, stepped out of them, and put her arms around Jack. "Let's not talk about Tucker. It's bad enough being around him and the rest of them all day. At night I'd rather pretend they don't exist."

There was a knock at the door.

"The trouble is," Jack said, "they don't realize they don't exist."

Helen ducked into the bathroom while he answered the door, expecting one of the ADs with a revised call sheet. But it was Moha, wrapped in his black burnoose. He pushed into the room.

"I have something to show you," he whispered. "Can you and Helen meet me in the screening room?"

"It's midnight."

"This is the only time I could arrange it."

"What?"

"A movie. One I made about the Berber tribes. It may change your mind."

"Change it how?"

"You'll understand once you see it." He seemed to strain to convey urgency without raising his voice.

"Okay, go on down. I'll be right with you."

"Please, don't make any noise. And if somebody's in the hall, hurry back here. I can't let anyone else know. If the Minister finds out . . ." He made a gesture of hopelessness with his hand.

When he left, Helen leaned her head out of the bathroom.

"Did you hear?" Jack asked.

She nodded.

"Look, he knows you have an early call. He'll understand if you stay here."

"No, I'm coming."

Switching off the lights, Jack opened the door, then quickly shut it when he heard somebody in the hall. On the second try they made it to the staircase landing and paused in the darkness before going down to the third floor. Once more they stopped, made certain no one was around, and crossed to the screening room.

Moha let them in before they had a chance to knock. After locking the door behind them, he clicked on a pocket-size flashlight and began threading a reel of film into the projector. The air was stale and smelled of cigars, cigarettes, and the flatulence of the movie company.

"How'd you get the key?" Jack whispered.

"Fatih." As he adjusted the spindle, Moha's sharp features were half in shadow, half in light.

"He a friend of yours?"

"No. We have known each other since we were boys, but we haven't been friends for a long time."

"I wouldn't trust him."

"I don't. I bribed him."

"Still he might tell someone we're here." Helen had folded her arms, but couldn't stop shivering.

"No," Moha said. "He'd get in trouble for taking a bribe. I can prove I paid him, and it was in dollars. It's illegal to have foreign currency."

"I suppose he's saving for his trip to America."

"That's what he told me."

"He's making a mistake," Jack said. "I doubt Nichols has any intention of taking him to California."

Moha stepped back to check what he had done. "It will be worse if he does go."

"Why?" Helen asked. "You said you liked the States."

"Most of the time I did. But I was in school. Fatih, he'll work in somebody's house or a restaurant, and he won't have anyone to boss around. Before long he'll realize that, as much as he's ashamed to be a Malitetan, that's what he is and that's how everybody will treat him—as just another nigger. He should stop pretending to be French or dreaming about becoming an American."

"Have you told him that?"

"Yes. It's no use."

When the projector was ready he motioned them to sit down. "I'm sorry there is no sound track. I hope you don't have trouble following it."

The film whirred, and a series of descending numbers flashed on the screen. The opening shot was of a stretch of crushed pebbles so vast and flat it was impossible to judge distance or perspective until six men on camels galloped right to left, racing just ahead of the dust they had raised. Their faces were masked by black *lithams,* their *gandurahs* fluttered at the hems and sleeves. From their necks flapped leather pouches and ceremonial swords. Each man held the reins in one hand and an antique, ornate musket in the other. On signal the muskets were fired and six plumes of smoke flagged behind them as the camels and riders sprinted off screen.

"Of course it would have been better in color," Moha said. "But that costs much more than I had."

The camera panned a campsite on a mountainside where thick-trunked cypresses seemed to have sprouted from solid rock. The tribesmen had pitched tents under the trees, and Moha moved among them in quick cuts that contrasted the fierce-eyed, veiled men with the women, whose faces were uncovered and who wore silver loops in their ears and Hands of Fatma around their necks.

The women were dyeing their palms with henna, plaiting the hair of young girls, and shaving little boys bald except for topknots. A group of men played camel-hide drums, xylophones of hollow gourds, and simple stringed instruments. Then the women clapped and sang and several men danced, stamping dust from the ground, waving their arms and thrusting their heads back and forth. Soon they were reeling, their *gandurahs* puffed with air, and they crouched and leaped, unsheathed their swords and flailed at one another. Some of the swords went wild, drawing blood, splattering the pale sand. But when the women quit clapping and the drummers stopped, the dancers dropped their swords and embraced.

Zooming in on one man's bloody hand, Moha faded into a shot of an infected sore. Flies swarmed over it, jostling for places. As the camera pulled back, there was a baby with a swollen belly and a head lolling on a flimsy stalk of neck. The sore—the size of a fifty-cent piece—was on the baby's forehead.

Jack felt Helen draw up straight beside him, but she said nothing.

Several skeletal camels clomped across the *hammada*, a parody of the opening scene made eerier by rippling heat distortions. One camel stumbled, pitched forward, slamming its jaw against the stony ground. It managed to get its hind legs underneath it, but the forelegs wouldn't bear the weight and it went down again, flopping onto its side, its nostrils quivering in a close-up that dissolved into a shot of a camel carcass with a gaping mouth, no tongue, and empty eye sockets.

Sitting under a stunted tree, a woman stripped leaves and bark from the limbs, chewed them into a pulp, and tried to feed it to a boy who might have been eight or nine but appeared to have the malleable bones, big head, and transparent flesh of an embryo. His lips and nostrils had shriveled from dehydration; his skin was cracked and covered with sores; his mutilated face was already a death mask.

"Did he die?" Helen asked in a small voice.

"He must have," said Moha. "There was very little water and no food at all."

Minute black dots moved over a washed-out surface. They might have been beetles on a blank sheet of paper. But then a telescopic lens brought a woman and several children into focus. Scuttling over an immense dune, sifting the sand through their fingers, they lifted their hands to their mouths. A close-up showed them catching and eating bugs.

Beneath a tattered lean-to an entire family, from infants to grandparents, stared impassively at the camera. If the kids' eyes hadn't bulged so hideously it would have been impossible to tell these people were starving. Oblivious to the dust that swirled around them, they looked like statues carved from sandstone, no less immobile than the two bodies stretched out in front of them. Both the living and the dead were being mummified by the desert.

"From the time they are born they are taught to show no negative emotions," Moha said. "You know when they are happy, but not when they are sad or scared or suffering. They believe it is undignified to complain. That's why they waited so long before coming into the camps. And they knew they wouldn't get much help there."

Swinging away from the family, the camera swept over hundreds of other bodies with skin like ancient parchment.

"Because of the soldiers I couldn't get close. But the telephoto lens gives the general picture."

"Is that the camp I saw?" Jack asked.

"No, it's farther west. But they're all alike. They feed them a little bread and powdered milk and maybe some soup—just enough to keep the strongest ones alive. The children and old people die first."

In the dunes far beyond the camp a sleek feral dog and a fat vulture appeared to be playing tug of war. They had dug a body from a shallow, sandy grave, and while the vulture was pecking at the fingers of one hand, the dog was gnawing at a foot.

The film ended by repeating the shot of galloping camels, guns going off, and the Berbers leaving the desert empty of everything except dust as white as bone meal.

The three of them sat silently a moment. Then Moha switched on the flashlight and moved up beside them. "Of course it is very amateur."

"It works," Helen said. "You can always add a sound track."

"That's not all that's missing. It's much too static. And the irony, the whole idea of showing what the tribes used to be and what's happening to them now, it's too obvious. But I was in a hurry and I wanted everybody to understand."

"There's no way they won't," Jack said.

"I thought a movie would be the best way—maybe the only way—to save them. Once people in the States see it and know about the famine, they'll send food and medicine. Can you ask Tucker to look at it?"

"I'm sorry, Moha. I don't think he'd help no matter what you showed him."

"Then we must get it to someone who will." He spoke in a low, tense whisper. "Surely you know somebody."

"Even if I did," Jack said, "there isn't a plane until next week. And who's going to smuggle it out for us?"

"Isn't there any way to get it out overland?" Helen asked.

"Very hard," Moha said.

Impossible, Jack would have said from what he recalled of the crew's escape plan.

Helen found Jack's hand and held tight. "We'll be finished here in eight weeks," she said. "I'll take it to New York. I have friends at the networks who'll know what to do with it."

"Eight weeks," Moha said. "That's too long. And it will take time to broadcast the news and organize relief. By then a lot of people will have died. And many more will have lost their herds and had to move into camps." He flicked the flashlight off and on, off-on. "Something has to be done now."

"Jack told you, we have money to give. Won't that help?"

He continued to toy with the flashlight, and during the intervals of brightness Jack noticed the boy's face—deeply troubled that his movie hadn't changed things, that the risks he must have taken had been wasted. "You'd better go back to your room," he said.

At the door, Jack gripped Moha's arm. "I know you're disappointed, but the film, it's damn good."

He shrugged.

"Jack's right," Helen said. "It's wonderful."

"What difference does that make?"

In the room they undressed, switched off the lights, and got into separate beds.

Helen said, "I feel like crying. But like Moha said, what difference would that make?"

When Jack didn't answer, she rolled onto her side, her legs rustling the cold sheets. "The whole time I was watching, I was wondering what I'd do if my boys had those horrible eyes and sores all over their bodies. I kept thinking I'd do anything to save them. I wouldn't just sit there. But seeing those women, I knew there was nothing they could do. That has to be the worst part—to know they need just a little food, a little water, but not be able to get it. Not to be able to do a goddamn thing."

"There is something we could do."

"Jack, I told you what would happen."

"I don't mean you. Give me the names of people in New York and I'll leave on next week's flight. This movie of Moha's, I think it might do it. It'll show what's happening here, no matter what the government or the Embassy or the studio says."

She reached across to him. "But what about the job, the money?"

"I guess I'll just have to do without."

"That's fine to say now, but what if your wife drags you into court?"

"Sybil's no monster. I'll work something out with her."

"What?"

"I've got a week. I don't have to decide everything tonight. Look, you'd better get some sleep or you'll feel like hell in the morning."

"I feel like hell now." Despite her efforts not to, she had started crying. "Seeing those kids, Jack, it made me sick. I keep asking myself, 'Why don't you take the film and fly back?'"

"It'd ruin your career."

"You're not worried about your career."

"I don't have one."

She sat up. "Goddamnit, don't talk like that. Like you don't have anything to lose."

He went to her. "It's okay. Whatever I lose, it can't be worse than staying here. I'm tired of looking the other way, keeping my mouth shut, doing anything to keep this job."

"What'll you tell Tucker?"

"Nothing about Moha's film. I hope you won't mention it to anybody either."

"Of course not. But he'll ask why you're going."

"I'll just say I'm finished."

CHAPTER IX

Jack and Helen woke in the dark at 5 A.M. Both had headaches, their mouths were parched, and the air tasted chalky and made their skin tingle. When Helen crossed the prayer rugs in her panty hose, sparks of static electricity crackled around her feet.

After a breakfast of coffee and aspirin they went down to the lobby where the air was harsher, heavier. The sun had risen now but they couldn't see it; the sky was shrouded by a dense fog that had turned the trees and shrubs the color of a sepia photograph.

Leaving Helen in the make-up room, he found Tucker, Moha, and Wattle out by the pool. The water appeared to have been sprinkled with pepper.

"What is this?" Jack asked.

"*Brume sèche*," Moha said. "The wind carries dust into the air. Sometimes it stays there."

"Whatever you call it," Wattle said, "how long will it last?"

"Impossible to say."

"I think there's enough light," Tucker said.

"Oh, really?" Wattle gave him a dubious glance. "This'll play hell with the cameras and bugger up the lenses. Don't we have a cover set?"

"Not till we find a house for the medina scene."

"Well, there's a day and forty thousand dollars wasted."

"No, let's go on out to the airport," Tucker said. "This stuff's liable to lift."

Wattle shrugged. "It's your show, old man."

When the four of them had returned to the lobby, Jack signaled to Moha and they went up to his office, neither of them speaking until they were in the room. Jack sat at his drafting board, glanced at a few sketches, then at Moha.

"I'm leaving on the next plane," he said. "I'll take your film to New York."

"Does Tucker know?"

"Not yet."

"Are you going to tell him why you're leaving?"

"No. I'd better not. Helen'll let me have a list of people to contact. Once they see the movie, I'm sure they'll want to help. I'll do everything I can to make them hurry."

"Shall I bring it to you?"

"I'll tell you when."

"This is very good. This is what I hoped for," he said, but seemed more concerned than pleased. "I have another favor to ask. In America, don't mention who made the film. Not to anyone."

"They're bound to ask where I got it."

"Say you did it."

"I'm no film maker. They'll know that's a lie."

"It's very amateur. They'll believe you."

"But I'd like you to get the credit."

"If Benhima learns I did it, it won't be credit I'll get."

Then Moha put his hand on the drafting board, fooling with pencils. "About your expense money. Are Helen and you still willing to give it?"

"I suppose so. You sure it's worth the trouble?"

"Yes. I thought it over. You were right. A few thousand dollars might do a lot of good in the camps until outside help arrives."

"But you said it was dangerous. I don't want you taking more risks."

"I've met some men. They swear they can get the money to where it's needed."

"Who are they?"

"I can't say. But they're willing to help."

"You trust them then?"

"I'm told by friends that I can. I'm not sure they trust me. They want the money right away."

"It's in Helen's room. I'll get it for you."

"Wait. They want it from you. They said they'd like to talk."

"About what?"

"I don't know. Maybe just to thank you."

"Look, I'd hate like hell for something to go wrong and have it foul up our chances of getting the film to the States."

"I'll be with you. Don't worry."

"I'm not." He was more than worried; suddenly Jack felt cold, watery ripples in his stomach. But he knew he couldn't expect Moha to take chances he refused. "When do we go?"

"I'll be back this evening just after dark. Wait for me in the lobby."

After Moha left, Jack pushed back the drapes, letting in a pale mocha light. Although he switched on a lamp, the room still looked as though a thunderstorm were threatening. After an hour of trying to work at the desk, he moved into the bathroom where the fluorescent bulbs were brighter and the air not quite so gravelly. He dragged in a chair, propped the pad on his knee, and bent forward to draw. The awkward position—or perhaps it was his apprehension about this evening—soon cramped his spine into a curving rod of pain.

He was taking a break, hanging by his fingers from the bathroom doorjamb, when Tucker showed up. Knocking once, he barged in with a bottle of scotch. "Fetch a couple ropes, bubba, and we'll both hang ourselves. I see the headline in *Variety* now, 'Director and Art Director Die on Location in Suicide Pact.'"

"What happened, you all quit early?"

"No, they're still out there eating dust." As Tucker fell heavily onto a chair, the scotch frothed in the bottle. "But I decided to come back and have a bath and a nice quiet lunch and kind of mellow out this afternoon. It was either do that or stay there and stomp shit out of Wattle. Know what that little cunt said?"

Jack was rubbing his neck.

"He said, considering the great contributions he's made, all the suggestions and innovations and so forth, he thinks he deserves a credit as co-director. Claims if I don't give it to him he'll go to the union and demand a hearing."

"He have a chance?"

"Doesn't matter. Either way I'll look like some kind of candy pants who can't even control the people working for him. I should have put a boot right up his ass."

"Why didn't you?"

"Yeah, why didn't I?" He pondered this a moment. "Well, fuck it. This is my day off. Let Wattle worry about filming in a god-damn sandstorm." He uncapped the bottle. "Like a snort?"

"I've got a lot of work to do."

Tucker didn't take the hint. Tilting the bottle, he swallowed twice, then wedged it between his legs. "It ain't turning out like we expected, is it, bubba?" Because his eyes had watered from the whiskey, he looked as solemn as he sounded.

"I guess you could say that."

"Damn right I could. When I saw you back in Cannes, I thought we'd cycle on down here, work hard during the day, and do a little drinking and bullshitting at night. It's sure no fun this way. What are we gonna do about it?"

Jack hesitated. He doubted there was any use talking, but decided he had to try. "Seems to me there's only one thing to do. I don't need to spell it out for you again."

Although Tucker had slouched in the chair, apparently loose-limbed and relaxed, his right knee pumped up and down.. "I wouldn't be too sure of that. What's clear to one man's cloudy to the next. Life's a funny old dog and I—"

"I don't know where you've been looking," Jack cut in, "but I haven't seen anything to laugh at lately. If life's some kind of dog, it's one vicious son of a bitch."

"Been meaning to tell you, bubba. You're losing your sense of humor."

"Yeah, that always happens when I'm around people who are dying."

"Oh, for Chrissake," he said and sat up straight. "Don't pretend you never knew this sort of thing went on. Back in Texas did you lie awake every night crying about all the wars and epidemics and catastrophes going on somewhere halfway around the world?"

"We're not halfway around the world. We're here. We're in it."

"What the hell's the difference?"

"The difference is there are things we can do. Ways we can help."

"I keep telling you, there's no way."

He was tempted to mention Moha's film, thinking Tucker would know what could be done with it. But the most accurate measure of the distance that had widened between them was that he feared Tucker might turn the boy in. This fear itself was so awful, Jack didn't want to believe it and came close to sharing the secret to prove he was wrong. But he couldn't take the risk. Instead he asked, "Is this movie really that important to you?"

"Not just this one. The next one and the next and the next." He flourished the bottle. "We're talking about my life. Don't act so fucking superior. Would you give up painting to save those people?"

"Yes."

"You're lying."

"I wish there was a way to make you believe it."

Lowering the bottle to his lap, Tucker stared at Jack a moment. "I don't like to say this, bubba. But maybe that's your trouble. Maybe that's why you never got anywhere. You don't want it bad enough."

"You're probably right. I didn't realize it before, but there are things I value more. But what about you? What's your limit?"

"Can't say. I just know I haven't reached it."

"I'm curious about something. Couple weeks ago you told me what baseball players say when a guy gets cut. 'He died.' What do they call it when somebody actually dies? Do they say, 'He failed?'"

"Getting too heavy for me, Professor." Tucker hauled himself to his feet. "Specially on my day off. School's out." He closed the door quietly behind him.

From the balcony he stared down at the garden, which still had the brown and beige tones of an antique daguerreotype. As one of the bellboys strolled over to the wire pen to check on Lisa's gazelle, he scuffed up khaki clouds of dust. Jack couldn't force himself to work any more today. He was too agitated and the weather made things worse. For hours a storm appeared to have been building; now it had broken. Although no rain fell, the dark sky pressed down against the dunes and soon the wind was blowing a gale.

Going to Helen's room, he changed into warmer clothes and, gathering their money, stuffed it into an air mail envelope which he slipped inside his shirt. Then he wrote her a note. Because he thought it unwise to mention where he was going, with whom, and why, he simply asked her to eat dinner in the room so everybody would assume he was with her.

At five-fifteen he put on a poplin windbreaker, went down to the lobby, and waited by a window, hoping Moha would show up before the company came back from the airport. Instead of checking his watch, he kept an eye on the dust that hissed in under the front door, streaming across the tile and piling up in a corner—a miniature dune like one at the bottom of an hourglass.

A bellboy with a dustpan and broom was sweeping up the sand when somebody rapped the window behind Jack. It was Moha swaddled in a burnoose, grimacing against the wind. He motioned for Jack to come around and meet him.

Although prepared for the cold and the blowing sand, he had not expected so much noise. The storm roared at anything strong enough to stand up to it, ripping down bunches of dates, thrashing the trees, smacking the dead birds in the net against the wall.

"I brought you a burnoose." Moha had to holler.

"Don't need it. I'm warm enough."

"Wear it. Nobody will recognize you."

Slipping the burnoose over his head, Jack let the heavy wool fall to his ankles and pulled the hood up around his face. Then he followed Moha through the gate and into an immensity of howling darkness. He felt asphalt under his feet and saw the hazy lights of Tougla ahead of him. Otherwise he was adrift, every sense distorted, and as cars sped past, sounding their horns and raising cyclones of dust, he had to fight his temptation to freeze in the middle of the road or to race straight at the headlights—anything rather than plunge off the road into the emptiness on either side.

Avoiding the lighted streets of the European quarter, Moha

entered the medina where the alleyways shut off the wind and sand. But Jack thought that, awful as it had been to wander through the outer dark, it was worse to be in this maze of stinking tunnels. At night the medina seemed more primitive than tents or thatched huts. A nest now, not a town, it was almost subterranean and struck him as subhuman, the dwelling place of insects and animals.

He stepped on something soft. It snarled, clawing at his ankle, and he cried out, stumbling into Moha.

"Careful. People are here to get out of the storm. Stay close to me."

"Jesus," Jack said aloud. Then he whispered the word and wound up repeating it to himself—the expletive becoming a feeble prayer against the dark. Tripping over outstretched legs, sensing warm bodies all around him, he put a hand on Moha's shoulder and struggled against a childhood fear of being abandoned. He knew if he lost touch with the boy he would have no idea how to get back to the hotel.

Finally they stopped, waited a few seconds, then stepped close to a heavy wooden door. Moha knocked four times. Someone inside knocked once, and when the boy answered with three quick raps the door opened. They entered a courtyard where two men wearing the masklike veils of the Berber tribes spun them around, shoved them against the wall, and patted them down.

Finding no weapons, they led them across the courtyard into a room dimly lit by a lantern. The men carried Sten guns. It was one of few rifles Jack would have recognized, he had seen them so often in old war movies and recent documentaries about revolution. The British had mass-produced them and now, because they were cheap and mechanically simple, Stens were found wherever desperate, underfinanced wars were fought.

Dozens of them lined the walls. On a roughhewn table lay revolvers and Lugers, along with the walkie-talkie units and first aid kits that had been stolen from the film company. Jack turned on the boy.

"I took them to prove I could be trusted," Moha said. "They were testing me. And they needed the medicine."

"Are you in with these guys?" he demanded.

"No."

"Don't lie to me."

"I swear I'm not."

Three more men in *lithams* came through a door to a back room.

"Who are they? What are all these guns for?"

Moha didn't answer.

"You heard me." While trying to keep a calm face to the men, he snapped at Moha, "Who the hell are they?"

"I don't know. They said they'd take the *gourdes* and smuggle supplies into the camps. That's all I cared about. You said you wanted to help."

"I didn't say I wanted to throw in with the same guys who probably tried to blow us up at the airport."

But there was nothing he could do now except wonder how much money would go for food and medicine and how much for arms and ammunition.

When the men with the Sten guns returned to the courtyard, one of the tribesmen inside locked the door by sliding home an iron bolt. Jack experienced a sudden weakness in his ankles, his knees, at the pit of his stomach. A single lantern hung from a rusty hook in the palm-beamed ceiling, and as a draft set it swaying and the pool of light yawed back and forth, he felt he was at sea, floundering in a storm. But the air here tasted of ashes, not brine.

Moha said, "Let me have the money."

Jack passed him the envelope, and the man who did the talking gave it to one of the others. Then, gesturing with slender hands that had henna on the nails and palms, he spoke again.

"He asks why you're doing this," Moha said.

"You know why. Tell him that money is for supplies."

There was something unsettling about the way the man's mouth moved behind the cloth, the way his words emerged vague and muffled, while his gaze was direct, unblinking.

"He asks why other Americans aren't helping."

"They can't do anything without the government's permission. Look, let's cut this short and get out of here."

For a few moments, while Moha and the man talked, there was no translation, and the other two men stared at Jack. His hands were shaking; he pulled them behind the burnoose.

"He thinks there's more you could do," Moha said.

"I'm going to do more. I'm taking your film to the States. And Helen'll keep giving her expense money. That should add up to four or five thousand bucks."

"He has something else in mind. The plane each week, he knows it brings supplies for the film company. He says if you'll tell him when it's going to land—what day, what hour—he'll hijack it and have it flown to a field up north. From there they'll distribute the food and hold the plane for ransom."

"What the hell are you getting us into?"

"He didn't say anything about this before."

"Don't bullshit me."

"I'm not." At last Moha looked as frightened as Jack felt.

"Tell him it won't work. Tell him I have no way of knowing the plane schedule."

"He's sure you can find out."

"Even if I could, it carries food for thirty, forty people. Not enough to stop a famine."

"But a hijacking will bring attention to what's happening here."

Jack shook his head; everything on him seemed to be shaking. "I'm not getting into this. Somebody's going to get killed."

"A lot of people are dying already."

"Goddamnit, I'm not responsible for that."

"He says you are. He says anybody who doesn't help is killing them."

While he tried to think, the lantern creaked and guttered above his head. Lying seemed too simple, too obvious, but there was no choice. "All right, I'll ask around. Soon as I hear about the plane, I'll let him know."

The man appeared to smile. It was difficult to tell because of the veil.

"He doesn't trust you to come back. I don't think he means it. Don't be upset." Moha sounded more than upset. "But he says he could kidnap you instead of hijacking a plane."

"He's got the wrong guy. They're not going to give a dime to get me back. He should have grabbed one of the stars."

When Moha told him this, there was no doubt the man smiled.

"He thinks you're too modest. Somebody will always pay for a white man. Especially an American."

"I'm counting on you to convince him he's got nothing to gain by holding me."

Jack heard a high-pitched whine of hysteria in his voice. He glanced at the guns on the table within easy reach. Then at the three men. But that made no more sense than hysterical pleading. He couldn't shoot his way out of here, across the courtyard, and through the streets of the medina.

At last Moha said, "He claims he brought this up to prove he could do anything, even kill you. But he won't because he's grateful for your help. He'll be waiting for you to find out about the plane. If you don't, he'll come find you."

While the man told Moha where they should meet next and when, Jack knew the only plane information he intended to find out was how to get a seat on the next flight from Tougla. If he had his way, Helen would be on it with him.

But hearing a commotion in the courtyard, the three tribesmen turned to the door. Somebody was shouting. Then there was a single shot, followed by the tinny, fast stutter of the Sten guns. When the automatics stopped, a volley of louder shots crackled. In the room one of the men started to slide back the bolt, but the other two grabbed him.

Abruptly it was quiet and the man who had done all the talking picked up a revolver from the table and leveled it on Moha. The boy shook his head no and was about to speak when someone rammed a rifle butt at the door. The man swung around, firing four times through the wooden planks.

Then the door started to disintegrate; bullets and splinters ricocheted through the room. The man's head jerked forward, tearing away a scrap of his veil and splattering blood on the wall.

Jack dropped to the dirt floor, pulling Moha down with him, and crawled for cover. Another man was down too, legs thrashing, but he couldn't crawl. Grabbing the lantern, the last man flung it against the front door, filling that space with kerosene smoke and flames. Then he ran to the rear door, and Jack and Moha stumbled after him, staying low.

The door led to a second room which led to a third, each one dimmer and smaller, it seemed, than the last. High on the wall of the fourth room was a window the size of an air shaft. Leaping onto a barrel, the man beat loose the wooden screen and squeezed through it head first.

Moha went through next and was still on the ground when Jack clambered awkwardly onto the ledge and let himself fall. They dragged one another upright and dashed into the street. Hearing the man headed in one direction, they went the other, running blind through smoke and darkness, bumping into walls and people, shouting and shoving free of hands that grabbed at them.

When they reached a square, Moha said, "Go to the hotel."

"What about you?"

"I'll be all right. I'll see you tomorrow. Don't do anything until then."

"Where are we?"

He spun Jack around. "Stay on this street and you'll come to the European quarter." Then he left and had gone no more than a few steps before he disappeared.

Jack was rooted to the spot, battling his panic, blinking against the smoke. He could see blurred shapes and shadows, nothing more. When he heard footsteps behind him, he made himself move, arms extended, hands groping, finding his way by touch.

Blundering down a dead end, he tried to retrace his steps and lost all sense of direction. But the street was no longer covered and he noticed the sky was a little brighter off to his left. He pressed on until he spotted the arc lamps along Avenue de la Libération. Shrugging off the burnoose, he left it where it fell. It had provided him camouflage coming into the medina, but it was safer to walk out in Western clothes.

On the way to the hotel, he remembered the money, the thousands of dollars' worth of *gourdes* stuffed in an air mail envelope. He didn't know who had it—the man who had escaped or one of the two who had been hit. Worse, he couldn't decide whether there was any way of linking it to Helen and him.

His mind raced, his blood raced, and he wanted to run but held himself to a steady walk, dredging each breath to painful depths in his lungs. Without the burnoose he was much colder and his bruised knees throbbed.

He thought it had to have been soldiers, Benhima's men, who had stormed the room. Maybe they had followed them from the Sidi Mansour. They might have been watching Moha all along.

He fumbled for an alibi, anything to explain what he was doing out this late. He'd claim he had gone into town to scout locations. Lame as that was, soldiers might swallow it, but not the members of the movie company. They would have finished dinner by now and might have noticed he was missing. He needed a better story for them.

In the hotel garden the wind pelted him with dates and debris, and he was hurrying up a path, head down, when he bumped into somebody wearing a burnoose. Stunned, he thought it was Moha. But the man dropped something, sprinted to the wall, and hoisted himself over.

Lisa's baby gazelle stood up on wobbly legs, tottering toward Jack. The man must have been scavenging in the garbage cans when he spotted a better meal in the pen. Gathering the gazelle up in his arms, Jack went into the Sidi Mansour.

He searched the bar for Benhima, but the Minister wasn't there. Phil came over.

"I saw somebody nosing around the pen," Jack said. "By the time I got there he was carrying off this little fella."

"Jesus, thanks. Lisa would have had a fucking hemorrhage."

"Where's Benhima?"

"He hasn't been around."

"Have you seen Helen?"

"They're upstairs in a meeting. Something Tucker wanted to talk over. They wouldn't let me and Roberta in." Phil took the gazelle. "Lisa better buy a cage and keep it in her room from now on."

Jack stood at the bar and ordered a scotch. He wanted everyone to see him and assume he had been around most of the night.

"You look like you walked into a windmill. Where you been?"

Nichols sat with Tallow, Schwarz, and Fatih, all of them drinking martinis.

"In the garden." Jack combed a hand through his knotted hair. "Somebody was making off with Lisa's gazelle."

"Making *out* with Lisa's gazelle! Well, that's Maliteta for you. No holes barred. Right, Jerry?"

Fatih grinned and forced down a sip of his martini.

"The truth now, Jerry," Tallow demanded. "Would you rather stick it to a goat or a woman?"

"I am no farmer. I have nothing to do with animals."

"So it's chicks for you all the way. What's this Malitetan twat like?"

"Yeah," Nichols said. "Do they lower their veils? Or just lift their skirts?"

Fatih frowned. "You do not understand. Here it is not like in America."

"No shit," Schwarz said. "I never woulda noticed."

"You mean nobody in Maliteta fucks?"

"Not before they are married."

"Wait a minute. You saying you never been laid?" Tallow asked. "A good-looking kid like you with a mug just like Jerry Lewis?"

Fishing the olive from his martini, Fatih said, "You forget. I have been to France."

"Don't gimme this 'I been to France' bullshit. Did you score or didn't you?"

"Don't let Marvin razz you." Nichols slung an arm around the boy's neck. "Couple months from now we'll be in Malibu banging beaver left and right."

"Yes, I am looking forward to fucking an American woman."

"Me too," Tallow said.

"At this point I'd look forward to fucking a lizard," Nichols said.

Leaving his drink unfinished, Jack went into the lobby, sank down on a purple velours sofa, and tried to concentrate. He had to decide what to tell Tucker. Or whether to tell him nothing at all. Although he felt he owed him a warning—there was no imagining what the man who got away might do—he didn't know how to do it without endangering Moha. And himself.

A Land Rover pulled up to the front entrance and the Minister bustled in with one of his soldiers. After they had brushed off their uniforms, Benhima sent the soldier away and strode over to Jack, smiling. Grains of sand sparkled in his tribal scars.

"A terrible night to work outside." He pointed to the couch. "May I?"

"Sure." Jack felt his chest tighten.

"And what about you?" Benhima sat down. "Have you been outside?"

"Yes, in the garden for a few minutes. Somebody was stealing Lisa's gazelle."

"Did he get away with it?"

"He dropped it and ran."

"I warned her she'd better eat it while it's tender. Every week will only make it tougher."

"She plans to raise it as a pet."

When Benhima laughed, his pink tongue curled. "You Americans, you have such a wonderful sense of humor." He tucked one plump leg up under him. "Have you seen your friend Moha tonight?"

There was no safe answer. They might already have caught him and implicated Jack. "No."

"And not this afternoon?"

"Wasn't he on the set?"

"I don't know. I wasn't there." The Minister had yet to stop smiling.

"Maybe he'll be here for the movie. Tucker's showing one of his old ones. Want me to tell him you're looking for him?"

"I thinks he knows. He'll turn up sooner or later."

"He'd better if he expects to get paid." Jack put on a smile to match Benhima's.

Again the Minister laughed. "Yes, I remember this sense of humor from television in New York. I was there two years with the UN."

"Sounds like a nice assignment."

"No, New York is awful. Know what the problem is?"

Jack shook his head that he didn't.

"Too many lazy niggers."

"We don't call them that."

"Of course you do."

"Not me."

"But other Americans do. I heard it all the time. It doesn't bother me. In Maliteta we know the difference between a bad nigger and a good one, and we know how to deal with the bad ones. Now because I enjoy your jokes, Mr. Cordell, I'm going to let you have some advice. Don't go outside at night."

"Not even in the garden?"

"Not even in the garden."

"Are there *fellaghas* around again?"

"Somebody might mistake you for one."

The crowd was filing out of the bar, heading for the staircase.

"The movie must be starting. Are you coming?" Jack asked.

"Yes, I like Mr. Garland's films."

As they were climbing the stairs, the soldier who had been sent off earlier fell in beside them, whispered something to Benhima, then did an about-face and marched back down to the lobby.

While the Minister continued discussing Tucker's movies as if there had been no interruption, Jack held tight to the railing. His first impulse was to give an excuse and get away, find Moha and warn him. But it was impossible to guess how much Benhima knew. If he suspected Jack had been with Moha, why would he let him remain on the loose—unless he counted on him leading the soldiers to the boy?

Helen had saved him a seat. "Where've you been?" she asked.

"Running around the garden, rescuing Lisa's gazelle. Some guy thought he'd swiped a full meal."

"I was worried. I thought—"

"So was I. It's blowing so hard out there I could barely stand up."

She looked at him.

Shaking his head slightly, he reached over and squeezed her hand. "How'd it go at the airport? Get anything done?"

"A few takes inside the terminal. My part of the scene's finished. I've got tomorrow off."

He was grateful when the lights went out and Helen and he could quit staring at each other.

The film, Tucker's second, was about a woman's softball team

that toured rural towns playing exhibition games, supposedly for
charity, really for whatever they could rip off. Set in the forties,
it lingered lovingly on wood-paneled station wagons, cigarette
ads that showed men in uniforms, and the lacy underwear, black
garter belts, and silk stockings the girls peeled off in the locker
room. The point, as far as Jack could tell, was that films which
served no larger purpose at least provided a repository for cul-
tural trivia. But Tucker studied each scene, each frame, like an
accountant double-checking his figures, trying to discover where
he had gone wrong and what he could do to remedy the disaster
at the bottom line. Jack wondered if anything could break that
tunnel vision, the obsession that reduced Tucker's interests to
what could be seen through a camera's eye.

Then he heard a distant explosion. When the shock wave hit
the hotel, rattling windows and doors, the screen went blank and
the sound track died on a long-drawn-out vowel.

"What the fuck was that?"

"Felt like an earthquake."

"It's those guys with the rockets again."

"That was no rocket. Had to be a bomb."

People bounced to their feet, shuffling and babbling in the
dark. Tucker shouted at them to sit down. "Whatever it was, it
was miles from here."

"Yes," Benhima said. "I'll go find out what happened."

"I don't like this," Phil said, and there was a sound like a
leather purse unsnapping.

"For Chrissake," Lisa said, "put that thing away before somebody gets killed."

Helen leaned close to Jack. "What is it?"

"I don't know."

His first thought was that the house in the medina, full of ammunition, had blown up in the fire. But what could have delayed
the explosion this long?

"I mean what's wrong with you?" she whispered.

"Tell you later."

When the lights blinked on, they burned at about half their
normal intensity. The spindle on the projector rotated slowly and
the sound track warbled like a record run at the wrong speed.

"They've switched to a generator," said one of the grips. "Better cut it off. There's not enough juice."

Benhima returned, smiling cheerfully. "Everything is all right. It was an accident at a relay station. Repairmen are on the way. But it would be best if you went to your rooms."

The lamp on the end table was so dim they could see the filament glowing feebly in the bulb. Helen climbed into bed without undressing and pulled the covers up to her neck. "Now please tell me what's going on. I got your note. Where have you been?"

Too agitated to sit still, Jack stayed on his feet, pacing. "In town with Moha. We met some men he said would use our money to help the tribes. They took it, but then claimed they had this plan to hijack the plane that brings in our supplies. They asked me to go in on it with them. 'Asked' is the wrong word. They threatened to kidnap me if I didn't."

"Oh, God."

"It gets worse. After I told them I'd help—just to get out of there—somebody tried to bust into the house where we were. Benhima's soldiers, I'm sure. There was a lot of shooting and a few guys got hit. One man and Moha and I beat it through a back window."

"Where's Moha?" The shivering seemed to have gone inside Helen; her voice quavered.

"I don't know. We split up." Finally he had to sit down. "Baby, we've got to get the hell out of this country."

"Shouldn't you warn Tucker?"

"I've *been* warning him. But if I tell him about this he'll ask what I was doing there. Who was with me. That'll put Moha and me in a worse spot than we're already in. You know how Tucker's been. He's locked into this deal. I wouldn't put it past him to turn us over to Benhima."

"You're overdoing it."

"Look, after tonight I'm not betting on anything. Not with your life and mine."

"What are you going to do?"

"Moha said he'd meet me tomorrow. I'll wait and talk to him. I think we'll have to take him with us when we go."

"How?"

"Maybe we could bribe somebody at the airport." This sounded as improbable to him as a line from *Terms of Peace*. "But one way or the other I'm leaving and I want you to come with me. Right before we go, when I'm sure Moha's safe, maybe I'll warn Tucker."

"I told you what'll happen if I walk off this film."

"Jesus, can't I convince you either? It was bad enough when we knew people were starving. Now they're killing each other. Pretty soon they'll be killing us. I don't believe that explosion was any accident. Do you want to be around when they set off a bomb in the hotel or in your car?"

Throwing back the covers, she got out of bed. "I'll have to think about it."

"I thought you had been thinking about it."

"I have. I don't want to talk about it any more. It doesn't do any good." She pushed by him, into the bathroom.

CHAPTER X

Next morning there was no make-up call for Helen and, since the electricity was still off, no recorded cry from the muezzin. They slept late and woke well rested for the first time in weeks. Considering what had happened last night, Helen seemed buoyant, cheerful. But Jack knew better than to press her. Although they needed to make plans, he decided to wait for Moha.

Putting off breakfast, he went in to shower and, after a moment, she followed, asking him to help shampoo her hair. There was something more domestic than sexual about being together under the hot spray, slippery with soap. It reminded Jack of family life, the sunny reassuring side of it, and he remembered giving David baths, scrubbing his tiny, hairless body and being filled with an emotion—part love, part longing—for which he had no name. Maybe Helen knew the name for it. Maybe she had similar memories. Souvenirs, as Fatih would have said.

But they soon reached the point where the rough companionable scrubbing ceased being domestic and became an act of tenderness. After Helen had rinsed off, Jack began to soap her again, and although they had been touching one another the whole time, she had no trouble recognizing the changed intent.

Raising herself on tiptoes as she had the first night, she rubbed against him, then lifted one long leg and caressed the back of his calf with the high arch of her foot. Her shoulders were pressed to the cool tiles when he pressed into her standing up, trying not to think what he would do if she refused to leave with him, if he lost her.

Almost immediately after they called down for sandwiches and coffee, there was a knock at the door. Jack expected a serving boy, but it was Moha and Hal Nichols—Moha in his burnoose, smiling, seemingly unperturbed; the PR man in a green denim leisure suit looking annoyed.

"Tucker wants you and Helen on the set," Moha said.

"What for?"

"He didn't say. He just told me to get you and Hal and come right back to the airport."

"A script conference is all I can figure," Nichols said. "But why me? That's not my turf."

"Why didn't he call? I need this free time." Helen couldn't conceal her irritation.

"The airport phones aren't working."

"Let us eat first," Jack said.

"I'm sorry. They're on lunch break, and Tucker asked to see you before they start shooting again."

On the way down to the lobby Jack looked for an opportunity to speak to Moha. Or to get a signal from him. But he stayed in front, walking with Nichols.

"Have you seen Benhima?" Jack finally asked.

"He's on the set."

"He was looking for you last night. He tell you why?"

"I already knew."

In the garden the wind had died and the dust had settled in a frostlike powder on the trees and shrubs. A Land Rover was waiting for them.

"Isn't this Benhima's?" Nichols asked.

"Yes."

"Where's the driver?"

"I'm driving," Moha said.

Nichols sat up front. Jack and Helen climbed in back. Behind them, in the luggage space, were several goatskin water bags and a cardboard box full of tinned meat, bread, and cheese.

Moha swung right, toward Tougla, rather than toward the airport. "I have to pick up something in town," he said.

They passed the billboard of the President, and his face, filmed over with dust, looked porous, a composition of black and white dots like a newspaper photograph held too close to the eye.

With Nichols there, Jack preferred not to say anything else about Benhima. But since Moha had seen him and was using his car, he figured things couldn't be as bad as he had feared.

Helen must have assumed the same thing. She put on a pair of sunglasses and gazed serenely at the straight-edged geometry of Tougla.

"They ever learn what knocked out the electricity?" Nichols asked.

"A bomb," Moha said.

"No kidding. Benhima claimed it was an accident."

"They blew up the power line to Moburka."

"They?" Jack said.

"The Malitetan Liberation Front."

"Never heard of it," Nichols said. "But we'd be the last to know. The Chinese army could overrun the hotel before anybody told us the truth."

They skirted the town, speeding past several crumbled automobiles that had been cannibalized for spare parts, then abandoned like locust shells. On the road north, the whitewashed *marabout* dome was a creamy chocolate on the leeward side.

"Thought you had to stop in town?" Nichols said.

"A little farther."

"They'll be finished lunch by the time we get there. Tucker isn't going to like another delay."

"Let him wait," Helen said. "It's the first time in weeks I've had a chance to relax."

"This isn't what I'd call a scenic route," Nichols said. "But I guess there's one way to look at it. The whole country's like a dose of Quaalude."

Moha drove on through the dunes, which the storm had sculpted into crests as jagged as razorbacks. The fence of woven palm fronds had been buried by sand and in some spots the road was barely passable. But although their lean-to had been knocked flat, two soldiers were still at the checkpoint, crouching in the shade of a jeep.

Rolling down the window, Moha kept the motor running while the soldiers asked a few questions, glanced cursorily at Nichols, Jack, and Helen, then waved them on. They set off over the rugged *piste* that led to the Picture Rocks.

"Where the hell are we going?" Nichols asked.

"You'll see."

"I'll see, my ass. There's nothing here to see."

Jack tried to catch Moha's eye in the rear-view mirror. "We'd better turn back."

Moha said, "You're right, Nichols. There's not much around here now. There used to be people, but a lot of them have died and others had to move into camps. The ones left, the ones living under the pylons, they ran off after the explosion."

"Look," Nichols said, "you want to take a lecture group on a tour of this sandbox, be my guest. But count me out. I got work to do."

"What, another article on Lisa Austin's oriental philosophy?"

"Whatever game you're playing, I don't like it. Take me back to the hotel or I'll have you fired." Nichols was glaring at Jack. "Cordell isn't the only one who's got friends."

"They can't fire me. I've quit," Moha said in a quiet voice. "I'm going to drop you off and let you carry a message back."

"What are you, crazy? I'm no camel. I'm not about to walk."

"Once you reach the roadblock, the soldiers will give you a ride. Have them drive you to the airport. Then tell Benhima I'm holding Jack and Helen at the Picture Rocks and I'll kill them unless he does what I say."

"Moha, stop the car. Stop joking." Jack grabbed his shoulder, but he pulled free and brought a pistol out from under his burnoose. Steering with one hand, he stomped the accelerator, rocking Jack and Helen back on the seat. As they jolted across the *hammada*, stunted thornbushes scraped like fingernails at the enamel.

Moha had the gun barrel against Nichols' mutton-chop sideburn. "You want to jump out, go ahead. Just remember what I say. Jack and Helen will be safe as soon as Maliteta admits there's a famine and makes an international appeal for relief. Then I need a plane to fly me to Algeria. Understand?"

Nichols was frozen, too frightened even to nod.

"This is your big chance. Send off stories about the drought and famine and kidnaping and you'll make the front page."

"Glad to. Just lemme go."

"Tell them they've got until tomorrow morning. I have a short-wave set and I'll be listening to stations in London, Paris, and the States. I want a world-wide announcement."

"Right. I'm with you."

Moha pressed harder with the pistol, twisting Nichols' head around. "No, you're not with me. You're scared. I'd like to keep you, but you're no good to me." When Jack moved forward again, Moha said, "I'm warning you. Stay back."

Helen pulled him down beside her.

"Benhima isn't going to listen to you," Jack said. "He'll send soldiers and—"

"Not as long as I have you two, he won't. Tucker won't let him."

"He doesn't run things here. Put down the gun and we'll talk."

Nichols was still rigid, only his mouth and eyes moving. "We'll forget this and go back to the hotel."

"There's no way back now."

"If you've seen Benhima," Jack said, "if he didn't do anything, then you're safe."

"I'm telling you, it's too late."

"Then let Helen go. Keep Nichols and me."

"That won't work. Nobody cares about Nichols."

"You're right, kid. I'm just a messenger boy. Lemme go. It's a long walk."

"In a minute."

Glinting in the sun, the electrical pylons strutted for miles across the plain. But then they appeared to stumble, a column of toy soldiers tripping over each other. Two towers had tilted; a third was bent in half. The wires had snapped and, whipped by last night's wind, were lashed around the twisted stanchions. The next pylon was a mangled heap of steel, the girders scorched and doubled back on themselves. It might have been a massive piece of sculpture, some unsuccessful extravaganza by an amateur welder.

A soldier with a rifle over his shoulder stood beside the wreckage, looking bored and solitary as a guard in a museum. There was a jeep nearby, but the soldier, who wore a pointless camouflage uniform with green and orange splotches, must have had orders to remain outside, on the alert for more demolition squads. When he saw the Land Rover he stepped to the middle of the *piste* and flagged them down.

"Don't anybody be stupid. I'll do the talking." Steering with his left hand, Moha hid the pistol in the folds of his burnoose and braked to a stop, once again leaving the motor running.

The soldier—a boy really, no older than eighteen or nineteen —leaned his head into the Land Rover, more curious than suspicious. As he and Moha talked, flies crawled contentedly over his face.

"Hey!" Nichols shouted, jerking his thumb at Moha. "This guy's got a gun."

The soldier didn't understand, but he glanced at Nichols, who grabbed Moha's burnoose, ripping it away from the pistol. Nichols made another grab, this time for the gun.

It went off and the noise was enormous, reverberating through the Land Rover. Helen threw her hands up to her head, as if to protect her ears, and her sunglasses flew off. The soldier screamed, staggering backward. The concussion appeared to have blown both front doors open. Moha scrambled after the soldier; Nichols scurried in the opposite direction.

Jack wrestled Helen down onto the seat and told her to stay there while he went to see what had happened.

The soldier was slouched against the front bumper, sobbing and clutching his shoulder. Although Moha spoke to him in a soothing voice, he held the rifle now, as well as the pistol, and kept the boy covered.

When Jack came over, Moha turned one of the guns on him. "That's close enough."

"He needs a doctor."

"Nichols will drive him to town in the jeep."

"Let Helen do it. Don't drag her into this. Please, that's all I ask. Don't hurt her."

"No, she stays. Bring Nichols here."

Jack found him behind the pylon, face down in the dirt, his slack body trembling. Like Helen an instant after the shot, he had his hands pressed to his head as if to block out all sound. The lacquered flaps of his hair had flared out like wings.

"Stand up," Jack said.

When Nichols shook his head, his whole torso rocked back and forth. Jack flipped him over. There was a dark stain on his left trouser leg; he had wet his leisure suit.

"Goddamnit, get up."

"He'll kill me."

"I'll kill you if you don't. Why'd you pull such a crazy fucking stunt?"

"I was afraid what he'd do to us."

"You didn't have anything to be afraid of. He was sending you back."

"I thought I was helping you and Helen. I thought it was worth a chance."

"The best chance we had was talking him out of it. You blew that." Jack yanked him to a sitting position. "Now drive the kid to town and get him a doctor. Then make damn sure Benhima and Tucker have the story straight."

Nichols struggled to his feet, leaning against Jack.

The soldier had quit sobbing, but still had his hand over the wound. Blood oozed between his fingers, and the flies buzzed from his face down to it. Moha told Jack and Nichols to help him into the jeep.

"What do I say to those guys at the roadblock?" Nichols asked. "They're liable to think I shot him."

"He'll tell them what happened. I've explained to him what I want."

The soldier was walking unsteadily between them when suddenly he stopped and refused to go any farther. He called back to Moha, who removed the ammunition clip and tossed the rifle to Jack. "Put it in the jeep with him. He says if he loses it he'll be punished."

They stretched him out on the back seat, and Jack used Nichols' coat to plug the bullet hole. "He'll be okay if he doesn't lose too much blood."

Nichols was the one who looked wounded. Puffy face drained of color, he slumped behind the wheel, staring glassy-eyed through the windshield.

"Listen to me," Jack said. "I'm counting on you to give Tucker the picture here. Moha's no murderer, but he's cornered and he's jumpy."

Nichols said nothing.

"Tucker already knows about the famine. Do me a favor. Goose him along. Threaten to send the story out to the wire services." Uncertain he had gotten through, he grabbed Nichols' arm. "I don't want Benhima storming out here with a lot of trigger-happy soldiers and hurting Helen. Do you hear me?"

"Yeah. All right." He nudged the jeep into gear and drove off at a slow, jerky pace. His foot was fluttering on the accelerator.

In the Land Rover Helen sat up front; Moha had the pistol at her head. "In back," he told Jack.

Once they were under way, Jack said, "Take the gun off her."

He lowered it to his lap but kept his hand on it. Each time he had to change gears, he stepped on the clutch and told Helen to work the shift.

"There had to have been a better way, Moha. Maybe there still is." Jack desperately wanted to believe this.

"Benhima knows I was in that house last night."

"You said you saw him today."

"He didn't see me. I stole his Land Rover and drove to the hotel."

"Then how are you sure he knows?"

"After you and I split up, there were soldiers waiting at my house. A friend warned me and I got away. They were after me all night, arresting and questioning anyone who saw me."

"Does Benhima know I was with you?"

"I doubt it. Otherwise he would have arrested you."

"But, Moha," Helen said, her voice full of anguish, "after getting away from the soldiers, why do this? Now they'll know where you are."

"They would have found me sooner or later. And they're not the only ones after me. This friend who warned me, he's the one that put me in touch with the men we met."

"The Malitetan Liberation Front," Jack said.

"I guess that's who they are."

"Jesus Christ, don't play games. You're in it with them. Have been the whole time."

"No, I swear to you. They think I was working for Benhima, that I led them into a trap."

"Then why would the soldiers be searching for you?"

"That's what I asked. But no one will listen. Now my friend says the Liberation Front is after me too. If Benhima doesn't find me, they will. There's no place to hide. In a car or on foot, I'd never reach the border. This is the only way. Besides, I don't mean to save myself alone. I want to help the tribes."

"But why kidnap us?" Helen asked. "We're your friends."

"That's why. I knew you'd understand what I'm doing—why I have to do it. If I held anybody else hostage, I'd need to be on guard the whole time."

The boy's enormous naïveté had begun to infuriate Jack. "What you're saying is we owe it to you to let ourselves be kidnaped. To risk being killed, if it comes to that."

"It won't. There's no real danger for you. You shouldn't even look at this as a kidnaping."

"What the hell is it?"

"A plan, a way of doing what the three of us agreed had to be done. It'll spread news of the famine and save a lot of lives."

"Say we refuse to go along with your plan. What'll you do, shoot us?"

"I didn't mean to shoot anyone. The gun went off when Nichols grabbed it."

"Is it going to go off again if we don't co-operate?"

"Yes."

"Then we don't have any choice, do we?"

"I'm the one without any choice." No longer able to drive and talk at the same time, Moha hit the brake and the Land Rover bumped to a stop. In the vacant expanse of the *hammada,* the engine sounded as feeble as the fluttering wings of an insect. "I won't shoot you, but I might as well shoot myself. Without you, I am already dead." He handed Helen the pistol. "Here, take it. It won't protect me. I can't hold off an army with a revolver. You two are all that stands between Benhima and me."

Helen wouldn't touch it. The gun slid off her legs onto the seat.

"You want it, Jack?" He picked it up and offered it barrel first.

Jack took it; the metal was hot and oily. "Let's go back to

town. We'll talk to Tucker and Benhima and work something out."

"I prefer to die here."

"Don't be so damn melodramatic."

"You are my friend, Jack, and I don't want to insult you. But you talk like a fool. Like you're in America. What do you think they'll do to me for shooting a soldier?"

"An accident. Helen and I'll swear to that."

He shut his eyes an instant, evidently infuriated now by Jack's naïveté. "Even forgetting last night—which they won't—and the fact that I stole the Minister's Land Rover, you have to remember that Maliteta has been under martial law since the coup. The penalty for carrying a gun is death. And if the Liberation Front catches me, do you think they'll let me call a lawyer?"

Jack glanced at Helen, who looked more frightened than she had when the soldier was shot. Like Jack, she understood now the corner Moha was in and that they had helped put him there. What was it the boy had said when they offered money? The American way.

"Start driving," Jack said.

"I'm not going to Tougla."

"Drive to the rocks."

He jammed the Land Rover into low gear and rumbled across the corrugated track.

"Soon as we get there," Jack told Helen, "you're heading back to town."

"No, I'm in this too."

"Don't be stupid."

"I'm being practical. If I stay, it'll be safer for everybody."

"She's right, Jack. You said it last night; you have to kidnap a star."

"You're both nuts. Benhima may not negotiate. He'll try to outlast us—let us fry during the day and freeze at night. I don't want you going through that."

"But don't you see, they'll have to negotiate if I'm here? It'll cost thousands of dollars every day they fall behind schedule. And if anything happens to me, the film collapses or they have to reshoot all my scenes. Believe me, they'll bargain. Remember, the Malitetans have a financial interest too."

"This isn't Hollywood. Somewhere on the back lot at Warner Brothers. The Malitetans might decide to lose the money—and us—rather than give in."

"No, listen to me," Moha said. "No matter what the government would like to do, the last move is up to Tucker. If the President refuses to bargain, then Tucker can always threaten to tell about the famine. Whether he does it or I do, it amounts to the same thing. The news is going to get out."

Ahead of them the Picture Rocks broke the rippling line of the horizon, the ocher tints taking on depth in the afternoon light.

"Why here?" Jack asked.

"There's water, and nobody can get behind us. It's close to that camp too. If any reporters come, they can go see it."

"Your deadline's tomorrow morning. They might not get here by then."

"I'm prepared to wait longer. I brought food and blankets. I'll stay as long as it takes."

He had started to pull into the ravine when Jack told him to turn around and back in.

"That way when we're leaving we'll be able to see what's in front of us." He didn't mention that in case of shooting the gas tank was less likely to get hit.

The corridor was just wide enough to accommodate the full length of the Land Rover. After that it gradually narrowed to the point where a man could pass only by turning sideways. Leaving Moha and Helen to unload the supplies, Jack hiked into the rocks. Beyond the fifty-gallon oil drum, the path and the banks of the *guelta* were littered with candy wrappers, cigarette butts, and yellow film boxes. An empty wine bottle bobbed in the water. But he was relieved to see that the giant hunters in the murals were still striped with fierce reds and oranges, still stalking herds of game through lush fields and leafy forests.

Standing at the center of the canyon, the gun in his hand, he studied the concave walls and thought that Moha was right. Holed up here, they wouldn't run low on water, and there would be some shade during the day and protection from the wind at night. But he wasn't so certain nobody could get behind them. Soldiers could climb up from the other side and rappel down the cliffs into the grotto. They would have to watch for that.

Trying to recall everything he had read about terrorist kidnappings and how governments coped with them, Jack wondered what else they should watch for. In the States and in Europe, they brought in cameras and sound equipment to monitor a kidnaper's every move and word, psychiatrists to analyze his mood, snipers to cut him down if he made a misstep. But it seemed unlikely Maliteta would handle things that way, and it was such a reasonable demand Moha had made—no money, no release of political prisoners, just an international appeal for famine relief —Jack thought they had a chance.

As he returned to the Land Rover, he dragged the sawed-off oil drum to the narrowest spot in the ravine and wedged it between some rocks, barring the path. That wouldn't stop anyone, but moving it would make enough noise to alert them.

Sitting on the rear bumper, Moha and Helen chatted as they ate lunch. They might have been on the parking lot of a football stadium. Helen was even wearing a loose-fitting rugby jersey. Jack couldn't decide whether to be annoyed or amused by their insouciance.

"Any more ammo for the pistol?" he asked.

"Two boxes." Moha pointed to them among the meat tins, water bags, and blankets, which he had stowed in the shade. On top of the pile lay a metal film can about the size of a pie plate.

"Is that your movie?"

"Yes."

"Better put it in a safe place."

Moha balanced it in one hand, testing its weight. Then he gathered up the hem of his burnoose, reached around, and tucked the can between the waistband of his Levi's and the small of his back.

Jack gave him the gun. "If you have to fire it, careful not to hit these rocks or we'll have ricochets buzzing all around us. Now where's the short-wave set?"

"There isn't one. I just wanted them to think we had a way of checking whether they made the announcement."

"They might bluff you, lie to you."

The boy looked a bit sheepish; obviously he hadn't anticipated this.

"Well, it doesn't matter that much," Jack said. "The important thing is to get out of here to a country where you can show your movie."

"Do you think I should tie you both up?" Moha asked.

"Better not." Although that might have added a convincing touch to their charade, Jack didn't want to be helpless if things suddenly fell apart.

An hour later two jeeps thumped across the plain toward the Picture Rocks. Jack told Helen to stay behind the Land Rover while Moha and he moved up to the mouth of the gorge.

When the jeeps were a hundred yards away, Moha glanced at him.

"They'll stop," Jack said and felt his stomach start to flutter.

When they were fifty yards away, Moha glanced at him again.

"Fire a few warning shots. Keep them low—way in front where they'll see them."

The boy's hand was shaking as he raised the pistol and pulled the trigger four times in quick succession, kicking up sand. One jeep braked and spun broadside. The second swerved to miss it, tilted to the right an instant, then stopped.

Tucker was in one of the jeeps; Benhima and half a dozen soldiers scrambled out of the other. The Minister sent the men charging forward, firing on the run.

"Get down," Jack shouted, and Moha and he dropped to the ground as bullets rang against the bumper and grille of the Land Rover, puncturing the radiator and shattering the windshield. Moha returned fire without aiming, trying to force them to take cover.

When it was silent, Jack lifted his head. Four soldiers lay flat as lizards against the dusty gravel about twenty yards away. Benhima was hollering at them, but they didn't answer or move, and Jack was afraid they had been hit.

Seeing Tucker sprint from his jeep to Benhima's, Moha shouted, "Call off the soldiers or I'll kill Helen and Jack."

"Are they all right?" Tucker asked.

"Yes. Get the soldiers away from here or they won't be."

Benhima began hollering again, and the soldiers wormed their way backward until they were behind the jeeps. Jack and Moha hurried to Helen, who had curled into a niche in the rocks, hugging her knees to her chest. She was trembling badly.

"You okay?" he asked.

She nodded. "I just didn't expect all that shooting."

"Neither did I." But Jack knew now the soldiers hadn't been aiming at them. Water and oil gurgled from the Land Rover. They wouldn't be going anywhere in it.

The Minister was still shouting in Arabic.

"What's he saying?" Jack asked.

"That I have no chance. That I should give up."

"Tell him what you want and what you'll do if you don't get it. Speak English so Tucker understands."

Moha had barely started when Benhima cut him short. "The government does not negotiate with terrorists."

"Is that final?"

"Yes."

"Then I'll kill them now."

"Wait!" It was Tucker. "Let's talk."

"Why, if the government refuses to negotiate?"

"I saw Jack, but we don't even know whether Helen's alive. Bring her around where I can see her."

Moha glanced at Helen, and she nodded yes.

Jack motioned them to stay a moment. "Hey, Tucker, warn Benhima and those men. There's a gun at her head." Then quietly to Moha, "Grab hold of her."

He held her elbow as if to help her cross a street.

"Not like that. Like you mean it. Make sure the safety's on."

Collaring her with his arm, jabbing the pistol against her cheek, he shoved Helen along in front of him. She stumbled a few steps, then went limp.

When Moha tightened his grip and gave her a rough shaking, Tucker rushed around from behind the jeep. "Stop! Don't hurt her."

"I won't if I get what I asked for."

"Give us a chance."

"You've got until tomorrow morning."

Then, half dragging Helen, he backtracked until they were hidden by the Land Rover.

An engine rumbled, and one of the jeeps swung around and headed toward town.

"Good. They must be sending word to Moburka," Moha said. "They won't agree to anything without the President's permission."

Jack thought it just as likely they were calling in reinforcements. But he said nothing and kept watching Benhima, the soldiers, and Tucker, who had taken off his bush jacket, tossed it over his shoulder, and stood amid wavering rays of heat. "Need anything in there?" Tucker asked. "Water? Food?"

"I've got plenty," Moha said.

"I'm coming closer so we don't have to shout."

"Stay where you are."

Tucker took a step.

"Come any nearer and I'll shoot."

He raised his arms. "Look, I'm not carrying anything. Just wanted to talk. Thought I could help."

"You want to help, make that announcement and put me on a plane to Algeria."

"That's out of my hands. But while they're working on the details, we could talk."

"You're wasting your breath. Benhima's the man to talk to."

"Be reasonable, Moha. We're doing all we can. But these things take time."

"And time's money, isn't it?" Moha hollered. "If you don't hurry, you'll run way over budget. If I blow Helen Soray's head off, what'll it cost to reshoot her scenes? Go on back to Benhima and tell him how much you both stand to lose."

The sun had swung around to the west, its light slanting into the ravine, shrinking the patches of shade. The three of them could have sat with their backs to the tailgate of the Land Rover or gone deeper into the gorge, but then they couldn't have watched the field. So they stayed where they were, feeling the skin on their faces tighten, their tongues thicken. Unplugging one of the goatskin water bags, Moha drank from its hoof, then passed it to Helen, and she to Jack. Although it had a foul tarry taste, he forced down a few mouthfuls. By the time they spotted the trucks, jeeps, and taxis trundling toward them, the ravine was an oven, every stone radiating heat.

Four trucks parked bumper to bumper in front of Benhima's jeep, barricading it from the rocks. Then the taxis and jeeps pulled in, disgorging more soldiers and civilians among whom Jack noticed several men from the movie crew. They unloaded a generator and half a dozen Brutes which they set up on tripods and aimed over the hoods of the trucks toward the ravine. When the encampment was nearly complete, the Meal Mobile arrived.

"They won't go hungry, will they?" Helen said.

"Neither will we," Jack said. "But we need to put more pressure on them. The lost shooting time won't start to matter for a few days; before then we're all liable to have sunstroke."

"I could claim I'm not giving you anything to eat or drink."

"That might work."

Moha called for Tucker, who squeezed between two trucks, carrying a battery-powered megaphone. "What can I do for you?" Although amplified, his voice sounded natural, unstrained.

"What's the answer to my demands?"

"Afraid that's not my department."

"Whose is it?"

"Benhima's. He sticks to what he said. The government won't negotiate under these conditions. Set Helen and Jack free, then we'll talk."

Jack thought the megaphone wasn't the only change. Tucker's attitude, like his voice, now seemed neutral. He might have been a hired spokesman, and Jack suspected somebody had coached him what to say and how.

"I thought you'd like to know I'm not letting them eat or drink until the negotiating starts."

Lowering the megaphone, Tucker glanced back, and a lean pale figure rose from behind the trucks. Even at this distance Jack recognized Reid Gorman. Obviously when the news reached Moburka, the Embassy or the Malitetans had dispatched a plane. But why Gorman? he wondered.

Tucker swung around to Moha. "You said we had till tomorrow."

"You have until then to make the announcement and fly me to

Algeria. The way you talked, nothing's being done. So they'll go hungry and thirsty until I see some results."

"We're bringing in newspaper and TV people. And a plane for you."

"I'll take the one Gorman came on."

"It's too small. Doesn't have the range."

"Find a bigger one. Helen and Jack'll be waiting."

"At least let them have water. You don't have enough, I'll send some in."

"There's plenty for me."

"Weather like this, they need a gallon a day."

"I know. Unless you get moving, they might not last long enough for me to shoot."

The urgency returned to Tucker's voice; he begged Moha to be reasonable.

"It's working," Helen whispered. "But why's Gorman here? And where's Benhima?"

"He's out there," Jack said. "But it seems to be an all-American show now."

"Good," Moha said. "They'll get things done."

Jack agreed, but wished he knew what. The soldiers had fanned out in flanking positions, and he realized how easy it would have been to overrun the three of them.

Losing its heat and shape, the sun blurred at the edges as it sank. When it was no more than an oblong of fire balanced above the horizon, the rocks too lost their warmth and a chill wind blew through the gorge.

Then the wind suddenly increased and there was a loud clattering noise. Whipping up a tornado of sand, a helicopter dipped toward the ravine—so close Jack could see the pilots. They weren't in uniform and didn't appear to be Malitetans.

He raised his arms, as if begging to be rescued, but said to Moha, "Shoot at it. Don't hit it."

He fired twice, and the helicopter skittered back behind the rocks.

"Were they trying to land?"

"No, I think just getting the layout here. Grab Helen and hustle her around front. Warn Tucker you'll shoot her if you see another helicopter."

The moment Moha had her in a hammer lock, she began sobbing and kept it up as he shoved her to the end of the gorge, the gun at her head. "Call off that helicopter," he yelled.

"It's gone," Tucker said.

"I see it again, I'll shoot her." Helen's legs buckled, and he jerked her up straight.

"Do what he says," she wailed at Tucker.

"Take it easy on her, Moha."

"Why? You ask for favors, but all I see in front of me are soldiers and guns. I ask for a plane, and you send a helicopter to spy on me. If you rush me, you'll find a dead actress."

"We're not going to rush you. We're doing everything to meet your demands." Because of the dryness or his bad nerves Tucker's voice broke and it came across as static. Switching off the megaphone, he moved back behind the trucks.

As the sun slipped below the horizon the western sky was striped with varying intensities of red—a tantalizing light show that revealed the full beauty of the desert every evening in the last instant before nightfall. When it was dark, Moha climbed into the Land Rover and punched on the headlights. One beam worked, illuminating very little of the space between them and the fortress of trucks, jeeps, and taxis. But then the generator sputtered and caught, and the carbon-burning arc lights burst on, bathing the entire area, deep into the ravine, in the harsh phosphorescence of a prison yard.

While the three of them wrapped up in blankets and ate a dinner of cheese, bread, and cold meat from cans, they caught from across the way the aroma of roasted meat and coffee perking in the Meal Mobile's nickel-plated urn. Jack wished he had a cup. He was exhausted, his nerves were raw, his powers of concentration shot. Still, he had to keep trying to imagine what Tucker and Gorman might do, and what Helen and Moha were capable of.

"I know it sounds crazy," Helen said, "but I'd be more frightened if we were here in the dark and didn't have so much company. It's like they're protecting us. It doesn't seem possible they'd want to hurt us."

"It's not you they want to hurt," Moha said.

"Nobody's going to get hurt," Jack said. "But I think we'd better sleep in shifts. We'll rotate every four hours, with two of us awake all the time. Helen, why don't you turn in first?"

"It's not even nine."

"Get some rest anyhow. You'll need it later. Go back where the light won't bother you."

"I'm not going too far." She kissed Jack's forehead, then found a dim protected corner and rolled up in her blanket.

After a while, when her breathing was deep and steady, Moha whispered, "She is a good person. I'm sorry I dragged her into this."

"Well"—Jack paused—"we're in it now."

"I knew I could count on you, but I was afraid she would cause trouble. I was wrong."

"What would you have done if she'd taken the pistol and told you to drive to town?"

"The same thing I did with you. I wouldn't have gone. She'd have had to shoot me."

"She could have kicked you out and driven back herself."

"That would be the same as shooting me. It's over for me in Maliteta. No matter what, I'm a dead man here."

"Take it easy." He squeezed the boy's shoulder. "Tomorrow night you'll be in Algeria and—"

"And I'll never be able to come back."

This gave Jack another pause. For him, as for the others on the film, Maliteta was more a temporary condition than a place. It was just somewhere to work, a backdrop for his personal problems, a daily counterpoint to his nights with Helen. But Moha was losing a home, perhaps his future.

"I know it's hard to leave," Jack said. "Especially like this. But you'll start a new life."

"Doing what? To an outsider all these countries look the same, but Algeria will be different. They might not grant me political asylum. They certainly won't let me make films. The government will have its own directors and it won't take chances with a foreigner whose politics may be wrong."

He knew better than to suggest that Moha return to America. After this, he'd be confined to those marginal countries whose names changed with regimes, whose borders shrank or ballooned according to the mood of a dictator or the meandering course of a river, and whose slow, colorless strangulation was seldom noticed, but whose periodic splashes of blood made headlines and scared off help.

"I know it sounds easy for me to say. But you're young and things change. A few years from now Maliteta's liable to have a new government and you'll come home a hero."

"I never cared about being a hero. I just wanted to make movies. I thought they'd help."

"Don't be so hard on yourself. You *did* make a movie." Again Jack gripped the boy's shoulder, unsure he could get through to him any other way. "And it's going to help."

At midnight they woke Helen, and before he bedded down, Moha gave Jack the gun. Holding it in his lap, he regarded it as a prop that added the one authentic touch to their otherwise amateur performance. Or maybe it was more like a Hand of Fatma, which you clung to not in the belief that it would conquer evil altogether, but in the hope of warding it off a while longer.

Helen nuzzled against him, and together they gazed across the brightly lit field. A shadowy figure stood on the hood of a truck, changing a carbon rod that was fizzling in one of the arc lights.

Then somebody screamed in the gorge, the noise echoing and re-echoing behind them. There was a splash, then a thump, like meat smacking against cement.

Moha sprang to his feet, the covers falling around his ankles. He stumbled over to Jack and Helen. Grabbing the gun, he fired into the air. "Get up close to the Land Rover," he told them, and when they hesitated he shoved them, shouting as he ran, "What's going on? Somebody's back near the *guelta*."

There was no answer from across the way. But even where he was, Tucker had to have heard the moaning, the noise magnified by the grotto.

"I'm warning you, you better do something," Moha hollered.

Jack could feel the boy shivering beside him. Helen was shaking too.

"What do you want me to do?" Tucker finally asked.

"Tell him to strip naked and come through the ravine with his hands on his head. If he's carrying a gun or tries anything, I'll shoot Helen first, then him."

When Tucker repeated through the megaphone exactly what Moha had said, the three of them in the ravine glanced at one another.

"Is it an American?" Moha asked.

"What?"

"You're speaking English. Is it an American?"

"I'll have the Minister translate."

"Is it an American or isn't it?"

Tucker handed the megaphone over the hood of a truck. But as the Minister spoke in Arabic, the man continued to moan and there was no sign of movement in the gorge.

"He must be hurt too bad to move," Tucker said.

"Who is it?" Moha insisted. "What was he doing?"

Tucker didn't bother answering.

"How many men are back there?" Moha asked.

"Lemme bring in a doctor."

"You're crazy. You must think I'm crazy."

"But if he's hurt—"

"That's not my fault. I didn't send him in there."

"You want him to die?"

"I told you what I want. Do that, then you can take care of him."

Jack, Moha, and Helen retreated into the ravine to where they had been before. The moaning was much louder there.

"What do we do?" Helen asked.

"Nothing," Jack said.

"We have to do something. Listen to him."

"It could be a trick. The whole thing is some kind of trap."

"Moha's right. The guy might not be alone," Jack said.

"I'm not going to let him die. If neither of you'll help him, I will."

Jack grabbed her. "Don't start this. We've got to stay together. Stay calm."

"Look, I'm willing to go just so far. I'm not going to sit here while somebody's suffering."

"Hold it down. They'll hear us. We don't know whether he's hurt or not. Like Moha said, he could be faking."

"I'll find out." She tried to pull away from him.

"No, I'm the one who should do it," Moha said.

"What, and leave us here?"

"We'll all go," Helen said.

"That doesn't make sense either," Jack said. "It'd be easy for them to get the jump on us in the dark. I'll go."

"You'd better take the gun," Moha said.

"No, I don't want anybody to see me with it. That'd give the whole thing away. No matter what happens, no matter what you hear, don't you two come in after me."

Neither the arc lights nor the stars penetrated this far into the corridor, and Jack had to work by touch, sliding his feet forward, feeling for loose stones and chuckholes. Then, as the gorge got narrower and he could reach both walls, he used his hands as well as his feet, probing his way deeper into the rocks, experiencing at each step the terror of a nightmare repeated. It reminded him of running blind through the medina last night, only now he was moving toward the danger instead of fleeing it.

Or was the greatest danger behind him? Someone might have set up a diversion near the pond to give the soldiers a chance to come charging across the field.

When his knee banged the sawed-off oil drum, he fell back, hitting his head against the wall, and for an instant the darkness brightened with pain. He held himself still until the ringing died and he was steady on his feet again.

Jack called out, "I'm coming in. I don't have a gun. I'm coming to help you."

After repeating himself in French, he pulled the oil drum from the crevasse and squeezed through, advancing by touch until the gorge widened and he no longer had the walls to hang onto. In the grotto the moaning was all around him, and he had to guess at its source.

"Is anyone else here? I want to help. Answer me." Washing over him in waves, his own quavering voice frightened him.

To orient himself, he raised his eyes to the rim of the walls—a crenellated line with solid black below and stars above. Then, shuffling forward, he tripped, landing full length on a body.

Jack cried out, recoiled, rolled over, froze. He lay there what seemed to him a long time, listening to the moaning, straining to hear anything else. Then he forced himself to reach back and touch the body. Wherever he put his hand, there was a gummy wetness. Nearly sick at his stomach, he touched the man as a lover might, moving from his face to his neck. The chest felt lumpy, stuffed with broken sticks, and the arms and legs were twisted at odd angles away from the torso.

He knew the man had broken bones and maybe a fractured skull and internal injuries. There was no way Jack alone could drag him through the ravine without hurting him much worse than he already was.

"This guy needs a doctor," Jack said. "If there's anybody here, come help carry him."

There was no answer, no movement at all in the grotto.

"I can't do it by myself." That set off another echo.

Easing away from the man, Jack stood up and returned through the corridor. He wedged the oil drum into place and called ahead to Helen and Moha, who were huddled in blankets, watching the field.

"Did he say what he was doing?" Moha asked anxiously.

"He wasn't in any shape to talk."

"Didn't you help him?" Helen said.

"There's nothing I could do. I couldn't risk lugging him through the rocks in his condition."

"What's wrong with him?" she asked.

"I think he fell off the canyon wall."

"Are you sure there's no one else?" Moha said.

"I didn't see anybody. But it was damn dark."

"Are you going to let them send in a doctor?" Helen asked.

"We couldn't be sure he was a doctor," Moha said. "He might come in armed. What would a doctor be doing out here anyway?"

Jack knew what a doctor would be doing here—waiting for something like this. Besides Benhima and the soldiers, the people from the Embassy, the helicopter, the film crew, the Meal Mobile, and all the sound and light equipment, no doubt there were doctors, medical supplies, even an ambulance across the way. It angered him to imagine how much effort and money were being wasted here when the real trouble lay five or six miles north.

"It'll be daybreak in a few hours," he said. "I'll carry him out soon as it's light."

"But, Jack—"

"Helen, I'm sorry. We can't have anybody coming in here. Now please let me get some rest."

He stretched out beside her and shut his eyes, but it was to cut short the argument, not to sleep, and as he lay there listening to the moaning, still alert for other noises, it wasn't just fear that kept him awake. Recalling the urgency of Tucker's telegram— "Save my life!"—he wished he could express his own desires as succinctly. But he was worried as much about Moha and Helen —even the man sprawled by the pool—as he was about himself. Whatever might happen to him seemed less threatening than the thought of bearing the responsibility for somebody's death. Or assuming responsibility for their lives.

At last he did sleep and dreamed he was in his studio, too cold to climb out of bed and stoke the fire. Then he woke shivering, certain he was at the Sidi Mansour and the muezzin was calling. But it was Tucker squawking through the megaphone.

Jack sat up. Although the sun hadn't risen, the sky was suffused with a lemon-colored light. "When did he stop moaning?" he asked Helen.

"About an hour ago."

"Do you hear me?" Tucker demanded. "Lemme send a doctor in before it's too late."

"No," Moha hollered. "Jack will bring him out. He'll carry him to the middle of the field and leave him there. Have two of your people pick him up. Just two. If they try anything or Jack runs for it, remember I have a gun and I have Helen."

Jack crept through the ravine as cautiously as he had last night. Every few steps, he stopped and listened, but there was only the chill morning wind and his own uneven breathing. Lifting the oil drum from the crevasse as quietly as he could, he flattened himself against one wall, edging along until he had an unobstructed view of the area around the *guelta*.

Encrusted with blood, crawling with flies, the man lay crumpled not far from the water, directly under one of the high, overhanging walls.

Jack glanced up, then ducked back. Two men were on the rocks, peering down into the canyon. But when he made himself take another look, he saw it was a pair of vultures, one of which spread its wings and for a moment remained as motionless as the topmost figure on a totem pole.

Passing the *guelta,* Jack noticed something glint in the shallows—a rifle fitted with a telescopic sight. The barrel appeared bent, but that was water refraction.

Although he couldn't summon up much sympathy for a sniper, he hoped he wasn't dead. Crouching down, he cupped his palm in front of the mashed nose and swollen lips and felt a warm, faint exhalation.

The man wore crepe-soled jogging shoes and a dark blue warm-up suit. His face was blackened by burnt cork; now blood, gashes, and bruises added to the disguise. Jack searched his pockets but found nothing to identify him. Nothing at all except big brass cartridges. Then, folding back the collar of the jogging outfit, he noticed the American label.

Hauling him to a sitting position, he heard bone scrape bone. Then he raised him to his feet, took the weight over his shoulder, and carried him across the canyon and through the gorge to the narrow places. Through these, he had no choice but to wrestle and drag the man, whose arms and legs, hinged at half a dozen new joints, flapped against the rocks. His scabs split open and blood poured from cuts on his head, face, and hands.

When the ravine widened and he took the body across his back again, the man groaned once, then fell quiet.

"Tell them I'm bringing him out," Jack called to Moha.

"Is he dead?" Helen asked.

"No." He pushed by her before she got a close look.

Topheavy, teetering one direction or the other at each step, he staggered past the Land Rover and onto the rubble-strewn field. Halfway across, he squatted and lowered the man toward the ground. His feet and hands swung down with sickening thuds and his head would have hit next if Jack hadn't cradled it.

Thighs twitching, he got up and glanced at Tucker who, with the megaphone at his mouth, resembled some absurd, overweight cheerleader. Behind him, half hidden by the truck, stood Benhima and Gorman.

"For Chrissake," Jack shouted, "do something."

He returned to the rocks, his fingers glued together with blood, and watched two soldiers roll the man onto a stretcher.

"He's going to die, isn't he?" Helen asked.

"I don't know."

"I have never seen anybody so busted up," Moha said.

"Before you two get carried away feeling sorry for him, he's a sniper. His rifle's back in the pond. He was climbing over the rocks to take a shot at us."

"Do you think Tucker knew?" she asked. Then answered her own question. "He had to have known."

"You'd better remind them of the deadline before they get any other ideas."

The boy nodded.

"How much longer do you believe your friends will last without water?" he hollered. "I'm waiting for that announcement."

"A plane just landed in Tougla," Tucker said. "It's loaded with newsmen. They'll be here in a few minutes. Tell them what you want and they'll spread the story."

Jack thought Moha should demand to go to the airport to meet them, but then realized the greatest danger would be getting from here to town and onto the plane. Their chances would be better if the newsmen made the trip with them. The more witnesses, he reasoned, the less likely the government was to lead them into an ambush.

"What about safe passage to Algeria?" Moha asked.

"The plane they came on will take you out. Now please give them something to drink."

Moha glanced at Jack, who shook his head no.

"Not yet. Not until I talk to the newsmen."

"You're making them suffer for nothing."

"No, not for nothing. Now they know what it's like for the people in the camps."

As they ate a breakfast of cheese and bread, Helen said, "In a way I wish I was hungry and thirsty."

"The thing that matters," Moha said, "is that they believe you are."

"But I feel like a fraud. None of this seems real. Not even after seeing that man . . . that sniper."

"It only has to seem real to them. The important thing—"

"The important thing," Jack broke in, "is to get out of the country. Don't get so caught up talking to these reporters that you forget that. There'll be plenty of time to talk later.

"Another thing. Once we're at the airport, insist Helen and I leave on the same plane with you. If you're not holding hostages, there's no telling what they might pull. Tucker's going to argue about this, but don't give in."

When they heard a dull grumble, they moved up to the rear of the Land Rover and watched several cars advance over the *hammada*, driving side by side so their windshields wouldn't be cracked by flying gravel. They parked near the Meal Mobile and more than a dozen men climbed out, gazing at the Picture Rocks from behind the trucks. They wore civilian clothes, many of them carried cameras, and they had long hair, beards, sideburns, and mustaches—unmistakable badges of the media.

"Okay, tell them what you want," Tucker said.

"What I want is for the government to admit there's a famine and put out an international appeal for help."

"They've been briefed about that. Why don't you give them a little background on yourself and the Liberation Movement?"

"That has nothing to do with it. I'm not part of any movement." Although the morning chill hadn't quite burned off, Moha's face was moist with perspiration. "Just make the announcement and get me a plane to Algeria."

"Look, these people flew a long way. They'd like to hear the whole story in your own words and they need pictures. They're asking can they come around to this side with me."

Moha turned to Jack. So did Helen. He nodded yes, preferring to have them in the open where the newsmen could see everything and he could watch them.

As they clambered between the truck bumpers and fanned out around Tucker, there was a constant click of cameras. Several men shouldered video cassette recorders, aiming at the ravine.

"Tell them what's on your mind," Tucker said, as if Moha were expressing some petty personal grievance.

"For years there's been a drought, and the government has done nothing. Now people are dying. In camps a few miles from here they don't have—"

"Hold it. They're having problems picking up your voice."

Moha spoke louder. "They don't have much more food and water in the camps than in the desert."

"We're still getting a lot of static, and there's an echo from the rocks. Can we come closer?"

Jack shook his head no.

"Stay where you are," Moha said.

"It's for you I'm saying this. They're having trouble hearing you."

"You didn't have any trouble hearing me before."

"It's a matter of not getting a clear recording. And it's hard to shoot any decent footage with you hiding in there. Step around front where they can see you."

"I don't like this," Jack whispered. "There are too damn many of them."

"That's good. It's what I wanted. With so many, they're sure to send the news out everywhere."

"They don't need to see you to do that. Let's get to the airport. We're not here to put on a show."

"Yes, we are," Moha said. "Like I told Helen, it has to seem real to them. And pictures could make the difference between a big story and just another incident in some country nobody knows how to pronounce."

"It's not worth it."

"It'll be all right," Helen said, "if we do what we did yesterday. He can use me as a shield."

"I'm coming around," Moha hollered. "I'm bringing Helen with me."

"Hold on a minute." It was difficult now for Jack to keep his voice low.

"Don't worry," Helen said. "I've got this role down."

Moha grabbed her in a hammer lock, pushing her along in front of him, until they reached the mouth of the ravine and he brought her up short, yelling, "Hear me now?"

Across the field a few men nodded that they did.

Jack stepped up onto the rear bumper of the Land Rover for a better view.

"There's a drought and famine," the boy began again. "Unless people get immediate food and medical attention—"

"You're in the shadows," Tucker said. "A few more steps forward."

Moving a yard or two beyond the cover of the rocks, Moha started yet again, leaning into each word for emphasis, his damp curly hair gleaming in copper highlights.

Jack was tense and sweaty too and when he heard a noise behind him he assumed it was the wind driving sand through the gorge. But he turned to be sure, saw nothing, and was turning back when he caught sight of something above him in the rocks —a large dark shape like one of the vultures at the *guelta*.

Face blackened by burnt cork, dressed in a midnight blue jogging outfit, the man carried a rifle with a telescopic sight. Realizing Jack had spotted him, he lifted a finger to his lips, then knelt on one knee and shouldered the rifle, aiming at Moha and Helen, who were pressed into a single rigid figure.

"Get down," Jack screamed. He leaped from the bumper and ran around the Land Rover. "Behind you!"

Moha swung away from Helen and looked at Jack, more confused than frightened. Then his forehead exploded. The shot knocked him backward and the pistol flew from his hand. A second shot doubled him over and slammed him to the ground.

Helen was staggering in a circle, glancing around wildly, repeating one word, "What? What?" When she realized what had happened, her legs folded under her and she sat down hard, hugging herself.

Running across the field, Jack yelled Tucker's name. His friend raced out to meet him, and when he was close Jack took a looping, roundhouse swing that caught him on the point of his jaw and put him down.

He was going after Benhima and Gorman when a couple of reporters grabbed him. Jack punched and clawed at them until a hairpiece came off in his hand and he went weak with shock. As they wrestled him to the ground, he recognized a French gaffer and one of the bit-part players wearing a false mustache and sideburns.

A soldier hurried over and held a gun on Jack; Tucker shoved him aside. "Don't hurt him. He's hysterical. He hasn't had any water, is all."

Jack scrambled to his feet, lunging a second time. But Tucker caught him in a bear hug, and it might have looked as if he had fallen. "Bubba," he whispered. "Bubba, get ahold of yourself."

"Why? Why did you do it?"

"It's okay. Helen's all right." Tucker's breath was warm and sweet with toothpaste.

Jack let himself be held a moment, then drew back and looked at him, at Benhima and Gorman, at all the men made up as reporters and cameramen and network stringers.

Someone handed him a canteen; he drank deeply, playing for time, trying to think. Although he felt everything had been blown away with Moha, he knew there was a lot more he and Helen stood to lose if he wasn't careful.

"You okay now?" Tucker asked.

"Where's Helen?"

"In the ambulance. The doctor's giving her a shot. Something to calm her down."

Across the way two soldiers were sliding Moha into a body bag. If he didn't make his move now, Jack doubted he would have another chance. As he started for the rocks, Tucker caught him by the elbow.

"You better let the doctor take a look at you too."

The others were already looking at him.

"There's something I have to get. Stuff Moha took from us."

"Someone'll fetch it for you."

"I know where to look. I'm all right. Water was what I needed."

He shook off Tucker's hand, crossed the field, and reached the soldiers just as they were zipping the bag. Jack asked them to stop. Then, kneeling, he stared at the rumpled shape in the rubberized shroud. Telling himself it was no worse than touching the wounded sniper—he had stomached that and had to do this —he lowered the zipper and slipped his hands inside.

Moha was on his belly. Jack lifted his burnoose and patted the small of his back. The film can wasn't there. Reaching higher, his fingers oozed through warm blood and he had trouble swallowing. When he felt a ragged wet hole the size of his fist, he yanked away and thought he might vomit. Still he made himself run a hand over the outside, testing every inch of the bag. But the film was gone.

"What are you doing, bubba?" asked Tucker. Gorman and Benhima were with him.

"He swiped some stuff from us. I can't find it."

"The soldiers will search the Land Rover. What shall I tell them to look for?" Benhima asked.

When he stood up, the ground swayed. "A ring and Helen's watch."

"Anything else?"

"I'll go ask her." He set off for the trucks.

"She's gone," Tucker said. "The ambulance took her to the hotel."

"Is there anything else?" Gorman asked.

Jack paused only long enough to lean down and scoop up a fistful of sand. He rubbed it into his bloody hands, scouring his fingers until they stung. He was trying so hard not to cry he thought his forehead would split.

CHAPTER XI

Helen wore the blank, inert stare of somebody who had been jolted from a drug-induced sleep. Her face chalky with dust, her dark hair tinted with the same beige talc, she sat stiffly on one bed, gazing through Benhima and Gorman, who had roosted on the bed opposite her. Holding her lifeless hand, Jack stayed beside her as she mumbled in answer to every question, "I don't want to talk about it. I want to take a shower."

"For Chrissake," said Tucker, who was on his feet prowling, "what do you guys expect? She's under sedation. You're not going to get anything debriefing her."

Finally they dismissed her, and while one of the make-up girls led her away, there was a lull in the questions, but none in the racket seething through the Sidi Mansour.

A plane, never intended for Moha, was waiting at the airport. Citing a clause about rebellion and insurrection, the insurance company had threatened to cancel its coverage—and therefore the movie—unless everybody involved left Maliteta at once. The studio had arranged an emergency flight to Marrakech, where a charter would meet them and fly them to Nice.

By the time Jack returned to the hotel, bellboys, grips, and gaffers had stacked all the luggage in the lobby. Helen's and his personal belongings had been packed by the wardrobe department and were ready to be driven to the airport.

But then Benhima arrived and ordered that nothing be moved

until the customs officials had checked it. He claimed they had a master list of everything that had entered the country and it all had to go out again; nothing could be left behind unless covered by a fifty per cent tariff, payable immediately. As the Minister of Culture, Information, and Art interpreted the law, this included not only cameras, equipment, and costumes, but props, set dressings, and building material.

For a while it looked as if they would be forced to ship tons of used lumber and molded fiberglass from Tougla to Nice, and Marvin Tallow was frantic when he thought of the numbers. But then Joel Schwarz suggested that the carpenters haul it all into the dunes and burn it along with anything else not worth shipping. Acrid columns of smoke, swirling with ashes, had risen in the dead air as high as the fifth floor of the hotel. The smell nearly sickened Jack, whose exhaustion had taken on the distortions of a dream.

"Let's start at the beginning," Gorman said. "Try to recall everything that happened."

"I haven't forgotten anything," Jack said. "I told you what I know."

"Go over it again and see if you can't remember a few more details."

Unlike Tucker, Benhima and Gorman had no reluctance to look him in the eye. Leaning forward, they studied Jack's face and appeared to listen for changing inflections in his voice. Their own faces were immobile, as fixed as contrasting masks—the American pale, smooth, and wasted; the Minister plump, furrowed with scars, and glistening black.

"What kind of details?" Jack asked.

"Anything that might explain the boy's motives."

"He told me exactly what he told you. He wanted to help the people in those camps."

"But why?" Benhima insisted.

He stared at the Minister, suspecting any question that obtuse had to contain some subtlety. But he couldn't imagine what. "Because they're starving."

"That's not true."

"I'm telling you what Moha said."

"Did he mention the Malitetan Liberation Front?" Gorman asked.

"Yeah, he said he wasn't in it."

"He lied. He was seen with them several times in the last week." Benhima's cicatrices swept up in a triumphant smile. "How do you explain that?"

"It isn't up to me to explain. But if he was with them, why would he deny it? Why wouldn't he credit the Movement with the kidnaping?"

"That's what we'd like to know," Gorman said. "Everybody's baffled. Here's a boy who was educated in the States and never showed any radical leanings. Then suddenly he kidnaps two Americans, shoots a soldier, kills a man—"

"He didn't kill anybody. That sniper slipped off the rocks. He didn't shoot the soldier either. Nichols grabbed the gun and it went off."

"Still, you get my drift. There are a lot of unanswered questions. If he wasn't in the MLF, how do you account for what he did?"

"I can't tell you anything more than I already have."

"Can't or won't?"

Jack stared at Gorman. "Can't."

"I think you better try harder."

"Hey, what the hell is this?" he asked Tucker.

"They need to get a few facts straight, bubba."

"The facts are Helen and I were kidnaped, and you all damn near got us killed. I'm the one that should be asking questions. Why'd you send those goons in there? They could have hit Helen or me."

"They're excellent marksmen, specially trained," Gorman said. "To be frank, Cordell, a lot of us find your attitude and behavior a little puzzling. Like your running out to warn Moha."

"We've been over this," Tucker said. "He was worried about Helen."

"A little puzzling," Gorman repeated. "Like your searching Moha's body bag and saying you were looking for Helen's watch. We all just saw she's wearing it."

"I was confused. At the end there I was sleepwalking. In shock."

"And you attacked Mr. Garland," Benhima said. "Why?"

Jack let a moment pass and when Tucker still wouldn't meet his gaze he said, "I thought he was somebody else."

Gorman raised his sparse eyebrows. "Who?"

"A friend I used to go to school with."

"Is that supposed to be a joke?"

Jack didn't answer.

"Let me get this straight," Gorman said. "Are we supposed to believe you were in shock when you attacked Tucker and accused him of killing Moha?"

"Why don't you ask Tucker what he believes?"

"I distinctly heard you say to him, 'Why? Why did you do it?' What are we supposed to assume from that?"

"Tell you what, why not assume I had just seen a kid ask you to feed a bunch of starving people. Your answer was to blow his head off. I think you'd be safe to assume that's what upset me."

"This is what I mean about your attitude, Cordell. You're twisting things around. You make it sound like our fault."

"No, it was my fault."

"Another one of your jokes?"

Benhima broke in. "Why is it your fault?"

He considered for a moment the rage and sick hopelessness he felt and all that he might have said. But he knew it would be pointless—dangerous for Helen as well as him. "I told you, I'm tired. I need something to eat and a few hours' sleep."

Tucker came close as if to grip Jack's shoulder and speak to him face to face, but he stopped short of doing either. "There's no use bullshitting around, bubba. They think you were in on it."

"You mean I kidnaped myself?"

"Kind of. They know you were . . . interested in those tribes. They think you and Moha hoked up this scheme to force the government's hand."

"A minute ago they were blaming the Malitetan Liberation Front."

"That's what we're coming to, Cordell. What part did the MLF play in your plans?"

"I didn't have any plans. Neither did Moha as far as I know. He seemed to be making things up as he went along."

Now Tucker did put a hand on his shoulder. "That man, the

sharpshooter, he said he saw you and Helen eating and drinking this morning."

Jack struggled not to blink, not to swallow, not to show any reaction. "Yeah, after you told him there were newsmen on the way, he let us have some bread and water. So what?"

"He says he heard you three talking all night."

"Sure, we talked a lot."

"He claims it sounded like you were in charge."

"That's crazy. We were just trying to calm him down."

"The man's right down the hall," Gorman said. "Want us to call him in here?"

"Go ahead. I'm not afraid to face him as long as I don't have to look at him from the wrong end of a rifle."

Benhima was buffing his nails on his thigh. "If you were stupid enough to go along with Moha and get him killed, that's your concern. My government is simply interested to learn more about the Liberation Front."

"You tell them everything you know, bubba, and they'll give you and Helen a break."

He tried to decide what kind of deal he was being offered. If they had proof, he doubted they'd be willing to bargain. And if they didn't, he hated to admit anything that might help them. "I've told you everything," he said. "They could call in one of their goons and have him knock me around, it wouldn't make any difference."

Tucker turned to Benhima and Gorman. "Like I been saying all along, there must have been a mistake."

"Why would the man lie?" Gorman demanded.

"I didn't say he's lying. He misinterpreted."

There was a knock on the door, and Marvin Tallow bustled in. "This customs crap is getting out of hand. They're laying charges on us left and right."

Benhima stood up. "I will make sure they are following orders."

"Is Jack free to go now?" Tucker asked.

"Free?" Frowning, Benhima clapped his visored hat onto his bald head. "No, he's not free to do anything more in Maliteta. He's being deported along with the rest of you."

When Gorman had gone off with Benhima, Tucker said, "We gotta have a talk."

"I listened to you talk all day and night at the rocks. I've heard enough."

"Goddamnit, I went to bat for you. I want you to understand."

"I do. That's the trouble."

In the lobby the purple velours couches and plastic tables had been shoved aside, and members of the movie company stood in line waiting for Benhima and two customs officials to rummage through their suitcases. Still in her rugby pullover, Helen sat on a steamer trunk, bolt upright, her thin shoulders shaking.

Jack hurried over, expecting to find her sobbing, but her eyes were dry. She wasn't making a sound. She was simply trembling and staring at Fatih and Hal Nichols.

"You promised, you promised," Fatih was saying.

"Hold it down. I've had enough people yelling at me today."

"You said you'd take me to America."

"I said I'd look into a visa for you. I did. Call Gorman when you have the price of a ticket."

"I thought you would give me a ticket."

"I'm a PR man, not Santa Claus."

"But you promised you'd find me a job."

"Right. You get to LA, there'll be one waiting for you."

Fatih grabbed Nichols by the lapels. "I don't have enough money. I'll never have enough."

"Sure you will. Keep saving and you'll make it. Now get your mitts off the jacket."

"I told the hotel I'm leaving. I wrote the restaurant in Marseilles I won't be back. I have said to everybody I am moving to America."

"You better tell them you changed your mind."

When Benhima and the customs officers came to Nichols' luggage, the Minister mumbled something to Fatih and he fled to the dining room, leaving on the lapels of Nichols' suede coat the imprint of his damp hands.

On top of Lisa's suitcases was a cage the size of a breadbox. The baby gazelle lay curled inside it, munching a candy bar which Lisa fed it through the wire.

"This cannot leave the country," Benhima said.

"What can't?"

"The gazelle."

"What about it?" she asked.

"It is a rare animal. What you Americans call 'endangered.' It is against the law to remove it from Maliteta."

"For Chrissake, I bought it from a guy who was going to eat it. You said I should eat it."

"Even so . . ."

When Benhima lifted the cage, Lisa seized his wrist. A soldier stepped in, but the Minister waved him off. He smiled. "I'm sorry."

"You knew I was taking it with me. Why'd you wait till now? You want it for yourself, don't you? You want to eat it," she shouted.

Tucker rushed over. "What's wrong?"

"He's trying to take my gazelle."

"It is the law. The animal must remain in Maliteta."

"Bullshit, I won't do it. It's mine."

Tucker signaled to Phil, and when Lisa saw her bodyguard she said, "Take the cage from this bastard."

"Take Lisa outside," Tucker said.

One hand extended toward the cage, the other on Lisa's elbow, Phil looked paralyzed.

"Do what I told you. What the hell are you getting paid for?" she demanded.

Tucker grabbed her and dragged her toward the door.

"Goddamnit, don't just stand there," Lisa screamed at Phil. Then, seeing this was hopeless, she said, "At least let me give it to someone else. If they're going to eat it, I don't want that fat shit getting any."

But Tucker hustled her out of the hotel.

They rode to the airport in three battered, filthy, smoke-belching buses. Then, standing at the edge of the runway, they stared in disbelief at the only plane around—a C-97 military transport.

Since there were no baggage handlers, they had to load it themselves, hauling the suitcases, trunks, cameras, and equipment across the heat-warped tarmac and storing them in the cargo hold. When they climbed into the passenger compartment, it wasn't much better than the buses had been. There were no plush reclining chairs, just benches along both sides of the fuselage and weblike shoulder harnesses instead of seat belts.

Hal Nichols buckled himself in and said, "Now bring me a vodka gimlet."

Nobody laughed. After the hatches had been shut, the air conditioning clicked on, but did little more than whip up the smell of cigarette butts and sweat.

Then they waited. The flight crew came aboard, and they continued to wait. Tucker went and talked to the pilot, and still they waited. More than an hour passed before the engines rumbled to life and they taxied with lumbering slowness down the runway.

Once they were airborne, every rivet and stud in the plane rattled and it was impossible to talk in a normal voice. Tucker, Schwarz, and Tallow sat close together, hollering in each other's faces, and Nichols listened, scratching notes on a yellow legal pad.

Although she had stopped shivering, Helen sat rigidly upright and said very little. Holding onto Jack's hand, she stared out the window where below them, close to the ground, rain clouds appeared to be building. But it was another sandstorm, pushing westward, carrying the dry mist over the High Atlas Mountains.

As they descended toward Marrakech the sky cleared and the palm grove looked startlingly verdant after the Sahara. Two storks left the town wall, stroking upward on long white wings. The plane circled the airport, the landing gear thumped from its underbelly, and they dropped slowly toward the macadam. Then at the last instant the pilot pulled up and swung the C-97 around, making a second approach.

Jack saw two men with a stretcher trotting off the runway. At that distance it was difficult to tell what they were carrying, but it looked like a large mangled bird, and he thought one of the storks had flown into a propeller.

It wasn't until they were in the transit lounge that they learned it was Fatih. Wearing his gravy-stained tuxedo, he had stowed away in the undercarriage and when the landing gear came down he had fallen. Somebody said he must have been insane. Somebody else said maybe he had his reasons—political ones—for wanting to get out of Maliteta quick. Hal Nichols said nothing. A few people cried—perhaps because they liked Jerry Lewis. Or because they didn't like seeing what was left of him lying on the apron of the runway, waiting for the Moroccan authorities to decide what to do.

Jack swore he wouldn't cry. He didn't want to upset Helen who, although she didn't cry either, had started to shake again. He found them a seat and told himself it was stupid to cry for Fatih when he hadn't cried for Moha. Tears were inadequate to the occasion and to his emotions. Yet he felt the same sick hammering in his head as he had that morning at the Picture Rocks and finally he had to go off by himself.

In the bathroom he stared into the mirror, then splashed his face with cold water. Since there were no paper towels in the dispenser, he returned to Helen with his cheeks as wet as they would have been if he had broken down. She didn't seem to notice.

After a three-hour delay, they boarded a Royal Air Maroc Caravelle and the flight was so smooth and quiet, Jack could hear Tucker, Joel, Marvin, and Hal whispering, several rows away.

In Tucker's opinion, handling the publicity was going to be the most ticklish part. Nichols agreed but expressed great confidence in his own skill and tact. Schwarz said now that they had a news story to sink their teeth into, he was sure the insurance company wouldn't cancel them. Tallow knew just the spot in southern Spain where they could find locations that matched the shots of Maliteta. More or less.

Now that it was too late, Jack wished he had gone ahead and cried. Or at least that he could stop listening, stop thinking about the utter uselessness of Moha's death and the full depth of his own failure.

For years he had had an urge—an obsession that grew more unreasonable with age—to be somebody, to do something, to accomplish at least one thing in his life that would last. Each time he fell short he had thought the worst agony was to be gifted with enough vision to see what he desired, yet to be incapable of obtaining it. But that pain was nothing compared to what he felt now.

Some men, he had heard since he was a boy, "just didn't have it in them." Although he had long suspected he was one of them, he had continued to grope inside himself, hoping to discover some alchemy of small elements that might add up. Now he knew he had been looking in the wrong place. Too preoccupied by his paltry self, he hadn't noticed that the world was outside, all around him, and with Moha dead and the movie gone, Jack feared he had lost his last chance.

They landed an hour after nightfall, and Nice Airport was slick with rain. Neon signs sent variegated snakes wriggling over the wet asphalt, creating the sort of set Donald Wattle dreamed of. "Eye-grabbers" everywhere. Billboards extolled the sun in Monte Carlo and the snow at Isola 2,000, the virtues of Napoleon's favorite brandy and the flavor of various cigarettes. In the terminal you could cash a check, send a candygram, or stand at the zinc coffee bar and drink an espresso. The perfume, liquor, and accessories at the duty-free shops looked as if they had been laid out with a camera in mind, and the crowds of tourists provided back action that couldn't have been better choreographed.

While the rest of them waited for the luggage, Tucker and Marvin raced upstairs to the overseas telephones, and Nichols bought and passed around London tabloids and the *Herald Tribune*. Although Jack had led Helen to a bench behind a pillar, Nichols found them and dropped copies of all the papers in their laps. Helen's picture—years out of date, the hair long, her face fuller—was on the front page. The headline in the *Trib* said, "Quick End to Kidnap Siege. Film Star Unharmed."

Jack skimmed an article which referred to Moha as "Mohammed Assiz Sefrou, the California-educated, self-styled revolutionary who wounded one soldier, kidnaped two Americans, and killed an employee of the American Embassy in the course of his rampage." Never mentioning his motives, his demands, the drought, or the famine, the story devoted most of its space to the film and a summary of Helen's career.

"You can't buy publicity like this," Nichols said. "We got a press conference set up tomorrow morning. Reporters are flying in from—"

"Who sent this out?" Jack asked.

Nichols grinned. "Who do you think?"

"Does Tucker know?"

"For sure."

"Did you send it from Maliteta or Marrakech?"

"Maliteta."

"So Benhima had to approve."

"Check. Hey, look, those reporters are going to be hot to talk to you two. The both of you better decide whether to break the news about your romance now or save it for later. Maybe right before the movie opens."

Scattering the newspapers from his lap, Jack shoved Nichols. "Get the hell away. Just go."

"What are you, nuts? I get you and your girl good press and you go berserk. I don't have to take this shit from you."

"You'll take more than shit if you don't get out of here."

Backpedaling, Nichols said, "Fuck yourself, Cordell."

When Jack started for him, Tucker shouted, "Hold it."

"Please stop," Helen said.

It was her quiet voice, not Tucker's, that brought him up short. She was on her feet, eyes unclouded for the first time in hours. "Don't bother about him. It's not worth it."

Tucker came over, his face moist, gleaming. Now that they had left the Sahara, he was sweating again. "What's with you, bubba? All day you been acting like you're training for the Golden Gloves."

"Did you see what he wrote? Goddamn lies! Moha wasn't any revolutionary. He didn't kill anybody. There's not a word about the famine."

"Hold it down." He steered Jack over to the pillar where Helen stood. "I'll explain in a minute. Marvin's got an announcement."

Marvin's announcement was that they would finish the film in southern Spain, near Almería. They'd fly down in a few days, right after Helen had her press conference and did some talk shows for English and American TV. Meanwhile he had made reservations for the creative types at a hotel in Antibes and for the crew at a pension in Nice.

As the conveyor belt brought in the suitcases, golf clubs, ten-

nis rackets, and swim fins, Tucker said, "Marvin booked a suite
for the two of you at the Hotel du Cap."

"I have my own house."

"Suit yourself. But I hope the phone's working. I want to be
able to keep in touch."

"I'm finished."

"What are you talking about?"

"I'm quitting."

"You can't."

"The hell I can't. It was bad enough we didn't leave Maliteta
when we should have. But to come back and lie—"

"I said I'd explain."

"Explain what? Why you coaxed Moha into the open so they
could kill him? Why you're still not telling the truth?"

Tucker's face darkened; he folded his meaty arms. "I'm waiting, bubba. Are you gonna give me a chance?"

"You had your chances."

"Let him talk," Helen said.

"I've heard enough of his talk. I'm leaving."

"Wait." Helen caught him by the elbow. "Those stories Nichols
wrote, they don't matter. Tomorrow we'll tell the reporters what
really happened."

"That's what I'm trying to explain." Tucker led them farther
away from the others, over to a rent-a-helicopter office that was
shut for the night. "It's not the time to tell anybody what happened down there. Maybe it'll all come out eventually, but not
now."

The blank stare returned to Helen's eyes. "I don't understand."

He reached up as if to rake at his beard, but then let his hand
slap to his side. "Look, the long and short of it is Benhima had
you by the balls. He wasn't about to let you leave unless we met
his terms."

"So you made another deal," Jack said.

"You're goddamn right I did. We were bargaining for your
life. Helen's too. They knew you were in on it with Moha. Gorman and I got you off the hook by promising to keep things
quiet. Why the hell else do you think they let you go?"

"They had no reason to hold us. No proof."

"Chrissake, they didn't need any, but they had enough. Nichols told how you sided with the kid from the start, and that sniper heard you making plans."

"I explained that."

"I didn't buy your story. Neither did they. Because what really nailed you was the money. The dough you gave that group of Liberation yoyos. Couple nights ago they shot some guy and found a wad of *gourdes* in an air mail envelope and figured it had to have been your expense money. They decided you were footing the bills for the whole outfit."

"That's not how it was," Jack said. "Okay, we gave money, but it was for food and medicine. We weren't in with the Liberation Front and we didn't know anything about the kidnaping. But once Moha had us, we didn't want him hurt. We were just trying to make sure everybody got out alive."

"I understand. But do you think Benhima would? You think he'd see any difference between helping Moha before or after the kidnaping? Don't blame me because we had to do a trade-off to save you two."

"Wait a second," Jack said. "The deal you made, I don't suppose it had anything to do with wanting to leave Maliteta so the insurance company wouldn't cancel the picture."

"I'm not claiming that didn't have *anything* to do with it. Just that the big worry was Helen and you."

"Bigger than your worry that Benhima wouldn't let you bring out the equipment and the cans of film you shot?"

"You son of a bitch! You love to paint my ass black, don't you?"

"Will you two please stop yelling?" Helen said. "The important point is we're out now. We can tell the truth and they can't do a damn thing about it."

In spite of his anger, Tucker lowered his voice. "We promised not to."

"We?" Helen asked.

"The studio and the Embassy were in on the agreement. I'm not going to shaft them after I gave my word."

"Your word?" Helen said. "What's so sacred about an agreement with a monster like Benhima?"

Tucker said nothing.

"I think I get it," Jack said. "It's the money. All those blocked *gourdes*. What happened, did the Malitetans let you change them back to dollars if you kept your mouth shut? Did they forfeit their percentage?"

Tucker still didn't answer, but his face darkened again.

"It wasn't me they had by the balls," Jack said. "It was you."

"It's the studio," Tucker said.

"You mean Maliteta had the studio by the balls? Or the studio's got you?"

"What difference does it make?" He was irritated by all these fine distinctions.

"None to you. But I didn't make any deal and I'm not keeping quiet."

"Nobody'll believe you."

"If they won't take my word, I'll draw them a picture."

"You haven't had much luck selling your pictures in the past."

Jack was surprised that that hurt, but he smiled. "What the hell, you paid me to do cartoons. Somebody should be willing to look at a few sketches for free."

"I'm coming with you," Helen said.

"It's your business who you go off with," Tucker said. "Just make sure you're on time for the press conference."

"Forget it. I'm off the film too." Taking Jack's hand, she started toward the conveyor belt where their luggage was trundling around and around.

Jack held back. "You better think this over."

"I have."

"I mean get some sleep and let that shot wear off and call your agent in the morning."

"He's right," Tucker said.

"There's no contract that can make me lie for you." Releasing Jack's hand, she set off on her own. He had to hurry to catch up with her.

Tucker caught up too, fetched a pushcart, and surprised them by helping pile their luggage onto it. "Listen, why don't you two take some time off and rest? You've been under a hell of a strain. Is it the press conference that's bugging you? We'll call it off. You don't have to lie for me."

"Keeping quiet, we'd still be lying for you," she said.

As Jack pushed the cart through customs, then out the door to a cab stand, Tucker stayed with them. Perspiration had soaked through his shirt; the rain couldn't make it much wetter. But it plastered his gray hair and beard to his sunburned face. "Jesus, don't do this to me. Do you realize what you're doing?"

Jack signaled for a taxi, and the driver climbed out and heaved their suitcases into the trunk.

"What is it, bubba? You want me to beg?"

He looked at Tucker and, in spite of everything, couldn't help feeling something for him—maybe simple regret at what might have been. "I don't want anything from you. I just wish you'd understand."

"I send you a telegram, I beg you to save my life, and this is what I get."

"What you hired me to do, Tucker, was help save your career —your ass, not your life. We left the people whose lives needed saving down there in the desert. That's what I wish you'd understand."

As the driver followed the coast road through an area that looked eerily like America, the dual-lane highway, kaleido-scopically bright, was lined by gas stations—Mobil, Shell, Esso—used-car lots, motels, supermarkets, miniature golf courses, and a gocart track. But then he swung up into the hills, onto the autoroute, and they were soon in Provence. Bushy oleanders had overgrown the median strip, their slender leaves shining in the headlights, and off to the side where the stony landscape, covered with thyme and lavender, climbed toward the Alps, there were broad umbrella pines and black spears of cypress.

"God, it's great to see trees," Helen said. "Even in the rain."

"I don't think I'll ever mind rain again. But it'll be cold in the house. Sure you wouldn't rather spend the night in Cannes?"

"I'm tired of hotels."

"And the phone, they cut it off when I didn't pay the bill."

"I don't care. I don't have anybody to call tonight." She glanced through the rain-beaded glass as they passed the toll booth at Antibes.

"I hope you're not doing this for me," he said.

"I'm doing it for myself."

"I mean I'd understand if you decided to finish the film. You've got other things—especially your boys—to worry about."

"No, I couldn't go on after what happened. I couldn't bear to let them use it as a publicity gimmick."

"But if it ends your career . . ."

She let a moment pass. "Maybe it's time I came to some kind of ending. Reading that crap about myself in the papers—the truth as well as the lies—it made me sick, ashamed. It seemed so petty."

"The trouble is finding somebody who'll believe us. Tucker was right. They won't take our word. Not without proof."

"We have proof." Reaching around under her rugby shirt, she yanked something from the waistband of her blue jeans and handed it to him. The film canister carried the warmth of her body.

"God! Where'd you find it?"

"Moha gave it to me last night when you were back in the canyon. He was afraid the soldiers were going to rush us. He said it'd be safer with me.

"Tomorrow I'll call my agent. He'll be furious I walked off the film. But he's sharp and he'll see that this is the only way to explain what I did. He'll show it to everybody in New York and on the Coast. If anybody can put it across, he's the one. What I'd like is for him to arrange for us to stop in Paris or London on the way to the States and call our own press conference and let reporters have a look at the film."

"This'll clobber them, kill them." Jack was still staring at the can, incredulous. "Why didn't you tell me?"

"There was never the right time. In Tougla I didn't want to take a chance. Then once we left and I didn't have Benhima to worry about, I wondered about Tucker. I didn't want to give him or anybody else a chance to throw their weight around. It'll be bad enough as it is."

"Bad how?"

"Oh, they'll probably have Nichols and other people leak stories about us. They'll call you the radical art professor. Maybe they'll get a quote from your wife or next-door neighbor making you sound crazy. They'll claim I'm on dope or something, and make any director think twice about ever hiring me."

"But we have the film."

"Yes," she said. "That won't keep them from putting out lies and it may not give us the last word. But at least now we have a chance."

The taxi left the autoroute at Mandelieu and headed into the foothills. Because of the darkness and heavy rain, they could see nothing except what was right beside the road—the wrinkled bark of the cork oaks, the brindled trunks of plane trees, an occasional vineyard or silver-gray olive grove. The mimosas had lost their blossoms, and they swept through the gutters like gold dust.

When they reached the village, the square was abandoned; only the *tabac* was open. Following Jack's directions, the driver splashed up a narrow lane which the storm had transformed into a spillway, floating leaves and sticks downhill. Jack told him to pull around front and leave the headlights on while he sprinted to the house through the downpour. After a good deal of swearing and kicking, he swung the warped door open and felt a cold, musty exhalation rush over him. He switched on a lamp, and a mouse skittered across the tile, disappearing under the jumble of furniture piled in the living room.

"We're going to freeze," he told Helen as he paid the driver.

"We'll find a way to stay warm."

She hurried in ahead of him, then abruptly halted. "Did somebody break in while you were gone?"

"No, I store things down here. I live upstairs."

He led her up to his studio where the damp army blankets still covered the windows and his canvases faced the wall. On the ceiling a wet spot had grown a coat of green fur. She moved to the center of the room, glancing uncertainly at the empty easel, the scorched stove, the mattress with a rumpled sleeping bag instead of a counterpane.

"You were willing to come back here alone tonight?"

"Sure. Why not?"

"Brave man. The place looks haunted."

"It is."

"Why'd you live like this?"

He shrugged. "I didn't want to be bothered about all the stuff downstairs. I had this notion that if I narrowed my life, if I shoved everything and everybody else off to the side, I'd . . . I don't know why, but I thought I'd become a better painter." He smiled ruefully. "I suppose you could say it's the bourgeois artist's method of systematically deranging his senses—rearranging the furniture."

She put her hand on one of the canvases.

"Don't look. Not tonight," he said.

"You afraid the method didn't work?"

"There's so much else to worry about, I don't have much fear to spare for that any more."

"I really would like to see them."

"Tomorrow. Want me to build a fire?"

"Don't bother. I won't be awake much longer." She went to the mattress and, stepping out of her shoes, slid in under the sleeping bag without undressing.

Jack put the film canister on the easel, then, after prying off his shoes, he too left his clothes on and crawled in beside Helen, hugging her for warmth.

Taking another look at the dim, drafty space that had served as his studio, she said, "Really, Jack, how did you stand it?"

"I thought it suited me. In the taxi you said maybe it was time you came to some kind of ending. Well, I thought I had come to one here."

They were silent then, and as their bodies gradually warmed one another, he felt a steady, strong pulse wherever he touched her. He saw it at her temple and her throat.

"Want me to go turn off the light?" Helen asked.

"No," Jack said. "Let's leave it on a little while longer."